Bridges

THE LIGHTBEARERS SERIES

JEN LOWRY

To Eli, My Love

CHAPTER 1

Crazy Little Thing Called Love

Mimicking the same little sweet whine as his, I turned into the beggar for the tenth time to tell Alex, "Stop begging!"

He would not leave me alone until I would relent to his wishes. Such a typical summer day.

Alex's chocolate-churned mocha eyes were wide as discs as he pulled at the hem of my t-shirt. "Please, please, please. Defeat this level, and I'll never ask you again."

I rolled my eyes as if to act aggravated, but I didn't mind. "Give it to me."

The game controller fits my hand like an old friend, and I crossed my legs on the couch to brace myself for the bouncing up and down of my ten-year-old brother.

Alex screamed as he flew punches in the air, missing my head by mere millimeters. "I knew you wanted to play. Kill those zombies, Jazz."

My body rocked from side to side, reminding me of our choppy boat rides across the inlet, and I left-handed him behind the knees to tackle him down beside me. He fell in place, waiting for me to get him unstuck. Alex always wanted mature rated games, which was beyond my understanding because they were always so tough for him, him getting stuck at least by level three. There goes big sissy flying into save the day and blast open a recon mission or decapitate vampires. Today, it was flesh-eating island zombies. Such fun I was having.

I had to admit spending time with Alex was a given for the summer. As I took down the zombies hiding in the forbidden mansion, I smiled at the reflection of his face on the flat screen. He was in awe of my skill and wished that I would stream. He was right. I was almost good enough to battle it out with Tucker and host my own Twitch. If I talked, that might have been a good life plan.

Speaking of the dreadlocked devil, he bounded in without knocking and said, "Hey, Grommet. What's up? Hey, babe."

He pulled my long, tangled hair straight out of my elastic band like it was nothing.

"Ow! Tucker, that hurt."

He winked as he made his way to our fridge, pulled out two Fizzes and plopped down beside me on his perfect spot to my right, making my body float again. I almost lost my balance off the couch and lost a life.

He grabbed the controller for me as I opened our drinks. "When did you get this one, Squirt? I didn't know it was out yet."

Alex didn't even flinch at all the names that Tucker had for him. In fact, thinking it over I'd never heard Tucker ever use his real name. When he first met me, he would always call me Jazz-line, and I had to constantly tell him it was spelled that way but pronounced Jazz-lean. He finally gave up and started calling me Lean Mean Green Machine, or Jazzy McMaster, or some weird name that made absolutely no sense. But that was Tucker, and we loved him for all of his silliness.

I told him, "We drove to GamesRCool last night and traded for it."

Tucker eyed me crooked, his blue eyes sparkling like the ocean. "Did you get it yet?"

I knew exactly what he misinterpreted, and it pained me to

reply, "No car, yet. Luke dropped us off when he went to pick up some new restaurant supplies."

He put the game on pause, reached his suntanned bicep around my shoulder and squeezed me to the point that I was sure I'd bruise. He never knew how strong he was.

"These things take time, Jazz. It's all about the perfect moment with the perfect ride, the perfect wave."

Tucker jerked away, pushed X, and started the game back without breaking his concentration. For Tucker's sake, I was glad Murrell's Inlet, our little beach town in South Carolina, didn't have the big waves because he'd kill himself out there being a loony daredevil if we inhabited a place with decent ones. We were lucky to boogie board on a windy day. The South Carolina ocean was so calm.

But that didn't discourage his surfing dreams, and as soon as we graduated, he has promised that he's off to the University of Hawaii. It hurt at the thought of him moving across the continent and leaving me. Tucker had been my best friend since I was five years old. One more year. I shook it off trying not to think of what was next. For him or for me.

He threw the controller at Alex. "Here, Booger breath. I'm done. Level four is ready for your little hands." He pulled me up from the couch in one swoosh. "I'm kidnapping your sister today."

I tried to stop him, but my bare feet were dragging across the floor, and I was digging in. "Can't. You know I'm watching Alex today."

Alex cut off the TV and soared off the couch landing square on Tucker's back. "I'm being kidnapped, too."

His face grimaced and he made sounds like a pirate as he flipped him over, his Adidas shorts sliding down to expose his RAW boxers. "But if Monkey goes, then we can't discuss what I really need to talk to you about. And it's pressing. Like now. I mean today."

Great. I thought. Another girl conversation. Getting through

Tucker's relationships was so taxing. That's why I never had one, other than the not talking part. But that was another issue altogether. I couldn't handle hard. It was painful enough being me let alone attaching someone to me like a leech. And when Tucker got a girl, she turned into a life-sucking amoeba, changing who they were to be who they thought he would want, within days. Then, he'd pull her away, flick her to the side, and find another willing leech.

I tried to pull Alex off him, but he was squiggling like one. "Okay, but we've got to drop him off first."

Alex, red-faced from the blood being drained to his brain, stomped his foot. "No way, I want to hear, too. Is it Lisa or Rhonda this time?"

Tucker shoved him through the door with a kick of his sandaled foot. "It's neither. Can we please go? This is important."

I looked down at my appearance and wished that I knew how to make it more presentable, but I wasn't equipped with that kind of information in my brain. It was too brainwashed by video games and horror movies to make room for girly thoughts on how to do my hair and makeup. Momma was always so swamped at Chica's, her restaurant that she and my stepdaddy owned, that she never had time to do the momma-girl stuff, like teach me how to apply eyeliner or blush. So, I was a mess most of the time. Maybe that was the real reason why I never had a relationship.

I pointed at the bright orange sugary stain on my shorts. "I've got to change. I'll be right back."

Tucker frowned. "Nobody cares what you're wearing."

"Exactly my point."

He looked at me confused. "Huh?"

I hurried down the tiny hallway of our beach villa, more like a tiny hotel looking setup with every single villa looking identical to ours with different shutters and doorframes. Thank God, that Tucker was the yellow one next to mine.

He yelled for the whole neighborhood to hear as he was

chasing Alex around in our tiny front lawn. "We're waiting, princess. Your carriage awaits."

It was more like a deathtrap broken down 4X4 Jeep that he had to sometimes beat with a hammer to get the engine running. I grabbed an old pair of blue jean shorts, tried to brush the tangles out of my curly mess of hair that fell down to my waist, but without a wash and the sand still sticking to it from our sun up swim at the ocean this morning, there was really no use, so I threw it back up in the ponytail again.

I was reminded again that my two guys were out there because they were about to get the cops called on them for disorderly conduct if I didn't come out and break it up. Sometimes I wondered why in the world Tucker put up with Alex and me. He was so different from us. He was my sun, and I was his moon. He loved the attention, the spotlight, the heat. He was the party. The reason everybody came to the party. I was the one who never went. I loved to hide in the dark. I loved the cool breeze as it floated to me at night. All the noise of the day attacked my senses, and it was so hard to explain that to Tucker. He would never understand.

When took off in Jeepers Kreepers, what we nicknamed his death machine, I held on for dear life as we skidded out into the lines of beach traffic. I screamed over Pork Rinds, his favorite alternative band blaring from his playlist, "Why do you put up with me?"

He turned the volume down a notch. "What are you talking about, woman?"

"Why do you hang out with me and Alex?"

He switched it off and turned a little too sharp onto Highway 17 as I grabbed onto the roll bar for dear life. We were farther down the coast from Myrtle Beach, but the tourist still packed into our little inlet, especially during the motorcycle rally.

Tucker said, his voice picking up the most serious tone as he could muster, "I love you guys. Plain and simple like that."

I said, "We love you, too, but it has to be more than that."

I knew that he loved us. He never left us without telling us. No matter how big and goofy he was, he had the biggest heart of any guy I knew. Well, he was the only guy I knew.

"What's more than love? I've loved you since the minute I saw you with your pigtails and overalls punching Joey Paine out cold when he tried to kiss you under the art table in kindergarten. That sealed you'd be my best friend forever."

I knocked his shoulder and my knuckles hurt a lot worse than his thick skin. He had his routines, and they were more than trying to catch a wave and a tan, it was to tone for his ladies. "I'm really serious."

He sighed and said, "Stop feeling sorry for yourself, Jazz. You're my best friend, and you have to put up with me for the rest of your life or the rest of this year anyway."

I knew he was referring to his college acceptance. He couldn't wait until early acceptance letters arrived. There it went again, my heart was in my throat, and I tried my best to push past the tears. Senior year would be harder than I ever imagined, and it had nothing to do with AP Calculus.

Tucker said, "Will you just shut up about this nonsense. I have something really important to talk with you about, and I need your help."

Tucker had so many girlfriends, sometimes more than one at the same time, with much dismay from my end, and he never listened to any of my advice anyway. I didn't know why he bothered to get me involved in his little childish escapades. But here I was again, dragged into another one.

"I'm in love, Jazz."

Alex asked, "What? With who? Is she hot?"

I'd never seen Tucker blush, but I was sure it wasn't that it was hitting 100 degrees; he was truly red in the face. Crab red. Tucker rounded the curve with a squeal of his tires and hit the employee parking lot with a spray of pebbles and rocks skirting away in fear. We both got out of the car, waiting on Alex who had his hands crossed in defiance.

He pouted. "You guys can't leave me hanging like this. Come on, Tucker. I want details."

And I was sure he did but Tucker was acting way too weird to discuss it in front of Alex. He never had problems showing off pictures of his girlfriends or parading them around in Chica's as if they were some new board of his. But this one must be different. It piqued my curiosity, to say the least.

Momma was in the back, as usual, sweating it up, running up and down the line, pushing out orders and tackling lobster tails in one swish of her long, tanned arm. Everyone in town treated my chef-owner momma like royalty. She had a four-star establishment down by the waterfront, a daunting task to some with all our competition, but not for my momma. She loved the challenge and always strived for the best service, food, and atmosphere. She had a handsome, younger prince who adored her and treated her like a queen. Momma had her life. Sometimes I wondered if she ever included Alex and me in her perfect equation. It never felt like that anyway.

She gave Alex a quick hug and a peck on his full curly dark head, shaking it all out of order. She smiled at me and gave me that knowing look. It was lunch hour. They opened 11-2, then closed, opened again 5-10. She needed the extra hand, and without being asked, I picked up the salads and headed out to the dining room with a bright smile plastered on my face.

Hidden away in the corner where the crowds of hungry customers could fade away behind us, Tucker looked so uneasy as he squirmed in our family booth always reserved for us.

I put on my server voice, "Do you want something?"

He squirmed again and whispered, "Hurry so we can talk."

I shrugged. "You knew what would happen if I came here. She needs me. Can it wait a little bit?"

He looked down at his watch as if he had somewhere to be.

"Yeah, I guess. But I need you."

He had never was so serious before. This girl must be something.

"Just tell me her name. Who is it? "

"Bree."

I ran through the juniors and half of the faces of the garden tools he'd dated in the past and that name wasn't in my directory. This girl was a mystery, and she had captured my best friend. It's not that I was jealous. I never looked at Tucker that way, even though Momma tried to encourage it more than once. To everyone else, I was sure they thought he was the finest thing to grace the planet. But he picked his boogers and farted way too much in front of me to see anything fine about him other than his fine smelling feet I swore he never washed. But I was a little stumped to see him this enamored, and then I wondered what he needed me for?

Momma needed me more, and for the next thirty minutes I helped her young college staff, Ruby and Peggy Lynn, catch up on lunch specials before crashing down in front of Tucker. Alex was running up and down the dock with his hacky-sack Tucker made for him, keeping our stepdad, Luke, busy laughing.

I pushed back my hair that had fallen out of my rubber band holder as I slid in across from Tucker. He leaned over, grabbed a strand and pulled on it. He always said he loved to watch it spring back in place.

"Okay, shoot. I'm here. Now, who's Bree?"

He grinned sheepishly. "You'll kill me."

"Oh, no you didn't." I kicked him under the table and he winced. "You didn't get her pregnant, did you?" We'd already had this scare last spring.

Tucker shook his head violently. "No way. I've not even touched her like that. No, it's not like that."

I sighed with relief and fell back against the leather-cushioned booth. "Thank God. Tucker, don't go scaring me like that. What is it? What did you do?"

"She's a sophomore."

That's no big deal. Why would I kill him? "So, there are seniors that date sophomores. That's not the end of the world."

He continued, this time pushing the salt and pepper mills around in circles, spilling salt. I picked it up and threw it over mine and Tucker's left shoulders out of habit. He still wouldn't look at me.

"Well, I've got a genuine problem and you're the only one who can help me?"

I laughed. "If you want me to rub eucalyptus in your dreads again, sorry."

His face lit up again remembering it, too. "I wish it were that simple. I need you to go out with me."

Okay, that made me spill the saltshaker. I threw it over my left again. "What did you just say?"

He said, "Hear me out, okay. She's fifteen years old and her momma won't let her out of her sight without chaperones, so I really need for you to be like my wingman for our dates and I've got to be with her, and I have to have somebody. And I can't ask Billy, Jamie, or Frankie. They would scare her away from me the minute she spends time together with that rough crew. You are my moon. You are my moon and stars, please, please, please be my chaperone for the evening or summer, or the next year, please!"

I frowned, thinking about how that would go. "Are you serious?"

He grabbed my hand and squeezed. "Bree is different, trust me."

I trusted him with my life, and I knew that if I needed him, he'd do the same for me. So, of course, I could never say no, and now I'd be a granny chaperone.

"Okay, but wait, on one condition. If you start your kissing mess then you do it away from me. I don't want to be reminded I haven't had my first kiss yet."

His eyebrows furrowed. "Wait, I thought Joey Paine kissed you."

I couldn't help but laugh. "That didn't count. I punched him, remember. It wasn't mutual."

He leaned in closer. "Well, if I kiss you, will you be over it already."

He was so stupid and dramatic all the time. He needed his own one-man show.

"What would Bree say about that?"

Tucker leaned back, his voice confident and filled with emotion. "She knows about us and for the first time, it's okay. Thank God. You don't know how much of a difference that is."

"Ah-ah, I knew I got to those other girls and that was the reason that my popularity stunk. Nobody can stand it they are so jealous."

"The price to pay I guess, to be my friend. But Bree can't wait to meet you. She's the sweetest thing, besides you. When I told her about us, she was so cool with it. That's when I knew I could love her. That's why I've loved no one else. I couldn't help but love her anyway. She's it, Jazzy. Sorry you haven't found your it yet. I told you, I'd hook you up."

"My it would be some evil clown terrorizing me, knowing my luck. No hookups for me, thank you very much. Single and loving it."

He frowned and turned to look out the window again. My social status was always a concern for him. My school experiences had been less than lack-luster. Filled with studying, tests, reading, and hiding. No friends by lockers, no friends at lunch, no friends. Filled with teachers and Tucker. That is when Tucker could get away from his football crowd long enough to make plans with me after practice. No girls to talk with, to share secrets with, no guys to kiss. High school wasn't as it was in the movies for me. High school was a day-by-day existence to get me to graduation. What was so awful was that I didn't know what came next?

Momma was as concerned as Tucker was, I was sure. When she got a second to spend with me, it was always the inquisition. Why can't you be more like Tucker? Where is your personality? Where is your voice? What happened to you? Repeatedly. Tucker motioned for Luke, and I watched him pull Momma out of the kitchen. They were both headed this way. Great. An intervention.

Momma smiled and kissed Tucker on the cheek. "I heard about your date tonight, Jazzline. It sounds wonderful."

I sighed. Great, they already figured I could not say no. "Sure."

Luke started in with his fatherly like voice booming a little too over the top. He had no children of his own, so he fell into us half-grown, but he did a decent job, to be honest. "Your mother and I think this is a fresh start for you. You need to get out and have fun. We want you to experience life. Going on this double date will be a confidence booster."

My mouth gaped open. "Double date? Tucker?"

He squirmed in his seat. "I forgot to mention that. Bree's parents won't let her go out unless her older brother goes. She has two brothers. I haven't met them yet, so I don't know what you're getting yourself into. but I'm sure if they are anything like Bree, you'll love him."

Momma chimed in, trying her best to put it on thick in front of her crowd. "It will be fine, Jazzline. You don't even have to like him. You have to go. One step towards dating this one guy will lead to other guys, and other guys, and soon you'll have a record of accomplishment like Tucker."

I laughed at that. Not in a million years could I ever catch up with him. Tucker beamed. "Thanks so much, Mrs. Chicand, for believing in me. I have changed this time. Brianna is the one."

Momma's eyebrows rose. "I can't wait to meet her tonight. Jazzline, don't even think about coming to the back and helping. We have it all covered."

I threw up my hands and sighed. Great. My actual first date, double date or whatever, and I would be at Chica's. Couldn't Tucker be more creative than that? I needed to queue Netflix's romance categories and try to get Tucker the hookup. At least I would feel right at home. The big goof.

Momma handed me a wad of bills. I wasn't the girl that had a credit card with her name on it even though I could have if I asked. I wasn't the girl that even had a bank account. Material objects meant nothing to me. But Momma was handing me money for something, and I was sure it wasn't for my dinner.

Luke smiled and pulled me out of the booth. "Now get prettied up like your momma. We can't wait to see you fixed up. We're sure you'll be stunning."

Tucker said, "I'll get Alex. I can't wait to put him through all of this pain and torture. It'll be hilarious. Come on."

The wad of money was crushed between my tiny hand and his large calloused one. I murmured a thank you to Momma and Luke, and we were off hunting our little man to kidnap him yet again for a prettied-up day of fun.

When we made it inside Jeepers Kreepers, Tucker wished he were with a serial murderer I was sure, after I let him have it. How dare he try to push me towards a double date, which was different words than chaperone? And how dare he force a makeover.

But there I was, going into Studio 7, being dropped off by an elated Tucker who was past cloud nine.

I called out to him, "She better love you, you moron."

He grinned that boyish grin that every girl dreamed he'd flash her. "I'm betting on it."

Alex rolled around in the receptionist's chair flipping through entertainment magazines as I was being tortured to death, plucked, and hair blown. I couldn't help but visualize all of the girls in the world that enjoyed this kind of abuse. Then, it hit me. I was alone. I had no one to impress.

The makeup stylist commented that I had a soft, natural face. When I finally caught sight of myself, I saw nothing like the Jazzline I knew. It was a definite improvement before walking in.

Alex was spiking his hair out with some stolen moose, and I gave him the evil eye for us to leave before they noticed him. Tucker was right outside with front curb service, and he even jumped out and opened the car door for me. I gave him the most peculiar look.

He laughed. "I know. I know. I'm practicing for tonight. That hair, though."

I blushed for some silly reason. "Stop it. Who's this girl anyway?"

After a few beating-with-a-hammer attempts to start Jeepers Kreepers, he fired up the ignition, and we sped off heading to the mall. I told him to make a U-turn because I slipped the rest of Momma's money in a charity bucket at the counter of the salon. There was no way I would get a new outfit, too. Having my hair probed and eyebrows plucked was enough for a girl for one day. This girl, anyway.

Alex was back immersed playing his handheld video game, and Tucker began to tell me the whole story of how he met Brianna MacKenzie on the beach two weeks earlier. They had been on the phone every waking second he could talk to her. She was his love. His one true soul mate. Had he been dipping into his Momma's romance novel stash stuffed by the toilet or watching Lifetime? Where was my surfer-wanna-be, Rastafarian, alternative-loving player?

"So, where does she go to school?" Her name was still not familiar.

"St. James Academy. And her parents are filthy rich or something like that. She lives down at Pawley's Island on an oceanfront mansion. Sounds like a dream to me to be the poor surfer in love with the rich girl who has the entire world but chose me."

"What's with the parents and why do I have to be your chaperone? Like this really happens anymore?"

"I'm her first boyfriend, and her parents are super-freaky strict. She has to introduce them to me tonight, and I'm about to lose my mind. I've met no girl's parents before. And you have to come, too. See, they've been to Chica's. That was an in for me. That was a way to get them to even let me take her out. Nice to know you have influence somewhere in the world."

I tried my best to gain my composure. "Meet the parents, too? Come on, Tucker."

He knew how awful I was at talking.

He patted me again like a school kid. "It'll be fine. I'll be right there. Jazz, you've got to work on yourself. You take yourself way extreme and put yourself in a cardboard box under the pier. It's almost like you're some hermit crab."

I couldn't help but laugh at him. "You mean a hermit?"

He was so ridiculous at times, but to be honest, this time he was right. I never talked unless I was forced to. I never pushed a conversation or carried one through. People somehow read I was closed for business, and they left me alone, often hiding behind Tucker's massive frame and boisterous personality enough for the both of us and two more. That was where I liked to be.

"Whatever. You know what I mean. Everybody at Sea Side has to know that you're cool to be with me, but you're a freeze pop around them. They can't even get to see who you are because you won't let them."

I sighed, staring out at the traffic before me wishing that it would hurry up, so we could avoid this conversation. "But you know who I am. Isn't that enough."

Tucker frowned. His face was plastered with that concerned look again, and I hated it. "No, it's not. We'll be seniors, Jazz-a-licious. Seniors! You've spent all these years with nobody but me and little shrimp here. What'll happen after high school?"

He would be a marine biologist far away on some blue island shore. Me? I knew it wouldn't be a culinary school for sure, but Momma didn't know that, and I wasn't about to go there.

"No clue."

"I'm leaving, Jazz. You've got to open yourself up to other people, or I'll be worrying about you when I'm not here."

"What? Do you think I need a babysitter? I'm not the ten-year-old here."

He smirked. "Well, sometimes you act like it. You'll love Bree. You really will. She is kinda like you. She's different."

"What are you trying to say? That I'm different?" My eyes

twinkled at him because even though he was pushing my buttons, I could never be mad at him.

They chimed in, and I couldn't help but laugh. "No. You're weird."

Maybe it wasn't normal to be so closed up. There could be other life forms out there that could relate to me, and we could be friends and hang out.

Tucker dropped Alex off at Chica's, then me at the house to change. I needed to put together an outfit but my black work pants and one of Momma's blouses would have to do. There was no way I would get dressed up for this.

The doorbell rang. It couldn't be Tucker. He never rang doorbells. Then, it hit me. Tucker had left me here stranded for this stranger to pick me up. When I opened the door, I tried my best to smile but it all came out wrong.

The guy was not what I expected, but then again, I didn't quite know what to expect. I didn't even know his name. He held out his hand to me, and I wasn't sure what he wanted me to do. Would he shake my hand or kiss it? So, I did nothing but stand there in front of him and stare. I thanked God that I knew for certain that this guy wouldn't be the one. It would make it a whole lot easier to get through the night. Then, I would get Tucker Lane for this. He'd be owing me big time. Like for the rest of his life.

CHAPTER 2

The Tide Is High

His lip moved to the side in this peculiar way, and I knew that he was just like me, trying to smile but not knowing what it looked like. His wire-framed glasses reminded me of Harry Potter, and when he spoke, his voice came out a little squeaky.

He coughed it away. "I'm Bree's oldest brother, Colin MacKenzie. Are you ready?"

He didn't ask my name, and I knew he couldn't have cared less.

I got up enough nerve to speak, admiring his choice of car. "What kind of car is this?"

He gasped. "You don't know about classic cars? This is a 68 Chevrolet Camaro, mint condition."

I looked for the Jeep, but it was long gone. Pawley's Island was about fifteen minutes away from my house. I hadn't gone there much, just passing through to go to Georgetown a few times with Momma for kitchen supplies. But Pawley's Island wasn't a place I would frequent. Tucker, either. He'd met Bree here. Wonder what she was doing down this far from her prim and proper, uppity-scaled universe.

We didn't speak a single word as we drove down Highway 17,

and I was so relieved. The silence wasn't even awkward. It just was. Thank God that he wasn't a talker and asked me stupid first date questions. It was a silent drive, no music playing, with the rushing of cars around us.

When we arrived at his house, there was a grand entry gate with security codes and mechanical iron gates. He followed tiny lights up a cobblestoned driveway that rose and then fell to a magnificent castle-like mansion sitting right by the sea. It was like something from a fairytale, and if I were the romantic type, I was sure I would've been swept away. I raised my eyebrows at Tucker as we all walked in together to a foyer that was as large as our entire houses combined.

When we were inside, I couldn't help but stare at the little girl that was standing beside Tucker. Her face was heart shaped, doll-like. Her hands swayed as she spoke, and she bounded up against me, flinging her arms around me as if she had missed me for a lifetime. I stared wild-eyed at Tucker as she gushed about how happy she was to meet me. How she'd heard so much about me. How she couldn't thank me enough for doing this for them.

She giggled and pointed down the hallway as Colin disappeared around the corner. "He's not the sociable type, Colin. But he is a sweet guy once you get to know him. He's into his computers. I'm sure he told you all about it on the way here."

I smiled at her. The silence was golden. I would've taken the sound of cars over the sound of tech talk any day. Then, I saw movement at the staircase. A guy was springing up them two steps at a time. His hair was long and dark, flowing way past his shoulders. It was thick, and I wondered what it would feel like to put my hands through it. My hand flew up to my cheeks, burning to the touch. I was sure I'd taken off the first layer of the professional makeup but didn't care.

Tucker looked to Bree who was staring at me. Her eyes had changed. The blue had become more vibrant like the color was pooling darker clouds in her eyes as we watched. Her smile was radiating from within her, and I felt like she could burst forth in a ray of light.

I looked to Tucker, and he shrugged. "Baby, are you okay?"

She hugged herself as tears fell down her cheeks. "Oh, Tucker. This is so wonderful. I would've never thought it could happen." She was an exploding burst of sunshine, and I knew why he loved her. His sun to her rays. They were the same. And just as confusing, because why she was crying in the middle of her first date entrance made no sense at all.

He laughed and looked at me. "Man, I've never had a girl so excited to go out with me before."

That was the perfect cue for Mr. and Mrs. MacKenzie to walk into the room, with a still nervous looking Colin at their side. Bree pushed the tears aside, ran up to her father and mother and swung her arms around them. She whispered something to them and instead of looking at Tucker, they caught my eye. Both of them stared at me with this dazed expression.

Feelings of inadequacy and awkwardness evaded my senses. Something was going on, and I could feel it in my spirit.

Bree then brought them to Tucker. "Momma, Daddy, I'd like for you to meet my boyfriend, Tucker Lane, and his best friend, Jazzline Chicand."

Tucker held out his hand to shake theirs, and Mr. MacKenzie stuck his massive hairy arm to clasp his. Tucker winced, and I wanted to laugh. This would not be easy. I'd love to see Tucker sweat this one out. I felt a little sorry for him as we were leaving. It was an interrogation. It was you-better know-she-is-fifteen stare. You better get her in by ten. You better stay chaperoned, or you're dead. Bree was stammering and pouting, her cheeks turning a sweet pink, but she endured it to go out with him.

I had to make it to the Camaro, and for the first time in my life, I preferred Jeepers Kreepers to any other car in the world. No words were spoken, and before long we were at Chica's. We were being waited on and getting goo-goo eyed from all of the employees. One idiot server even took a picture of me I was sure they would post it on my locker in the back. Or worse yet, on our social media. I'd kill Tucker. Then, I'd go after the server boy. Thou Shalt Not Kill. Christian faith, hold me up.

When the little lovey-dovey date was over, I was almost sick to my stomach. This time because I saw a true connection between the two of them. There was a way that Tucker looked at her I couldn't describe. It was in his eyes. He didn't have to say a word to her. He leaned in a little, and she'd shift her weight, and they'd be right there, no space. They melded into each other as we walked out of the restaurant, and her tiny hand wrapped between his massive one like from an old movie scene. It was too strange and intimate to see, and I couldn't help but turn away a little embarrassed.

I was walking out with the loopy computer geek brother who happened to not once allow me to talk for the evening. I'd heard enough about computer upgrades and system requirements for the new program he was writing for an early admittance summer program to MIT once Bree got him to talk. I never thought we'd get him to shut up. I didn't know where MIT was, but I was sure it was up north somewhere. Far enough away from here that I'd never see him again.

He thought he was escorting me to his car, but I stood by the Jeep holding on to the door handle until my knuckles were a solid white. I was sure that Tucker could sense my foreboding, and he looked to Bree for approval. She smiled up at him with innocent, adoring eyes and asked for me to come along as if it were her idea. I loved her already. How could you not? I wanted to take her aside to put in points for Tucker and tell her he was a goofy, yet adorable big Teddy bear, but I didn't think she needed a Tucker tutorial. She was already his.

On the ride back to her house, Bree told us more about her family. She had two older brothers. One had just turned eighteen, a senior at St. James and was the one with the long dark hair flying up the staircase. Why wasn't I hooked up with him? Why some guy about to leave for college? But then again, I didn't want to be hooked up with anybody, so it had better be with the older one because something about the other one...

Then, she leaned in against Tucker and whispered, "They're perfect for each other. If only. Oh, I wish and pray."

I asked, "What? Who?"

She sighed. "Oh, nothing. I want to thank you so much for going with us so I could spend tonight with Tucker. It has meant so much to me."

She smiled at Tucker, and I felt the Jeep swerve. I knocked him in the head to get his attention back on the road and off her soft, blue eyes that mirrored her love for him. She was just a kid. We were too young for all of this. You couldn't feel like that, could you?

He grinned at me through the crooked mirror. "Whatever I can do for you, name it."

I frowned. "Never, and I mean never, let me alone with that guy again."

He held up his two fingers. "Scout's honor. But really, Jazz. How can we pay you back?"

"Go buy me a car."

He bellowed out a big one. "Yeah, right? You'd miss ol' Jeepers if you had to leave her. Admit it."

The cracked seat was cutting into my leg. Sure, I'd miss her and all her smells. All I wanted was a car of my own to get me and Alex around without haphazard driving and speedy deliveries. Why did it have to be so difficult?

Bree asked, "Have you tried asking for one?"

"Of course not. I don't think I should have to do that."

She looked confused. "But why not?"

I shrugged. "I don't know. Maybe it is a given when you turn sixteen you get a car."

She frowned. "But I thought you were seventeen."

I threw my hands up in the air. "Exactly my point."

She went back to the first question. "But if you ask, then it's out there in the open and it can be either yes or no. There, it's that simple. Ask."

Tucker squeezed her shoulder. "It's not that easy with Jazzy-old-girl. She doesn't talk much. She doesn't demand or ask or fight or speak to anyone. I'm surprised she talked to you. She is just Jazz."

She turned to me then, her full attention on me, her gaze intent as if what she was about to say would be life changing. "How can you not speak, when you have such a lovely tone to your voice. It's almost melodic, like a slow Jazz song."

Tucker added, "Oh, she has a voice. You ought to hear her sing. Go ahead, Jazz. Sing for her. But she only sings when she thinks nobody is listening or when she gets nervous and stuff. It's getting worse lately, and I haven't figured out why."

I swatted him again in the head. "Stop it, both of you. I'm fine like I am."

She grabbed my hand and squeezed. Her gesture felt way too mature for a girl of fifteen. "How can you ever let the world know who you are if you don't let them see? I know what I see, a beautiful strong woman, and I know that you deserve it. You remind me so much of him, it's ridiculous."

"Him? Tucker? No way. We're like the complete opposite!"

She said, "No. I meant my brother. You both deserve it."

I asked, "Deserve what? A car?"

Bree leaned through the window of the car and punched in the security code. She stepped out of the car and skipped up the steps holding out her hand to Tucker as she did so. She called out to me as I waited in the car for them.

"You deserve a life, Jazzline Chicand. Go get one. I dare you."

Then, she kissed Tucker full on the lips, rocking him back against the brick entryway before the light flickered on and off, and she pushed him aside. He stood there for a moment dazed then held out his hand to shake Mr. MacKenzie's hand. I waved at him as I pushed down a giggle. His large muscled arm waved back in an awkward motion, and he pulled Bree along with him through the massive iron gated door.

Tucker fell in the seat beside me. "So, isn't she a dream?"

I climbed in front, kicking off my shoes and resting my feet against the dash like always. "Yeah, she's a nice little girl."

I emphasized the little, and he snarled. "You know you like her. I could tell."

In fact, I did. "She's nice, and I can see why you love her. Who couldn't? She seems perfect for you, Tucker. Be good to her. Don't let it be like the others." The others included cheating, lying, fast, stupid fights, and all that corny crap that never amounted to anything.

He squealed out of the driveway. "Don't worry. I don't need the talk about this one. She's my baby girl, and I love her for sure. With you and her like that, talking, it did me some good."

"Well, I'm thrilled for you, Tucker. And I wouldn't mind another chaperone escort, as long as maybe it's me and Alex. The whole double dating thing isn't my style. Keep that in mind next time."

He grinned. "I know. You don't have to warn me again. Maybe this time it'll be enough for them to see I can take her out alone, and they can trust me."

And I would have thought so, too. But not for the MacKenzie's. I even pulled in Alex to meet them the next night, tagging along on their dates for the next week. Every night it was somewhere different. We went midnight bowling, found ourselves on the boat ride at Brookgreen Gardens and walking through the zoo. We ate brick oven pizzas at Bovine's and danced like maniacs at Charlie's to the Twisted Brothers knockoff band. It went on and on until I was just about sick of seeing all the sappy love exchanges, I felt like being thrown in a demon hole would have been better for my self-concept than going on another Tucker-Bree outing. But I couldn't say no, and Alex fell in love with her, too. We were going along fine until Momma got involved.

Bree spoke right before it was time to take her home, "Let's go by Chica's."

Tucker smiled. "Oh, yeah. I almost forgot."

Alex was asleep in the backseat with me. There was no way any sane person could do that with all the jumping and jarring, but Alex's little body seemed immune to it. Get him still when the stars came out, and he was out.

"Where now?"

Tucker was trying to maintain a level of seriousness in his tone, "Your mother would like to have a talk with you, young lady?"

I pleaded, "Don't take me by Chica's. It's close to closing time and I'd be forced to do hard labor."

Bree grinned, showing her rows of aligned white teeth. "No, it's nothing like that. We've already laid out the plan. We have to be there to witness it."

I had no clue what she was talking about, but whatever it was they couldn't help but show the excitement on their faces. It was as if they had been scheming this for a while now and were at the final push of watching their baby being delivered.

Momma flipped the closed sign when we drove up to the parking lot. How convenient. Another ambush. She even had Luke with her at our table with a full basket of breadsticks, a weakness of mine, placed strategically to soften me up.

I couldn't help but sigh. "Okay guys, what is this about now? No more dates, okay?"

Tucker still had Alex in his arms, and he transferred him to lean up against Momma. He didn't even wake up. Momma started, "I didn't know that you wanted a car, Jazzline? All you had to do was ask. You seemed fine riding around with Tucker everywhere."

Wait? What was this? No ambush? Relief flooded over me like a soothing wave. Was it a car conversation? When I told them they could get me a car, I was joking. They took it and paved the blacktop for me. How lovely.

"But there's a catch," continued Luke. There it was. I knew that it couldn't be that easy. "Jazzline, we're all a little concerned for you, that you aren't out with other teenagers. And your..."

Momma added, finishing his sentences like she always did, "Confidence and self-esteem seem so low to us. We want you to snap out of it."

"I didn't know that you guys even noticed." I couldn't believe that an up could spiral to a down in two seconds.

She mumbled, "We'll let you pick out any car you want if you promise us one thing."

Any car? That would be a hoot. I could see myself going to a Bentley dealership or maybe snatch a Red Ferrari with those doors that pop up at the sides. "Any car?"

Momma said, "Yes, but with one condition."

I braced myself. "Let me hear it."

Tucker jumped in like the Flash. "Be in a summer play program with me and Bree, and you have to have a speaking part. Put on the play in front of an audience, and you have to want it. It's for charity, if that makes you feel better. I know that's your thing."

I thought I would lose my stomach then, and I pushed the garlicky plate away from my proximity. "You're kidding me, right?"

Momma smiled and patted my hand. "Well, it's settled. First Take starts tomorrow morning at nine. I've seen the rehearsal schedule and planned for extra help around here. You'll be out with other people your age, talking, and having a blast before you know it. I've got Alex all figured out. You don't worry about a thing."

Tucker was already sliding out of the booth, pulling Bree along behind him, smiling like the Joker. Harley Quinn and the Joker, those funny little schemers. "Thanks, Mrs. Chicand. See ya later, Luke."

Bree giggled. "Bye, Jazz. See you in the morning."

I stood there stammering. "Wait. I didn't say I would."

Momma pushed me along towards the kitchen doors, and in a singsong voice, she replied, "But you didn't say no either. You'd better get to work if it's luxury you're after. There's a lot of dishes to clear away."

Now, Tucker and Bree were halfway down the coast making out, and I was up to my elbows in leftovers. Didn't they know the thought of being in some performance was like sending me to a firing squad? What they were asking me to do was way too impossible for me. But, then again, it wouldn't hurt for me to be a little more open. I was thinking about that a lot, well more like every night after watching Bree and Tucker and getting dropped off at night to walk up to my entryway alone. I needed to stop hiding. It was time.

But that? Come on. That was total exposure, out there, and a speaking part? And why did Tucker want to be in some play? Was he giving up summer football workouts with the team for this? That didn't take long for me to figure out. Bree must love this. She had that theater look about her. Okay, she was in the play. Tucker needed me there so he could be there, and they thought they'd throw in the car thing for leverage for me. Maybe they meant well, but in all honesty, they seemed like selfish little schemers at that moment. As I wiped leftover fettuccine sauce off my hands, he better be glad he was far away from me or I'd strangle him.

CHAPTER 3

Let It Be Me

"Come together boys and girls," shouted Dot Hammond, an exuberant, bouncy-haired director of First Take Productions. "We have so much planned for this summer, the largest production to date, so much to look forward to. I want you to visualize a transformational summer. Close your eyes."

She gave us the look like she meant for us to do it, so I did it.

"Your first step inside. Your first voice. Your first call. Your first applause."

She kept on with the firsts, and I couldn't help but smile at her ability to dramatize a situation. But if I thought, let my mind be free and go there, it was like she was talking to me. This would be a lot of firsts for me. Could I do this?

"Now, who is ready for Summer in Love series?"

Oh, great. A love story. Why couldn't we be doing a comedy or better yet a tragedy, since my life was turning out to be one?

It was amazing how many tanned and beautiful arms shot up around the room. These future cast members were not first timers with Dot. She was their leader of this little band of thieves, and they all seemed at ease rocking back and forth in the luxurious reclined theater seats. I turned to watch Tucker's expression in all of this, but he was so engrossed in looking at his Bree that I don't even think he cared.

I wished I'd had a moment alone with him so I could pick at him about this but that wasn't possible these days. I kind of missed my pre-Bree days with him. But I knew that he loved her, and I was happy for him. I wasn't the best friend that would grow green with envy and try my best to split them apart. I'm sure that existed in the world, but it wasn't my style.

Bree leaned across him and whispered, "You'll love her. She's a wonderful director and very inspiring. I know you don't get the theater thing, but trust me, it's magical."

Maybe I needed a little magic this summer. Looking around at all the other teenagers made it such a relief to me we were doing this at Pawley's Island territory and not down the road on my surf and turf. At least here, nobody would know me. Nobody would care to, either. I'd pop in the summer show, say some waitress line or something, like, "Can I take your order? Kiss my grits." And there would be a car in my driveway, that simple. I was already considering a Prius. A smile burst across my face like a lit fire-cracker.

Tucker sensed it in me and asked, "What's with the change?"

I shrugged. "Maybe I can do this. Maybe it won't be so difficult."

I wished I could have held on to that initial reaction. But when it was time to step out on the stage for the first audition calls for determining placement I freaked. And I mean, freaked out. My mind began to swirl, and I knew that I might even faint. Tucker started fanning me, and Bree pushed a glass of water at me, but it smelled stale, and I leaned into the bag that Tucker had prepared, flying around from his back pocket like a superhero move. Nice one. Throw up Girl and Plastic Bag Man would be our graphic novel names.

What an impression to make on a bunch of rich, private school kids. One haughty, perfect looking girl snickered at me, but when Bree glanced her way, she was silent and turned away.

Bree had an air of importance around her. She gave me a quick hug as she took my place to give me time to get it together. She stepped on to that stage as if a force outside of her was carrying her. I wasn't even sure if her feet even touched the black floor.

She purred, "Hello, Dot. It's nice to see you again."

I leaned in closer to the curtain and watched out at the faces of the other kids in the audience. There were all impressed with Bree. She was something else.

Dot clapped. "Oh, darling. What do you have prepared for me today?"

The audition was an open call for a musical Dot had not revealed to us yet. There was some secret show of love Dot cradled in her arms like a baby since she introduced herself that morning. All I knew was that we were to go up on the grand stage and sing and dance or do our thing, whatever that was, and she would decide where we were best fit to be. Bree didn't sing, but she danced across that stage like an angel with wings that only Tucker and I could see. She was amazing, and I caught myself holding my breath to the end. Tucker had tears well up in his eyes. Big baby.

Ms. Dot stood up and danced on her feet in place, screaming, "Bravo! Wonderful, darling! Truly!"

Bree danced off the stage and fell into Tucker's arms. He whispered something in her ear, and she smiled at him. The love between them was something special.

Dot called out Tucker's name, and he walked on the stage, not as confident, but he made it there, front and center standing on the tape in the floor marking center stage. She asked him what was his talent, and I was sure that he would go into some long monologue about his gorgeous tan and biceps, his surfing abilities, and his way with the ladies.

But I almost choked when I heard him say, "Loving Bree."

Just like that. It came right out of him, unashamed, in front of perfect strangers. She put both her arms around my waist and squeezed me. I wanted to shrug her off because my stomach felt too weak to even be touched, but I couldn't.

She leaned into my shoulder. "Look at my man out there."

And I did. And I laughed. We all did as he bellowed out, "Row your boat," like he meant to impress someone. The song was a hit with Ms. Dot because she screamed and applauded almost as she did with Bree's dance. I knew that it was my turn next, but I did the only thing I could do, crash and escape.

I told Bree I had to go to the bathroom a quick second but bypassed the ladies' room, trying to find an exit. At the end of the hallway was a room labeled prop and design and had a Do Not Enter sign blaring across it with a red marker. This room held all of her secrets to her show for the summer. I needed to know what I was getting myself into.

I slipped into the room but couldn't find a light switch. I could make out a few props, a boat, candelabras, a phantom mask on a statue, and then the heavy door closed in behind me. When I turned back to leave, realizing that none of the props would matter to me anyway because it wasn't like Tucker and I were into musicals in our free time, the door was locked. This couldn't be. Where was the light switch? I fumbled my way down the wall, nothing. On the other side of the doorframe, nothing. Panic began to swell and rise with me stopping at my throat where a scream was about to form, and I knew that I was going to lose it there in the dark.

I whispered, "Breathe, Jazzline. Breathe."

Instead of moving forward I slunk down against the door and prayed that I wouldn't get sick again. I texted Tucker and he would come to find me. Simple.

So, I did what I only know how to do as I waited. Sing. Words came to me, nothing I could do about it. "Let it be my time, let it be me. Being in this time makes me believe. Somehow, I will find him and he will make my life complete. Let it be my time, let it be me."

Then, something crashed in the room, and I heard a sharp curse followed by a pained grunt. Someone was there, and I felt paralyzed with fear. "Who's there?"

My mind went to a dark place and I swore if I got out of that room alive, I'd never watch another scary movie on the late night again.

His voice was low, "It's okay. I won't hurt you."

I panicked by the doorframe and my hand clasped around the knob trying again to force it open with no use.

I asked, "Where are you?"

He whispered again and this time I knew he was closer. "I'm right in front of you. It's okay, I promise."

He switched on a beam from his key ring and pointed it at the floor. I followed the tiny light as it made its way closer to me. He was tall. I was sure of that. His body was bigger than Tucker's, his shoulders were broad, and his hair was long in the shadows.

I was still shaking and held my hands around my waist trying to steady myself because I didn't want to fall in the dark.

"Did you hear me?" I prayed, God, please let him say no.

He said, "Yes, and it was beautiful. I don't know that one. What performance was it from?"

I didn't understand his meaning and was silent a little too long because he continued. "Is that from a musical? Which one? I thought I knew them all."

So, this was a drama guy. Great, computer dates to musical madmen.

I couldn't believe that he heard me sing. And, he'd said it was beautiful. "No."

He stepped closer to me, this time I could make out the shadow of his hand reaching out to me, but he never touched me. It was just out there between us as he spoke.

"Then, did you write it?"

"I sing when I'm nervous."

He laughed, and the sound of it echoed around the room. It was a deep laugh, and I felt myself get lost in it. His voice, his laugh, my heart. They were connecting in this dark place, and I knew that whoever was in front of me would be the one. The one. Here he was, and I couldn't even see his face. I didn't have to because his words were like music to me, beautiful and melodic. Washing over my soul and taking me to a place I'd never felt before. It was happening, and I was letting it. My mind was free, I was open to it, and I wanted to cry. He couldn't see me as the tears fell down my face. He wouldn't know what he had done to me in the dark by his calm whispers and laughter.

I'd grown soft. Bree and Tucker were influencing my brain and allowing me to believe that love could happen like a dream. Like how Tucker described it.

His said, "You sing like an angel. You are an angel."

God, why couldn't I be strong? The strong and silent type, not the weakling mute girl. His hand found mine, and the flashlight bounced off my Converse to the tile floor as he held firmly to my hand, pulling me through the crowded room. I could feel his strength in his giant hand, and it was so warm. His fingers entwined with mine, a perfect fit.

We were to be a perfect fit.

His thumb caressed the inside of my hand. "Why are you crying? It's okay. I know how to get us out of here. I know another way."

He'd found me vulnerable and alone like I'd felt all my life. But how could I say something like that to him? How could I even describe the feelings that were washing over me by him holding my hand? I followed the little light bouncing on the tiles as we made our way to the back of the room and out a second door, leading out a side exit.

The light in the hallway was brilliant, and I had to turn away. Tears were still there, wet on my face, and I didn't want him to see me like that. I wiped them away and tried to regain my composure. He still held my hand, and I found myself following behind him in the narrow hallway only big enough for one person to fit through. He was filling up space in front of me. Then, we were back. Just like that. Like I'd never gone. Bree was still there waiting. Turning her head this way and that, looking for me to return.

When she saw me, she smiled, but then it was switched to confusion when she saw us together.

I asked, "Did you get my text?"

Tucker pulled his phone out of his pocket, "Sorry, Jazz. I had it on mute."

I realized that I'd never had a chance to see his face. He was in front of me the whole time either in the dark or in the hallway. We were still holding hands, and I prayed he would not let go.

Bree whispered, "Seth MacKenzie, what did you go and do?"

He shrugged, taking my hand with him, up and down with his body movements, as if we were one. "I found her."

Did he mean it? Like, found her, like in me, the love of his life. Then he finished. "I found Christy." And he pulled me out on the stage with him.

Ms. Dot walked up on the stage to meet us. He was a MacKenzie. I'd come to love his sister over the course of our everyday adventures together, I knew that I'd fallen in love with him in the dark room.

He whispered something into Ms. Dot's ear, and she turned her back to me and clapped, startling me back to where I was standing, center stage, yet not frightened because he was still holding my hand.

She said, "There we have it, my young pupils. The cat is out of the bag, or the mask is revealed. Who can tell us the Summer of Love haunting retelling that will captivate our audience and leave them breathless for more?"

Being on the stage with the hot lights beaming down on me made it impossible for me to even see the audience.

Someone squealed out in the sea of seats, "I know!"

Others chimed in, "I know, it's The Phantom of St. James High!"

Seth led me off the stage to where Bree and Tucker were still standing. I went straight to Tucker, letting go of Seth's hand. Feeling it rip from me like an electrical shock, tingling against my fingertips.

He stood beside Bree, and I peeked around Tucker at him. He was whispering to his sister, and their heads were so close together I couldn't make out what they were saying. Tucker said for me to come on and follow him, but I wanted to stay by Seth. I didn't want to go too far, but I didn't have a choice. He grabbed me by the arm and moved me back down the side steps from behind the stage, and that was when I saw all of the faces of the cast watching Ms. Dot's elaboration on the details of our Summer of Love performance. They could have cared less that I'd been on that stage a second ago, crying my eyes out. Maybe they were used to performances like that. Maybe they thought it was part of the show.

We sat back down in the seats, and I felt the nervous energy flowing through my body, pulling me tight as a cord. I felt alive and on fire. I felt scared and confused. I felt. He walked out with Bree, arm in arm. Both of them so different, yet so alike that it was scary. He was so tall, at least six foot four, and she was five two. She was fair, with sparkling blue eyes and strawberry blonde hair that flowed around her as she walked. His hair was as dark as night, falling over like waves of massive curls hiding half of his face. He wore the black molded phantom mask on the right side of his face. So, he was the tall statue standing in the prop room when I had first opened the door.

As they made their way closer to us, I couldn't help but continue to stare at Seth. His shoulders hunched down as if he was trying to appear small in that huge frame, and it looked awkward and out of place to her graceful glide beside him. I could tell he knew my eyes were following him, but he refused to meet my gaze. She waited at the end of the row until I could move down so she could find her way beside Tucker again. Two people separated us but I still felt connected to him as if he were right here still holding my hand. Instead, I held both of mine between my legs, squeezing them to calm the feelings that were raging in me.

It was so hard to follow Ms. Dot's exaggerated movements

and swaying of her hands and all of her darlings, but it stood out when she began to call the cast list out. I didn't know the musical they had adapted, so my mind focused on what I did know.

Feelings of gratitude washed over me, and it had nothing to do with the car possibility. It had everything to do with that boy sitting crunched into the seat next to Bree, with his head down, watching the floor.

We would rehearse seven hours a day, every weekday for the next five weeks. The cast was being called out. Bree was Megan, the cheerleader dance team leader. Tucker was playing the part of a football star named, Rao. Seth was the Phantom of St. James. I'd already figured that out. He still hadn't removed the mask.

Then, Ms. Dot twirled around at her announcement. Bree held up her cell phone so her Momma could hear the news. "And the starring role of our leading lady Christy goes to, Jazzline Chicand. Oh, that's just a darling name. I can see it on our billboard now. That's a name that deserves to be in lights."

And I was sure that was the last thing I heard before my head cracked the seat in front of me as I passed out cold.

CHAPTER 4

Kiss on my List

Seth's voice brought me back. I could feel his hot breath against the cool of my neck, and I leaned against him.

He whispered, "It's okay, angel. It's all right. I'm here."

Then, my eyes popped open, and I could see the concerned faces around me. Bree and Tucker, Ms. Dot and a few of the other kids stood in the rows in front of me, peering down at me with worry. Okay, I went a little drama queen on them. Maybe I was cut out for this stage stuff, after all.

I pleaded with Tucker in a whisper as I managed to get back on my feet, squeezing his arm, making a mark with my fingernails. "Tell them, Tucker. Tell them I can't speak like that."

Bree rubbed my arms. "You'll be fine."

But I wouldn't be. A lead role? I just needed a speaking part, like pass the cheese, please. I felt like a complete fool with strangers watching every blink, every sweat bead pouring down my face, every rapid breath. And then, he was there, covering my hand with his and taking it off Tucker's arm. I focused on his eyes. They were the color of a tiger's, yellow, with twinges of light and dark brown, split in an unusual pattern. His eyes were like the flickering of a candle. Questioning me and probing without speaking yet I heard him. Because when he spoke, it was over.

Seth whispered close to my ear, "I'll be with you every day. I'll help you practice. I promise you. You'll not be alone."

I turned to Ms. Dot, and her encouraging gaze comforted me. Bree and Tucker were waiting for me to say something, anything. Seth was towering over me, and I felt my body leaning into him for support.

How could I say no? I felt my face try to form a smile. Signal received.

Ms. Dot exploded with glee. "Okay, it's settled then. Study groups begin."

I was still in a daze as we made our way with our heavy scripts in hand to the back of the theater. As I climbed up the incline, I couldn't help but see all of the empty seats that were waiting to be filled with a bright-eyed audience. An audience to see me and to hear me sing. Bree and Tucker didn't seem to notice. They were so into each other they wouldn't have cared who was in the room with them as long as they could be together.

We were in the far corner away from everyone huddled together in plastic, orange school desk chairs. Tucker and Seth looked silly in those seats, trying to get their bodies to fit. Bree was rocking back and forth in excitement, tipping it over. She leaned over and kissed her brother on the cheek, and he smiled at her. So, they were the close ones in the family. They seemed to speak to each other without even making a sound.

I heard her whisper, "I know."

Seth squeezed her hand, and a sad expression crossed his face.

Tucker waved the book. "Okay, Tootie Fruitie. Let's get this thing started."

I nudged him in the leg. "Please, Tucker. Please tell me that didn't happen? How can I do this?"

Tucker looked over my head to Seth's and smiled. He knew him. He'd met him and he'd never told me about him. I was really going to get him now. "I told you she didn't talk. Why did you put her in that position? You also know she can't say no."

"What else did you tell them about me?"

"Enough," said Bree. "All we need to know that we love you."

I wanted to pull my desk closer to Seth's, but I'd topple over and land on my face. I'd already made one scene today. I didn't want to fall right into another.

Seth shrugged. "I don't know. I'm sorry, but not sorry at the same time. I was in the prop room because Mrs. Dot had me looking for the lanterns, and I heard her sing. That's when I knew."

Bree frowned. "I've been trying to get her to sing for me for weeks. Tucker said she is amazing, and she should be on a reality show kind of good. How did you do it?"

They were talking around me as if I wasn't there, so I had to speak up to remind them. "I didn't know he was there."

Tucker crossed his arms. "Then, there. We have the problem solved. Did you see how it looked up there, Jazz? You really can't see anybody. You can imagine that no one is there."

I shrugged. "Or that everybody is naked. Yeah, I know where this is going. I've tried all of that before."

Seth said, "Or you can just let go."

Let go. Let go of my inhibitions and feel? I thought that was what I'd been doing since I met him.

Tucker responded, "That would be the day when monkeys really climb the Empire State Building."

Bree giggled. "I think you're supposed to say when pigs fly."

He put his arm around her shoulder and pulled her close. "That one's been used too much. I try to be original."

She kissed him and replied, "No. That was being original. Nobody has ever kissed me like that."

He joked. "Wait a minute here, dear. I thought you said I was the first boy you've kissed."

I held up my hand in protest. "Okay, enough. Let's look what you evil kanevils have gotten me into."

I tried counting the lines but I stopped after twenty-eight. Okay, this was serious. My voice was on the edge of a whiny whisper, and I hated the way it sounded. "Really, Tucker. I can't do this. You know I can't."

Bree said, "Well, it's about time you did."

Tucker closed the book and hit me square on the head. "Stop beating yourself up over this. I have connections. Seth and Bree will help us."

I looked to Seth then. He still wouldn't look at me, and his hands were gripping the script like he could have torn it apart.

Bree's eyes lit up. "I have an idea. Let's go back to the house and watch the old black and white movie. That might help since you've never seen the musical. Momma and Daddy flew us to New York last year to see it on Broadway. Remember meeting the Phantom, Seth. Wasn't it like the best night?"

Seth said, "Yeah, it was a night to remember."

Tucker stood up and stretched. "Let's go. I like that idea better than being here cramped up."

Bree pulled him down to her, still having to stand on her tiptoes, kissing him yet again. "Let me go clear it with Ms. Dot. I'm sure she will be fine with it."

We watched as Bree sauntered off in search of Ms. Dot who was rummaging through ruff totes on the edge of the stage with a study group. When Bree made her way there to her, they parted like the Red Sea. Ms. Dot handed her a few objects, gave her two pecks on the cheek, and she was back running towards us. How she could run in heels was beyond me?

She said, "Here. Isn't this cool. She said that we have to wear something from the costume department at all times when we're studying. To put us into character."

Tucker flipped a black Fedora on his head and frowned. "This will be hot."

She tickled him. "You're so hot already. You'll burn this place down."

My breath caught when she handed me a beautiful ring. It

was a cluster of costume diamonds so huge that it weighed my hand down when I put it on my finger. Seth stopped me, pulled it off, and slid it on my ring finger.

He said, "No, it has to be this one. It's a promise ring from Rao."

I said, "What, you mean Tucker? Oh, Jesus, help me now."

Bree laughed. "It's okay. You don't have to really kiss him. And you give the ring to Seth to wear around his neck. He is the phantom that lives in the basement tunnels of the school."

"So, who do I end up with at the end?"

Seth said, "Me."

Bree laughed. "Not really. Don't spoil it."

But was he talking about the play or himself? I wasn't sure. When he spoke it, he stared straight into my eyes, and I felt a shiver go down my spine. I found my voice through it, and it was another whisper.

"I see what your prop is."

I reached to touch the porcelain mask, and it started to fall from his face. I was so embarrassed. What made me act so bold? He grabbed it, and turned his back to us. I heard Bree let out a sigh, and Tucker turned away.

Tucker said, "Why don't we just take this stuff off and get it over with right here. Might as well, Seth. I'm telling you that it won't matter. I know Jazzy, and it will mean nothing to her. Besides, I look ridiculous in this hat with my dreads all hanging out, and I know that half-mask thing has to be frustrating."

Bree said, "Now Tucker. We aren't going to start this off by disobeying Ms. Dot. We play by the rules."

She must not have known Tucker. But maybe I didn't know the new one because he tucked his tail under his legs and sulked behind her, his hat sitting crooked on his head. Then, out of nowhere, he started to do a little tap dance and popped it off his head, making it land square back in place.

Seth laughed. There it was again. My heart skipped to the sound. I wanted him to laugh for me but if I tried to do a little dance, I'd probably trip and break my leg. I followed behind them as we headed to Jeepers Kreepers.

I started to climb in the backseat of the Jeep when I heard his voice behind me. "Jazzline, please ride back with me?"

My eyes found Tucker's and he raised his eyebrows at me and puckered his lips. Oh, he was asking for it.

I tried to sound nonchalant, "No, that's okay. I'm fine with Tucker and Bree."

He put his hand on my shoulder. "Please, I insist."

"Okay."

But when we made it to his car, I knew that it would be him and me. There was no way this would be okay. Tucker wouldn't be there to make him laugh. Bree wouldn't be there to carry along the conversation and fill in the empty spaces. I followed him to a front space marked reserved and stopped at a sleek, black BMW. This was so unlike his brother's car, that musty ol' vintage Camaro. This was smooth, and I thought of Alex. He would have loved this ride.

He frowned. "What's wrong?"

I shook my head. "I need my brother."

He opened the car door for me and took quick strides to get inside.

My cell phone rang to the tune of the Darth Vader march, and I smiled. I waved the phone at Seth. "That's him now. Hey, Alex. I was just talking about you. Wait, what's wrong?"

I held my hand over the phone and bit my lip. "Could you please do me a favor?"

I hated to ask him, but there was no way I'd let Alex be bullied by some teenage jerks out by the Marshwalk.

He never took his eyes off the road. "Where is he?"

That was fast. This guy was a quick study. He must be a mind reader or something. "How did you know?"

He shrugged. "I could hear him screaming through the phone."

"Oh, he's at my mom's restaurant. Could we please go get him?"

He switched on his blinker and turned around at the next light. Tucker would have swerved over through the median. This guy was at least considerate.

I tried to calm Alex down as he yelled out expletives. "Go find Luke. I'm coming as fast as I can. Well, not that fast, but I will be there soon. Love you, too."

"How old is he?"

I flipped to a picture of him on my phone and held it up for him to see. "He's ten, and he's my baby."

"But you would have been like nine years old."

I realized how I made it sound. "No, no. I didn't mean it like that. I look after him. We take care of each other."

He smiled again, this time it moved the mask, and he held it in with his right hand as he maneuvered in traffic. "How does a ten-year-old possibly take care of you?"

I smiled back at him, this time feeling it for the first time on my face like he was Tucker. I smiled at him, and he was a stranger. I was talking to him and having a back and forth exchange that felt like a natural conversation. It was so easy.

"He's my little man. Like my little sidekick, and he puts up with me."

Seth chuckled. "You make it sound like I would think it a chore."

I shrugged. "I don't know. You tell me."

He leaned over, reaching for my hand that was lying on my lap, and he grabbed it from its resting place and brought it over to him. "I'll let you know soon."

And that was it. We didn't talk again until we reached the restaurant. I tried to focus on what he had on his playlist, but I didn't recognize any of the music. It sounded strange, with harps and horns, and what sounded like a bagpipe that I'd heard played in the Christmas parade downtown. The singer's voice was melodic. I stared out the window and searched for Alex behind the restaurant.

And there he was. He was hanging upside down from the deck, tied by his feet through the white poles with rope. I screamed, "What are you doing? Where is Luke?"

He frowned. "Well, I didn't do it. Don't look at me, Jazz. Those creeps over there have been messing with me all morning."

I looked towards the restaurant and its wraparound windows giving a full view of the inlet to search for any signs of Momma or Luke, but they were nowhere to be seen.

I was furious. "So, this is how she has you covered! Oh, God! Alex, I won't leave you again."

He smiled, an empty spot showing where his tooth fell out the night before making him look even more adorable if that was possible. "It's not so bad. All this blood rushing to my head is getting me prepared to battle the Cobra."

Seth was confused again. It would take him years to figure both of us out, and I was praying that he'd stick around long enough to get it. "Cobras? Here, in Murrell's Inlet?"

I laughed. "No. His video game. Come on, Alex. You're coming with us."

Seth picked him up as I untangled the ropes, and he jumped on me, almost knocking me over. "Where to this time? Can we go drive Grand Prix? Can we do the waterslide park?"

He'd been referring to our daily expeditions with Tucker and Bree. "Not today. We're going to watch a musical at Bree's house."

He stuck out his tongue, and it was red where he'd been eating too many Fruit Roll-Ups and changed his voice to a pitiful rendition of a British accent, "A musical? Like with singing and stuff? Oh no, Jazzline. Not my cup of tea, thank you very much."

Seth looked up and down the Marshwalk. "Who did this to you?"

Alex peered around like a pirate searching through his imaginary eyeglass. "There they go. Over there at the next restaurant, out at the oyster bar."

Seth looked at me as his eyes narrowed. "Why don't you go inside, and let your mother know that we have Alex? I'll only be a minute."

I knew that tone and look all too well. Tucker used the same one when we were in eighth grade, and this one kid kept calling me stupid names every day. Finally, he had enough and punched him out cold on the ground and got suspended for a week. His mother wasn't the least bit upset since he was defending my honor.

I touched his arm and a shock wave went through me. "It's okay. You don't have to. It's not worth it."

Then, I realized the mistake that I'd made. I should have quietly taken Alex inside, but Alex got it this time and started to scream across the distance. "You better watch out. My sister and her boyfriend are coming over there to beat you up."

I scolded him. "No one is beating anyone up."

Seth was not even paying any attention to us as he took off, in great strides to reach the group of older teens that were still looking like they were up to no good. I wanted to follow behind him, but I knew that Alex would only go extreme fighting and try to jump in on top of one of their heads or something, He watched way too much MMA and played too many video games.

I guess the look on Seth's face meant business, and the attendant from Fresh Market Shrimp House stepped out and hollered to them, "What's the problem, here? You better leave before I call the cops."

The other boys scurried away like the yard rats they were. But not Seth. He confidently stepped toward the attendant, spoke and pointed, then exchanged handshakes. I knew he was talking about how he should have worried about what was happening to Alex earlier, and I saw the attendant's eyes drop a little.

When Seth made his way back to us, I was filled with mixed emotions all at once making me unable to speak, yet again. I couldn't control Alex anymore as he jumped up and down high-fiving Seth and jumping onto his back. He didn't seem to mind.

"You just walked like this. Walk it," laughed Alex, and Seth made exaggerated motions, "And those dudes flew. That was awesome."

Then, I was in awe of him. Here was a guy that I'd just met defending my baby. I loved Seth more at that moment than I did the second I heard him whisper in the dark. Could it really be love? Could I really feel this for someone I had just met? Then, flashes filled my brain of all the times I'd seen Tucker and Bree together, Momma and Luke, and I knew love did exist out there. Now, it was standing right in front of me.

Lord, let me not mess this up.

I pulled Alex off of Seth and shooed him into the restaurant to tell Momma he was going with us, permanently for the rest of the summer. He wasn't going to be out of my sight for long. I'd find him something to do at that theater if it was cleaning up or playing his video games or helping us rehearse. No matter how much he complained, it would be better than this.

Not only was Seth the new hero, but Alex flipped because he also had a chance to ride in his dream car. When we finally made it to the MacKenzie home, Bree and Tucker were parked outside the gates. They didn't want to chance to come in without us behind them for fear of Mr. MacKenzie. He was way too strict on Bree in my opinion but let him do his thing. I guess he was playing the concerned Dad. Like I would know what that felt like. Mine was never around to play any role.

When we walked in, we were told by the staff that their parents were out for the day, and Bree took us to the theater room where autographed posters lined the walls of all the Broadway shows in New York and Europe they had attended since they were children. Hanging beside one of the cases with collector's editions of South Pacific and The King and I props, I read a wall plaque from First Take Productions, which was sponsored solely by the MacKenzie family.

I turned to Bree and motioned for her to explain. "So, your family does the theater at Pawley's Island?"

She drawled in a cute, Southern accent, "Honey, we are the theater at Pawley's Island." She beamed. "Yes. Isn't it wonderful? Momma writes screenplays for a living for Hollywood. She wants us as much a part of what she does as she can so she created First Take Productions. She found Ms. Dot from one of her movies and she is like a part of our family."

Then, it all made sense. The leading roles, the commanding presence that Bree and Seth had in the auditorium. It was theirs. Man, I knew we didn't want for anything. But for a split second, I let my mind drift to the place where the rich people lived since I was standing on a Spanish marbled floor. What would it be like to have anything you wanted? Seth and Bree didn't seem all caught up in it. Even with the fancy sports car and the house and her clothes. She was just Bree.

And I couldn't wait to learn more about Seth.

Seth lowered the projection screen, and we were in our own personal movie theater. Throughout the movie, Bree couldn't help but give her personal take on each scene. It was almost as if I needed a notebook to record it all. Her family had lived the theater her whole life. Tucker and I tried our best to escape from the drama of ours. Right in the middle of the movie, Seth asked did any of us want anything. Bree and Alex jumped up for snacks, and he said he'd go and make enough for everybody. Then, he left, just like that.

I got up and stretched my legs. "I'm going to go check on Seth to see if he needs any help."

Bree frowned. "But you can't leave now. You have to see this next part."

I laughed as I made my way out into the main foyer. "I'm sure that I'll have weeks to figure this movie all out. I can't take in but so much in a day's time.

I could hear crashing and banging from what sounded like coming from the kitchen, and I followed the stench of burnt popcorn. Just like a rich guy to not know how to push buttons on a microwave.

He had his back turned to me, and I asked, "Do you need help?"

He was so startled that he dropped the sodas and they began to roll under the bar. The popcorn bowl slid off the tray and crashed to the floor in a metal thud. I couldn't help but giggle. I watched his hand reach for the mask that he'd dropped on the counter and secured it to his face before turning around to face me.

I said, "You don't have to be that serious about it, do you?"

He wouldn't look at me, but stood still as the drinks made a sticky puddle on the floor. "Apparently, I do."

He knelt down beside me, taking both of my hands from the floor and holding them between his. He whispered, "I..."

"What?"

He pulled me up, then bent down and began cleaning it up himself. He sighed. "I've got it."

I leaned against the stainless-steel refrigerator and actually thought of sticking my head in the freezer to cool me down and giggled.

He looked up at me then, those cat eyes searching me out. "You're different."

He finished cleaning up everything and threw another bag in the microwave. This time I reached around him and programmed it. No time for burnt kernels.

I asked, "How?"

"I'm still trying to figure this all out?"

"Me, too."

He sighed. "I've figured out that we're all meant to be that way."

I didn't follow. "What way?"

He turned his back to me again. "Different. But tolerance and love are not the same things."

I wanted to do more than have him tolerate me. "Do you want me to leave?"

Then, I knew that wasn't what he wanted at all because out of nowhere I felt his massive arms circling around my waist and he brought me up close to him. "Does it look like I want you to leave? I want to keep you right here. Just like this. Forever."

I closed my eyes and leaned in against his hard chest. My heart was so full of love for him that I wanted to cry again. Crying around him wasn't going to be my thing so I held it in, pushing it down as hard as I could.

We didn't even hear Bree come in at first. He stood there holding me in the kitchen, pulling his fingers through my hair, messaging my neck, never letting me move to look up at him. Never speaking a word. Then, Bree pushed us a little, and I thought that we would literally topple over.

She giggled, her face blushing. "Sorry, guys. I didn't mean to interrupt, but we're starving in there, and the movie is almost over. They're in the last opera. Come on."

Tucker announced, "Finally! Where've you two been?"

Bree smiled a knowing smile like she knew we were perfect for each other from the beginning, and I remembered the little remark that she'd made on the first date that we all shared. "I found the two love birds in the kitchen making out."

Alex screamed. "What? You were making out with my sister?"

Seth glared at Bree, then turned to Alex. "No, it was nothing like that."

Bree glared back. "I know what I saw. They were in there kissing."

Tucker clapped his hands, mimicking Ms. Dot earlier at rehearsal. "So, it's a done deal. The infamous first kiss for the books."

Seth didn't need to know all of that. He didn't need to know that I'd never been kissed.

I said, "Tucker, he didn't kiss me."

Alex said, "Wait till I tell Momma."

I glared at him this time and didn't have to say a word. He popped open his Grape Slurp and started to gulp it down.

Tucker asked, "Well, are you two a couple?"

I wanted to say yes but I couldn't find my voice.

He said it for me. "No."

My heart split into and I felt the dull ache filling the void again. And I thought that we were just beginning something.

He didn't look at me the rest of the movie, and when it was over, I was still in the same position, heart bleeding, and eyes unfocused. The genius idea of Bree turned into a disaster for me because I was no more schooled on what happened in The Phantom than when we started the movie.

CHAPTER 5

Open up and Say Ahh

Seth didn't offer to walk us out, gave Alex a high-five again, and disappeared down the hallway. Just like that. And I felt so empty and alone. What happened between us? He was holding me. I swear it. He was whispering to me. It was real.

When we settled in the Jeep, thunder began to roll. Great, he didn't have his top, and it was about to pour buckets.

Tucker fumed. "What was that all about in there?"

How could I describe all that had happened to me that day? I blasted the radio, and Alex began to scream along. For that brief second, I could mouth the words for him to see.

"I love him, Tucker."

As soon as he saw the turn, he slammed on the breaks and skidded off into our public beach access road. He gave Alex a ten to go buy us some ice creams by the pier. And then it was him and me. We beat the rain but it was coming. It was in the air. He rolled out the blanket we always kept stashed in a tote behind the bushes and waited for me to sit on it so it wouldn't blow away. The beach was deserted. Exactly in tune with my emotional state.

And that was when he started. "You can't love him. You don't know the half of what's going on. Trust me on this. Don't get involved with him. He's dangerous."

I crossed my arms in defiance, feeling like a small child. "I'm sorry if it messes up your perfect little love affair with Bree. And how is he dangerous? Seriously?"

He pushed sand over my sandals. "This has nothing to do with Bree. You don't even know him. You don't know about that family. I'm telling you, no."

"Honestly, I don't know him. No, I don't. But I know how I feel around him."

"That's lust. That's not loving someone."

"Is that what it is with you and Bree? And lust is a pretty strong word for me, and you know this."

"Exactly what I mean, Jazz. You wouldn't know the difference. You see this guy with a mask on, and you get caught up in the moment, and the next thing you are making out with him? I can't believe this. And, for the record, I love Bree with all of my heart."

I felt so sick we were fighting. We'd never fought. My feelings for Seth were real, even if I couldn't describe them or even understand them, and I would defend them to him at all cost. Even if it meant a fight with Tucker.

"It wasn't a make-out session. Bree was exaggerating. But it was more than that. I know he loves me, too."

Tucker laughed. I was glad he was finding this funny. "He can't love you, silly. He wouldn't even admit that you were a couple."

My heart stung at the mention of it again, and my face dropped between my knees. I didn't want him to see he'd stabbed me. I felt his sandy hand rubbing up and down my arm.

Tucker sighed. "I'm sorry, Jazz. I didn't mean that. Let's not fight about this. And let's go get Alex before we all get soaked. Trust me on this, okay. Loving Seth won't last. He's running out of time."

Alex was running towards us, chocolate dripping all down his arms. Then, out of nowhere, crash. Lightning struck around us, right between us on the beach. We froze.

"Alex!"

The ice creams were flopped down around his feet, covering his toes. His lips formed a perfect O.

Tucker screamed, "It's okay, Alex. Stay there."

We started to run to him. Tucker picked him up and carried him to the Jeep. Alex kept on and on about what happened, hating he didn't catch it on video.

"Tucker, why wouldn't he love me?"

As if I even had to ask. What was there to love? What could I offer him?

Tucker frowned again, and I could sense he was ill at the thought of me with Seth. He should have been ecstatic. It would have sealed his double date problem like sticky glue, but sounded livid instead. "He's different. You really should try to keep your distance from him. I don't want you to get hurt, and that is all that will come with him. Trust me."

Alex looked up at me. His fear was gone. I could tell he was trying to think of something grown up to say. "Well, I thought Seth was cool. But if he doesn't love you, well then, he's the biggest moron I know."

I squeezed his hand. "I love you, Alex. It'll be okay."

And I prayed that it would be. I prayed that I would have the strength to get up in the morning and move towards that theater. Bree would be there expecting Tucker and me. Bree was such an open, loving girl. Why couldn't her giant brother be the same way?

DURING REHEARSALS, SETH HADN'T COME TO SOME stark realizations overnight about his true feelings for me because he didn't even show. I hadn't slept at all, replaying the whole days' worth of drama over and over in my head like a cheap soap opera. Ms. Dot was already giving stage directions for the opening Friday night lights scene, and I tried to immerse myself in her every word.

I held the script in my hand and mimicking the cast like I'd done this my whole life. Until she looked to Bree and told her I'd need a mic for my costume or the world would never hear how wonderful I was.

That was when it hit me again that it wouldn't be just us. Me and Tucker playing around. Alex seemed to get a kick out of my current situation, and he was watching as he sat crossed-leg at the edge of the stage. He hadn't once even opened his game bag. They broke us up into chorus groups. And there was the solo where I longed for the attention of the star quarterback.

My eyes scanned the page, and I wondered how their mother could have written a part like this without even knowing me as if this was made for me. The lines were something I would have thought to say on my own, so it made it easier to memorize.

Ms. Dot pushed me towards the piano and placed the sheet music in my hand like a delicate piece of priceless jewelry. "Now, stop being so timid. You'll do it justice, dear."

I'd been fine all morning because the Phantom boy was nowhere to be seen. He already knew all of his lines by heart anyway. Bree did. She was playing my best friend in the play. It was as if she'd had all the parts already picked out for us for her perfect little plan for the Summer of Love. That whole angel line he fed me was a gimmick.

Ms. Dot waved her watch in the air exaggerating how we didn't have much time. By my calculations, we had another three hours and thirty-five minutes and four more weeks after today. She'd announced that our musical director had called in with a sick baby, and she couldn't come in for rehearsals, but her backup was on call and on the way.

He arrived and made his way over to the piano, sat down and flipped through a leather messenger bag stuffed with hundreds of pages of sheet music. He found When You Think of Me, a song I could have written myself, and placed his fingers on the keys without once even glancing up. Was she serious? Was I to sing while he played? I found Tucker's gaze and he frowned at me not even trying to hide his disapproval. Bree stepped forward and came to lean against the piano beside me. Ms. Dot hadn't moved a muscle waiting in anticipation to find out whether or not I would ruin her show.

The funny thing about me was that I loved to sing. I sang at home all the time. I sang Tucker's alternative songs. I'd sing to Alex while we played Ultimate Fight Showdown. I'd sing while washing clothes or vacuuming throughout the day. I'd taken chorus and music electives since middle school without ever having to sing a solo or even open my mouth other to lip sync. My teachers never knew that I could sing, but I learned from them without having to say a word. I could read sheet music. I was an apt pupil, except for the opening my mouth and saying, "Ahhh" part.

I was forced into this situation by someone I loved who claimed he would help me, but after day one, wouldn't even look at me. Not to mention I had predator eyes on me from two girls who envied my part in the production. I wanted to throw the script at them when I heard them whispering and say, "Be my guest. Forget the darn car."

But when his fingers hit the keys, I couldn't help myself. I was lost again.

When You Think of Me started as a whisper. I felt Ms. Dot's hand on my shoulder, and she pulled me back. She motioned for Seth to stop playing. Ms. Dot spoke in my ear, "Darling, you must sing for us. Please let's get through this together and with some dignity."

I knew what she meant. I was trying my best to hold on to mine without hurling on the tiled floors or her platform shoes.

He started again. This time I forced my voice to rise higher. The song was beautiful. I allowed the words to flow, "Think of me when there is nothing left to say when words can't even play out what my heart is feeling."

I was singing to him, and with each line I sang, my voice rose louder and louder until he couldn't help but look up at me. His fingers stumbled across the keys, but he kept playing, not once looking at the sheet music, continuing to play and never taking his eyes off of me when I'd gotten his attention.

At the end of the song, Bree hugged me, almost knocking me back. "That was perfect. Oh, Jazz. I never knew that you could sing like that. When Seth told me, I thought it was just because he, well, that he needed to find Christy for his last show to be perfect, but he was right."

Seth took the sheet music from the piano and stuffed it back in his bag then rose to leave again. This time Ms. Dot went to him and whispered. Then he was gone. Come and go. It would not be that easy.

Ms. Dot hugged me. "That was beautiful, darling. We don't need to run through it again. Do it just like that our opening night, and we'll have a hit on our hands. We have a masterpiece with you. A true diamond in the rough. How darling."

I traced the steps I saw Seth take towards the exit at the back. He slid into his car when I hit the sunlight.

"Wait!" I ran out to the car and put my hand on the doorknob.

I stood there for what seemed like the longest time before I heard the click of the lock. When I opened the door and stared at him. What was next? Would I beg him? Would I tell him how I felt about him? No, I just stood there. Nothing could prepare me for how his eyes searched out mine.

Then he spoke, "Well, are you just going to stand there or are you going to get in?"

So, I did. And we drove out of the theater parking lot and off towards his home.

CHAPTER 6

We've Only Just Begun

His mother as tending roses in the garden. She had every color imaginable, in ornate ceramic pots as tall as I was. Flowers were flowing over trellis after trellis. She pushed up the brim of her straw hat and wiped her brow.

She saw Seth first and asked, "What are you doing home so early, dear? Practice canceled? And where is Bree?" Then, she saw me cowering behind him and smiled at me. "Oh, hello Jazzline. Where are Tucker and Bree?"

I pointed towards the direction of the theater, still not able to find my voice.

Seth answered, "They have Alex with them at the theater. I just needed to come home and get a few things we forgot to take to Ms. Dot."

She waved towards the house. "Take a break. Maybe go swimming in the pool. Ms. Dot can wait until tomorrow for her costumes or props or whatever it is. You have all summer. I'll text Bree to bring Alex along with her."

I lingered on that thought. All summer to be with Seth. All summer to feel torture and pain if we didn't settle this nonsense right now and kiss already. He didn't answer his mom, and he didn't grab my hand like he did all day yesterday, but I followed him anyway as he sulked towards the house. He was upset. I could tell the way he carried himself.

He didn't stop in the family room or go to the theater like I thought he was going. We went up a winding staircase, and I tried my best to keep up with him. He was going two at a time, and I was walking slower to look at all of the family portraits that lined the walls in golden frames. He was so adorable as a child.

Bree always looked like an angel, always in a white dress and flowing hair. Seth as a teenager was so striking. I was sure he must be the most arrogant guy having heard it his whole life. But then, I saw that the pictures no longer included him. He wasn't there. Three pictures without him. Three years of his absence. Where did he go? And the look in his family's eyes had changed, almost like a great sadness had washed over their entire family like a shroud. He wasn't in the picture. It was the oddest thing.

But no stranger than his room. He led me into a dark room, walls painted black, with a baby grand black piano in the corner. There were no mirrors, and the windows were painted over. There was an organized desk, dressers and closets lining around the perimeter of the room and a large four-poster mahogany bed with dark blue drapes all around the sides. It was like a cave more than a teenage boys' room. So different from Tucker's with his surfing posters and band tickets or flyers lining the white walls he'd graffitied with spray paint. He pulled the seat from his computer table and swirled it at me, expecting me to sit down. When I didn't, he stared at me.

Seth started to pace back and forth in the room, his hands smoothing back his hair from his face. Then, he felt the mask and turned to sit on the edge of the bed.

I whispered, "Why are you doing this to me? Is this how you think you should treat a lady?"

He looked up at me, and I could see the torment edging to madness in his eyes. He spoke in that soft way I'd remembered in the dark, "What I'm doing to you? It's what you're doing to me. I want so much for you. For us. But I know things you don't, and it will change things."

I took shaky steps toward him, and his hand moved up to stop me. I wasn't intimidated, and I tried to push his hand down but he was too strong for me, so I did nothing but run into the palm of his hand. At the touch, my heart began to flutter, and I knew that I had to sit down. I turned and went back to the swivel chair and waited. Waited for him to speak, to say anything.

I had to do it because the silence was killing me. "Do you love me, Seth?"

He didn't answer. Only continued to pace the room, pulling his hair back in the way that I was accustomed to seeing him do.

I would say it all. "Seth, I don't know you, but I love you."

It was out there between us, and there was no turning back now. He would either laugh in my face or kiss me.

But he did neither. He was just there. I went to him again and put my hand out to grab his, now resting against his silk comforter. Seth's hand was so warm. He didn't push me away.

"Do you know how hard that was for me to say that to you?"

He looked up at me then. "You don't know me."

I sat down beside him, still holding his hand. "I have time to find out."

He pulled his hand away, and I could feel his body tense and fight me with all of his strength. "The truth is we don't have time. I don't know where to start."

I grabbed for his hand again. There was no way that I would give up now. I'd already told him I loved him. He would have to hear me out.

"I knew it the minute you took my hand in the dark you were mine."

He turned to me then, and his eyes teared with emotion. "Don't think I don't feel it, too. Jazzline, I feel too much."

"Then, just love me. Don't push me away. I want us to be... "

I couldn't say it. I refused to say girlfriend-boyfriend-a couple-a thing. I couldn't finish it. He was supposed to give me a speech, not the other way around.

He didn't let go of my hand this time. "I can't. There's no way. It wouldn't be fair to you."

Then, it hit me. He was already in a relationship. Why wouldn't he be, look at him? Every girl at St. James was crazy over him. I was sure. Like everyone at Sea Side was over Tucker.

"That's it. You have a girlfriend. I'm so embarrassed. Why didn't you tell me that before?"

His voice was barely audible. "No, it's not that. I haven't had a girlfriend since I was fifteen."

I didn't understand. If he felt it, too, and he was free, then why not? What was he so afraid of? Why was he so tightly closed off? Was he more like me than I thought? I would have been this way weeks ago.

"Well, then. Do you want me?"

It had to come down to that. If he said no, I swore I would leave right then. I would forget about the summer thing and the car. I'd take a freaking bike ride to school if I had to before walking into that theater again. Bump Tucker and Bree. Let them figure out their own chaperone problems. They could use Alex.

But he answered instead, "I want you more than anything I've ever wanted in my life."

"Oh."

He sighed, running his hands through his hair again. A nervous habit. At least he didn't break into song. "And I know I can't have you."

He could. He did. "Why? I'm right here, Seth. I've told you how I feel about you. I didn't even believe that love could exist before yesterday. Then, here I am with you, and I love you, and you say you can't have me. You're the one that's wrong. Because I'm yours already and you don't have to do a thing about it."

He turned to me then, a tear falling down his cheek, the one that I could see. "Do you really love me? Do you, Jazzline? Do you think you could?"

I whispered, "Yes."

Seth sighed and reached for the mask. "You'll change after this. And I'll have to live with it. But I can't keep pretending anymore because it's not fair to you. I didn't mean to take you in. Bree warned me, and now it's too late. Bree has already confirmed it and knowing that alone will make my life a living hell without you, but I just can't let it be."

He pulled the mask off his face and let it fall. It cracked when it hit the hardwood floor. His hands went to his face, and his hair fell to shelter him.

I sighed, moving closer into him where there was no space between us. "What is it? What's wrong?"

He choked. "This."

And he turned to me then, and it was not what I expected at all. His face. It was hurt. That wasn't the word. It was scarred. It was taken on one side. His right side was not smooth and soft as his left, it was not proportional. It was sunken in with hard lines covering and twisting like vines. His eyes held my face, trying to read my expression. Seeing if I would run. Flinch.

I held my ground. I loved him. Every part of him.

I shook my head. "So."

He laughed then, and it echoed around the dark cave.

I made him laugh, and I couldn't help but smile.

"So, that's all you have to say is so? I don't get you. You'll not faint at the sight of me?"

I reached up to touch his face, and he flinched. I didn't let it stop me. What I saw didn't bother me in the least. He was just Seth. Beautiful yet scarred, fragile yet strong. I wanted my voice to sound calm so I would assure him. I didn't want there to be a doubt between us.

"I love you. Don't you know it has nothing to do with your face? Don't you know that? I loved you before I saw you. I loved you when you whispered to me in the dark."

He crushed me up against him, and I could feel my heart exploding in my chest. I felt a painful noise escape his mouth, and he buried his face in my hair. His face without the mask. And he didn't let go of me for the longest time. We sat on the side of the bed, him cradling me in his arms. It was so warm and peaceful that I even felt myself drifting off to sleep. Since I hadn't slept the night before I was exhausted. Telling someone you love them takes a toll, too. And I was spent.

~

I DIDN'T KNOW HOW LONG I slept, but when I woke up, I was so startled. I felt a scream form but he sat up and shook me a second to remind me where I was. It was so dark. There was no light coming in through the windows. There was no light in the room. It was Seth's room, and I had fallen asleep in his arms. Had it all been a dream?

He whispered in my ear, "Do you have nightmares? Do I scare you?"

I put my arms around him again. "No, I forgot a second. I'm here with you, and that's the only place that I want to be."

He sighed as I leaned in against him. "Why are you doing this?"

"Promise I won't have to live everyday reassuring you what I feel for you is real. Trust me when I say that I want to be with you. It doesn't matter to me, Seth."

"Why not?"

I said, "My heart was yours from the minute I met you. You in the dark or the light, it doesn't matter. I loved you before I saw your face. I love you now. Forever and then the day that follows that."

He smiled. "You are the most beautiful woman I've ever seen."

I rolled my eyes. "And you exaggerate."

"Not in the slightest."

"I see you for who you are. I see you. I know how you make me feel. And that is enough for me."

"Won't I embarrass you? Won't you wonder what it would be like with a normal person?"

I laughed. "Normal? Show me one. And I don't worry about what other people think. People don't bother me in the least. I've always been that way. I don't talk much to them, anyway. Don't you know that already? I run with Tucker and Alex. There's no one else that matters. No one at all. But you."

He turned from me again. What would it take to make him see? If it was time, I had all the time in the world, and I was a patient person. Fighting out in silence had made me so.

"But waking up to this? Having this to look forward to?"

I said, "I'd be the happiest girl in the world. Just like I am right now."

He sat up and threw his legs off the side of the bed. "I guess that means we're going out then, huh?"

"Is that how you'll ask me? Don't I get a speech or something?"

He shrugged. "I don't really know about all this stuff. I guess I need to pay Bree to teach me a few lessons."

I wanted to reply especially how to kiss me since she seemed to have no trouble at all falling into Tucker and smooching him in front of the world, but I wouldn't dare speak it.

He pulled me up from the bed. I didn't want this to be over. Then, I had to remind myself that it had only begun.

"I love you just the way you are. Leave Bree out of this and just let us be." I began to hum... We've only just begun to be...

He smiled. "Are you nervous?"

I wasn't. "No, why?"

He opened the door, and the light was startling from the enormous five-tiered chandelier suspended from the vaulted ceiling. "You just started singing. I thought you said you sing when you're nervous."

I shrugged. "Well, I sing when I'm happy, too, and when I'm sad."

He laughed. "So, I really am going to live out a musical my

whole life? I thought that I was already doing that with Momma. Now you, too?"

His mother was standing by the foot of the stairs, dressed in a pale yellow suit. It had been a while since the rose tending. She said, "What are you doing with your momma?"

He stopped short. "Oh, nothing, just that I find it very amusing that Jazzline loves to sing. At random times. Kind of like someone else I love."

She smiled at me and looked to her son and gasped. I'm sure she was wondering what all had happened and why the mask was off, and why I was still holding his hand. But her eyes welled up in tears instead.

"We all love to sing around here, dear. Some not as trained as others," and she eyed Bree and Tucker down below, their mouths in that perfect oh my expression. She continued as she turned to sway back down the stairs, looking just like an older version of Bree.

"You'll fit right in here, sweetheart. Welcome to the family."

Where was Alex? Then, I heard him before I saw him. Hooting like an owl to hear his echo bouncing around him. Thank God. I let out a sigh of relief. I owed Tucker and Bree for this one. But no, I didn't. I'd given them the best summer of their life. They could repay me by giving me the best day of mine.

When we made it down the stairs Tucker was eyeing me, narrowing his eyes at Seth as if to say if you hurt her, you're dead. But I winked at him and let go of Seth long enough to give Alex a big hug. I picked up his tiny arm and twisted his Superman watch to read the time. It was six thirty!

I closed up the cape on the watch and ruffled his hair. "Are you hungry?"

He grabbed his stomach as if he were in pain. "I'm starving. These two knuckleheads didn't stop to eat. We rode up and down, up and down the blessed road about fifteen hundred times, and I could reach out my hand and touch McDonald's five times, but they didn't stop. It was killing me."

I imagined the pained, whiney afternoon they had with him, and it made me laugh.

Tucker's voice was low, still not knowing how to react to Seth and me together. "We thought you might like to go out or something? Like we could all go out?"

Mrs. MacKenzie patted Seth on the back, and he coughed. He turned to me. "Would you like to go out with me?"

Everyone was silent. I could feel all eyes on me. Breathless. Steady on your feet. You already told him you loved him. Why would you be so caught up with an invitation to go out to eat?

I whispered, "Yes."

Alex stepped in between us. "Is he still a moron?"

Seth laughed, and I covered my face with my hands and then buried it into his hair. "No, Alex. He's, well, I guess he's my boyfriend?"

I spoke it still as if I were questioning it, then I heard his voice announce it as soon as his father stepped through the door.

Seth's voice was strong and deep, "Yes. We're now a couple."

His father's eyes widened in surprise, and he went over to grab his wife's hand. "That's nice to hear, Seth. A girlfriend, huh? Bree, what do you think about this?"

He eyed me as if he had just met me, which was ridiculous since I'd been coming by, even if it was to wave from the back seat of the Jeep for weeks.

"I told you all it was perfect. You know what I say goes about these matters." She laughed but I saw their expressions and knew that she was serious. What was up with that?

He shook his father's hand in such a formal manner. "Yes, sir. Jazzline is mine."

The way he spoke, it sounded final. I was his. The words sealed it for me. It was official. We were forever.

CHAPTER 7
Endless Love

Bree announced, "We'd all like to go out on a date."

Mrs. MacKenzie said, "That's fine, honey. But, if you'd like to stay here, I could get Carla to whip us up some burgers. We could have a bonfire on the beach."

Alex rubbed his stomach and started to jump at the idea, but Bree stepped in between Alex and her parents. "We'd all like to go out, but separate, if that's okay with you, Daddy. Please."

He held up his hand to Bree. That was where Seth had learned that defensive move from. "Wait one second, young lady."

Seth touched his father's arm and asked, "Can I speak with you a minute in the study?

He didn't respond, but they walked in great strides down the hallway. Seth was as tall as his father, both with the same soft, golden eyes.

That's when Mrs. MacKenzie, who asked me to please call her Maura, made small talk with me in the hallway as Tucker and Bree planned what they could get into if her father agreed. She asked me about my mother and the restaurant. There was nothing to say except she was doing well, and that she stayed busy all the time. Then, she asked about my father. I told her he lived away, and we saw him over holidays every other year. The rotation cycle seemed to work well for them. I was so glad it was Momma's turn with us this year. Christmas was my favorite time of the year. Not having that with Seth would have been the worst.

She whispered to me, "I'm so glad you and Seth are together. We never thought, but I wish..."

I knew what she meant, and I jumped right in to reassure her, "His face doesn't bother me."

She hugged me, like the way Bree did, and it was nice. "You seem like a special girl. Do you have any gifts?"

That made me want to laugh. Was I? I answered, "I try to be nice to everyone. I go to church. I attend St. Mark's Methodist on the corner by my house. I drag Tucker with me, too. Do you mean gifts like musical gifts?"

She pointed at Tucker and Bree. "Never mind about that now. Tell me this. They seem pretty serious to me. Is there any reason I should be worried?"

With Tucker, I wasn't too sure, but I couldn't tell her that. "No. Tucker would never hurt Bree. He really does love her."

"I was afraid of that. Bree is so young, though."

"But she seems so old. She'll keep him straight. She's stronger than you think."

Maura grinned. "I'm more worried for Tucker. Don't let her tiny dancing frame fool you. She has a black belt."

I laughed. "Didn't know that. What else should I know?"

Before she could go into any more family info, Seth came back around the room with his father. Their conversation had turned to golf.

Mr. MacKenzie barked, "You are free, Brianna Rain MacKenzie. But I swear, if you touch her, well, you know what I mean, Tucker. I'll kill you."

Tucker held out his hand and shook it like he'd been awarded a million-dollar jackpot check. "Trust me, I know what you mean. And I refuse to die young."

Maura broke in between them, pointing at Alex to make sure that the conversation they were about to have stopped so young ears could not hear. She clapped. "Go on now, children and have fun this evening. Bree don't be out past ten. Seth, stay out as long as you like, dear."

Bree stomped. "Wait, that's not fair."

Her father interjected, "Okay, then fine. Eight. Or maybe you should stay in with Tucker and your momma and me? Seth deserves this night."

Her face was still red with anger, but she waved her hands in front of her, and then grabbed Tucker pulling him away before he could change his mind for real. "No, Daddy. That's fine. Tucker will have me home by ten."

Tucker promised. "Nine-forty-five."

She stepped on his foot. "No, ten."

She blew her parents kisses and left us in the hallway. I was sure they'd be clear across town before Seth could even get me and Alex to the car.

Seth shook his father's hand again and kissed his mother. She asked, "What plans do you have this evening?"

He shrugged. His eyes sparkling as he winked at his father. "I don't know. I haven't figured that one out yet."

Alex jumped in. "Let's go to Medieval Journey!"

I pulled Alex by the arm through the double doors leading out into the courtyard. "Can I ask you a favor? Can I have a first date with Seth, alone? We'll make it up to you, buddy."

This was my night and as much as I loved Alex and wanted him to be with us, this was our first date.

Then, I thought about what that meant to be on this date with him. Look at me. I was a disaster. My t-shirt was all wrinkled and I had on an old pair of blue jean shorts that were ripped along the seam. My hair was still pulled back into my typical black pony-tail holder, but strands were loose from sleeping.

I was sure I was such a mess and to know that I was going out with him tonight and I'd actually had a freaking makeover for his older brother at my momma's expense was hilarious. What I needed now was a full overhaul and no time to do it.

When we got inside his car I whispered, "Can you please take me by my house for a minute?"

He smiled. "Why? You look fine."

How did he know what I was thinking? "No, I don't. Just please."

I was sure I could improve myself enough to get by.

Alex leaned forward and said, "She doesn't know how to get made up pretty."

I swatted at him but missed.

Seth laughed. "Alex, she's your sister. You wouldn't get it. Everybody tells me how pretty Bree is, but she is just Bree to me."

Alex said, "Bree is hot."

Seth smiled at me. "See, your sister is hot to me." I felt the blush overtake me.

Then, Alex said something I couldn't believe came out of his mouth. "Well, wonder what you look like to her with your half-face and all like that guy off of Batman?"

I sucked in my breath sharply and a ripping sound escaped my lips like a zipper. I seethed, "Alex, take it back."

He frowned. "What? What did I say?"

Seth grabbed my hand and squeezed. He whispered to me, "It's okay. Really. I'm used to it. If you're going to be with me then you must have thicker skin than that. We'll get looks. You'll hear whispers. But you have to keep walking, and let it slide. Or it will tear you apart. Don't let it. Alex didn't mean anything by it."

He apologized. "I'm sorry, Seth."

Alex was silent in the back seat the rest of the way. We were about fifteen minutes from Pawley's Island but it felt like hours of silence down Hwy 17. I was going to have a talk with Alex. I was sure of that. Alex went in ahead of us, and I turned to Seth before we stepped inside. His behavior was too reserved for the first time in his life, and I think he understood what he had said and that it was so wrong. Maybe I wouldn't be too hard on him.

"Don't expect your house inside this tiny cottage."

He smiled. "I don't."

"Good, because I don't want to disappoint you."

He squeezed my hand. "I don't think you could ever disappoint me."

I pointed to Tucker's next door. "See how close I am to that loony-bin."

Seth laughed. "I like him, though. He's good for my sister."

And he was so right. "He's good for me, too. He's been my best friend since we were five years old. That's a long time to know somebody. I hope you understand that."

He reassured me. "I'm not the least bit jealous that you have Tucker. Why would you think that?"

I told him about Tucker's past girlfriends and how they all treated me at school like I had the plague or something.

"Me and Bree aren't like that. We understand. To be honest, it's nice to have the both of you belonging to the both of us. It's right."

How right he was. Tucker and I were the lucky ones. But my mind raced right back to how things would be so different for us when school started. Both of them at St. James. Then, graduation. I couldn't go there tonight. This was not about Tucker, for once. My night wasn't about him and me and Alex. It was Seth, and I had to figure out what to do with myself. I wished I would have brought along Bree for emergency aid, more like roadside service, but they ran off before my mind could even wrap around the fact that I was actually going on my first real date.

Alex pulled out his game bag and started in on an extensive run by run of all of his games and his favorite characters, throwing out his game magazines in heaps at Seth's feet. That would keep him busy for half the night. I could hear him telling Seth all about how beast I was gaming, and then Seth said he didn't play. We would have to change that one day. The cave could use a system.

My clothes were pretty much the same, t-shirt after t-shirt, shorts to jeans. My makeup was nonexistent because I didn't think strawberry swirl lip-gloss counted as real makeup. So, I knew that I had to raid Momma's room. It would thrill her that I had shown some interest in girly things and wouldn't mind the intrusion.

Her and Luke's room was nothing special. Just another extension of the hotel like atmosphere. As much money as she was turning around, I always wondered why we never moved. But we didn't. She said that she didn't care about all of the material things like cars and houses. Probably because she was never at home, maybe long enough to sleep, since she lived at the restaurant. She was saving everything for an early retirement where she and Luke were planning on traveling the world. Where did that leave Alex since he was still so young? I couldn't think about that either.

She might not have cared about luxury homes and such, but her wardrobe was a different story. She had a beautiful designer collection. I picked a silky black top. Seth was wearing a pair of jeans, so I didn't have to go all-fancy with one of my momma's dresses or skirts, so I slid on a pair of her dark jeans, and her strappy leather shoes. It was nice we were the same size.

Her makeup was so confusing with all kinds of applicators and colors to choose from. Where to begin? Why couldn't it be like paint by numbers or have color charts or diagrams or something in the cases? To be safe, I popped blush on my cheeks and used a darker true cherry lip-gloss. That was it. I sure wasn't going to try any of the liquid stuff or eyeliner. It would be terrible to have to go out with a bleeding eyeball and an emergency room visit. My hair was the easy part, brush, brush, brush, and a couple of fa-la-las and that was it.

Jazzline Chicand. At her finest.

Seth stood up when I came back in the den and the magazines slid right down to the floor. "Jazzline, you look beautiful."

I bit my lip. "Are you sure?"

"I'm sure that you are lovely."

Lovely. What a word to hear him say. I did feel lovely when he opened the car door for me and butterflies began to dance around in my stomach. This was it. The first date. There would never be another one. I would remember it forever.

~

When we got to Chica's, Luke was at the door speaking with the guest attendant but he fell silent and gawked at me as we entered.

I whispered, "Luke, can we speak with you a minute?"

He grabbed Alex by the arm before he bounded into a couple by the entryway, and we went straight to our reserved family table in the corner booth of the restaurant, hidden from view. I was glad because people were doing what Seth said they would, gawking, whispering, some louder than others, and I felt my face redden with anger. Not from embarrassment, but from anger. Alex went off to find Momma, the little tattletale.

Luke couldn't keep his eyes off of Seth even if he tried, and I put my hand through his arm for support. It was funny I felt like I needed it, and it was my family. "I'd like you to meet my boyfriend, Seth MacKenzie."

His eyes widened. "Boyfriend? Since when?"

Momma popped over with Alex, a smile flashing across her face when she saw I'd attempted to pretty myself up and she glowed when she saw her outfit on me. I knew she wouldn't be upset. But, then, she flashed her smile to Seth then it turned to something else. Strange. Did he always have this effect on people? Was I missing something?

She fell into the seat next to Luke, holding on to his hand until her knuckles were white. "Hello. I'm Jacqueline Chicand."

"It's nice to meet you, mam. I would like permission to take your daughter out on a date."

Luke asked for them both, "Where will you be taking her?"

"To Pawley's Club at The Sawgreens, then to a light show by the gardens."

Momma's eyebrows rose all the way to the roof. "Um, really? The Sawgreens?"

I didn't know where he was talking about, and I thought he

wasn't sure where we were going based on his conversation with his mother. I'd never heard of it but apparently, Momma had.

Then, she said. "Okay. Where's Tucker?"

I knew that she would have felt better if Tucker would have been with me. What was wrong with the parents around here? They didn't trust us?

"He's off with Bree somewhere. This is Bree's brother."

Momma's eyebrows rose again. "Okay."

That was it. Nothing more but two okays and a Tucker. Then, she rose and apologized for having to run back to the kitchen before it backed the orders up and it was over. Luke was left with us but only for a second because he slid out, giving his excuse of having to go fuss out the attendant. That left Alex.

I grabbed his hand. "Stay out of trouble."

He frowned. "Why can't I come?"

Seth sighed, and I could tell that he felt as guilty as me. "I really want to spend some time with your sister. But I promise you that tomorrow night we'll go to Medieval Journey."

My heart melted. Alex's eyes widened with excitement. That was like his favorite place to go, and I still didn't understand how he could go year after year and the same story would replay. He knew who would be the champion from the get-go, but he didn't care.

"For real?"

I chimed in. "Yep, we'll do that tomorrow, if, and only if, you promise to be good tonight and lay low."

He smiled. "Like this?" He grabbed his game bag and slid underneath the table. "Is this low enough?"

I knew as soon as we'd hit the parking lot he'd be up running around. "No, under there will hurt your eyes with the game. Just sit here and chill. I mean it, Alex. Don't make me worry about you tonight, and you'll be eating dragon soup in less than twenty-four hours."

He held up his two fingers like he'd seen Tucker do a million times. Neither one of them had ever been Boy Scouts but they thought the rule still applied to them. "Scouts honor. See, I'm here. Lying low."

His voice went deep, and I couldn't help but laugh as I could still hear him repeating lying low in baritone as we made it out the door. It reminded me of the Grease dance-off with the Born to Hand Jive song, and I started to mimic, "How low can Alex go?"

I made Seth laugh and the song was worth it. "Are you going to break out in song every time something reminds you of a lyric? Is this a happy date song or sad to leave Alex rendition?"

"Yes, I told you it is a ridiculous habit of mine, and this is still happy. I'll let you know if it changes."

"I'm glad I can make you happy. I never thought I ever could make any girl happy."

"Well, I'm not just any girl. I'm your girl."

"I could get used to that."

I started flipping through his saved tracks on his playlist. "What are Highland Expressions?"

He smirked. "Yeah, about that. I like Scottish Folk songs and traditional Celtic hymns. See."

The music was melodic, but the words were unrecognizable.

"It's in Scottish Gaelic. Not easy for a sing along with you. My parents are from Scotland. Dad came to the U.S. when he was about Alex's age. He went back and found Momma and brought her here. We travel back and forth all of the time. It's very important to us. To me."

That explained the shield at the entryway of the house and the tapestries. The castle and the formalities. The bagpipe music was peaceful and the sound of the angel from the speakers was soothing and rich. I might not have known what she was saying but it was moving.

How could I feel all of this so soon? My heart beat against the music and the hand drums. My thoughts were running wild and my hands wrung in my lap. This was all so new and exciting, yet felt so perfectly right.

My stomach growled, breaking into our silence, and we

laughed. We hadn't eaten all day. Poor Alex. I was sure he was lying low with some burger and fries. Momma would at least cook for him. She would do what she did best.

He pulled up to a gated community, Pawley's Pointe Clubhouse. I'd never been to a country club before, but I was sure I was underdressed, for sure. But he had on jeans, so maybe I was okay. The security guard holding the fort in the brick and glass building that looked the same exact size as my house waved him on through without even stopping us. He took me down a long winding road through massive trees and beautiful homes. Not as magnificent as his, but still, breathtaking just the same. Then, we pulled up to this immaculate Southern mansion that was The Sawgreens Restaurant.

"You took me all the way out here, and it's not open tonight?"

He waited, standing there like the doors were to open for him, and then they did. A man stepped out dressed in a tuxedo and smiled at Seth. "Good evening, Mr. MacKenzie. We've been expecting you."

"Thank you, Louis. I'd like you to meet Ms. Jazzline Chicand."

The man smiled at me, took my hand while bowing then escorted us through the dining room to a courtyard with a view of the inlet. It was so peaceful here. No customers, boats pulling up to the Marshwalk, beach music wafting in the air. It was like me. And just like him to be able to bring me to a place like this with no one around.

The best date spot ever.

"The chef is ready to prepare whatever pleases you this evening."

Seth replied, "Thank you. Please give us a few minutes."

Then, he disappeared through the patio doors. Seth led me to the thousand candles that had been lit for our date. The preparation in such a short amount of time was amazing.

"What do you think? Is this okay?"

I didn't respond. I couldn't find the words. I guess he could tell by my expression because he turned back to the menu and began to go through the delicious possibilities. Just reading about prime rib and sea scallops made my stomach squirm a reply. I held on to it and dared it to speak again. He smiled and motioned for the waiter. Like magic, he appeared.

He took our orders then left us alone. "Is this a place you come to a lot?"

"Sometimes we do. Our family is so busy with the business we usually stay at home. Momma makes sure we have plenty to keep us busy at the house. I went out tonight with you, at Chica's walking through, and you saw what happened. I didn't want you to remember your first date like that."

He smiled as he got up from the table and held out his hand to me. "I hope you like this."

I looked around, and I saw a woman dressed in an elaborate costume stepping from behind the building and making her way to the patio. She stood by the fountain and waited for us. He pulled back my chair and almost lifted me from the seat and took me to what appeared to be a makeshift dance floor on the lawn. Candles circled us on the wooden floor and the woman glanced at me and smiled, then began to sing a playlist of our musical.

He held me in his arms, my head touching his shoulder. He bowed his head to find his way to get even closer to me. I leaned into him as we moved in small circles.

I whispered after the second song was over, "Wait, if you're the phantom, that means you can sing, right? Can you sing? Will you sing with me?"

Seth laughed. "I've been told I'm not bad." He put his fingers under my chin and raised my head to meet his eyes. "I can't wait to sing with you. You really weren't paying attention to Bree the other day when she talked about our duet?"

I smiled. "How could I when you were in the room?"

He put his arms back around me and pulled me even closer to him if that were possible. "Well, you have to pay attention, my dear, because it'll be here so fast."

"And just like that I became an overnight sensation."

He whispered, "And the girl of my dreams."

I sighed into his chest and let the words fill my soul. I was his dream, and he was mine. But I never thought this would be the summer. This fast. That this would be my time. I didn't have to be silent, yet I could be when I had to be, and he didn't seem to mind. But I could talk to him, and I could feel him all around me and invading all of my senses at once.

Could I ever be like the woman in front of me? Swishing in that gorgeous beaded jeweled gown shining like the stars above? With such confidence and freedom to sing. I suddenly hoped so with all of my being. I hoped so for Seth and Bree. I wanted to show them that at least I would try. But I wanted it for me.

Then, our dance was over. Our dinner was being placed on the crisp white tablecloth of our tiny little table. It was delicious, and I couldn't wait to tell Momma about this place. She would come here the next weekend when it was open to the public. She'd get a replacement for two hours for this.

Then, we took a walk through the lit golf course to stand by the inlet. It was like we were in our own little paradise, and I never wanted it to end.

He said, "Bree is going to get married here."

I laughed. "She's already talking about marriage? Poor Tucker!"

"Not only does she talk about it, but she has her dress already designed, her bridesmaid picked out, which is you, by the way. She knows her colors. Everything down to the minute detail."

"Does Tucker know all this?"

He gave me a stern glare. "No, and don't go tattling. Bree would kill me."

Then, I wondered if Bree knew. "Does she know about Tucker?" I didn't want to think it, yet alone say it out loud. "About next year?"

"We've both been trying to figure that out. How will we survive with you guys not at St. James? We've even asked about transferring, but my dad won't hear of it. I don't know what it would be like for me, anyway."

I wasn't talking about senior year. He misunderstood. It was the after-graduation party that had me anxious. "Please, don't even contemplate that. I meant beyond high school? Does she know?"

He frowned. "What? That he's going to Coastal Carolina for Marine Science? She's okay with that. It fits right perfect into her little plan. She'll be eighteen when he is halfway through his degree program. They'll get married when he is a senior in college and then off to Sea World or something."

My mouth dropped open in shock, and I felt the tears well up again. He wouldn't stay for me, but for her? Then, I wanted to punch myself in the eyeball for even thinking it. It hurt a little he hadn't shared his new goals with me or that the conversation hadn't arisen. But then again, we hadn't been alone together in weeks. No matter what the reason, me or her, he was staying, and that was all that mattered. I hugged Seth. His family had changed my life in more ways than one, and they didn't even know it.

CHAPTER 8

Every Breath You Take

I didn't want to go home just yet. There was one more place to go, and since he didn't have a curfew and Momma never even thought about giving me one since this was a whole new experience for her and me, I would take advantage of this one night. I pointed to our side little street, and we made it down to my beach access. I was sure that there was a Jeep parked here about an hour earlier before Bree had to be whisked back home.

He said, "You know we have the beach at my house. We could've gone home." But that wouldn't have been the same. His family would've still been there, and I wanted to keep him to myself a little while longer.

I threw my shoes off and left them by his car as we made our way down the pavement to the old wooden steps. I went under the bush and pulled out my lantern and blanket. There was something about sitting out at the beach after dark I loved more than anything. I loved how I couldn't quite see everything that most people wanted to see, but I could feel it all around me at once. My hair whipping, my feet warm in the sand, the salt on my face. I felt so alive, and I wanted to share that with him. And it was so much more intense when his arm came around me, and I leaned into him. I heard the soft crash of the waves, and I felt the sudden urge to kiss him.

"Will you do something for me?"

He sighed. "Anything."

I turned his face to mine, feeling him hesitate when I touched him. "Will you kiss me?"

He didn't answer, just leaned into me and found my lips as the whisper was still lingering between us. His mouth was warm and full, and I fell into him. His hand cradled my face, and he kissed me until every thought seemed to disappear. It was dark, but his eyes strangely glowed at me as the lantern cast its light around us.

My first kiss was like nothing I could ever have imagined.

I put my hands on both sides of his face and pulled him down to me again. "I want you to kiss me." And he did again, and again.

He pulled away and stared at me. "I ... Jazzline."

He couldn't say it. I wanted him to feel the same way as I did. But even if the words couldn't come from him, I knew in my soul when he kissed me that he did love me. And I was sure that he knew I loved him.

But just in case he didn't, I kissed him lightly on the lips, closing my eyes and falling into his chest. "Seth, I love you."

He picked me up and placed me in his lap. He cradled me in his arms and stroked my hair. Being with him was the most natural feeling, and I rested in that knowing. Instead of moving me off his lap he somehow managed to stand up, holding me close to his chest as he picked me up with one arm, grabbing the blanket and swooping me down to catch the lantern with mine. He carried me all the way to the car and placed me back into my shoes.

Instead of conversations of love and how much life had changed since he met me. He went back to the musical.

"I'll email you the soundtrack in case you need some extra practice when I'm not around."

I wondered if we would get a kissing part. I sure could use

more practice time with him in that area. When he dropped me home, Momma came right out of the house on cue.

Momma looked me over since I had sand stuck on her expensive outfit, and said, "I want to apologize to you."

Seth looked puzzled. "For what? I should be the one apologizing for keeping Jazzline out so late."

She threw up her arm to brush that off. "No, don't worry about that. Jazzline has never had a problem taking care of herself. I'm sorry I acted like that at the restaurant."

Seth shrugged. "That's fine. I'm sure you weren't expecting me." Seth came around the car and moved forward with me by his side. "I want you to know that I'll never hurt your daughter. And I promise that I'll always take care of her."

Momma said, "I want you to know that I'm really happy that Jazzline found somebody. I am."

He was more than a somebody. He was everything. We were a super couple with that magnetic force energy that radiated from us, and it made me feel so blessed that I had found my other half to complete me. When I would study couples from the Bible, I always was fascinated by how they met or how God had created the one for the other. Our relationship brought to mind Isaac and Rebekah, seeing each other for the first time and falling in step with one another. It did happen. I was living proof that teenagers could fall in love and find the one for the rest of their life.

Momma and Seth talked as my mind wandered, and I looked out the window to see the Jeep home. Momma said that she had to go on in for bed, but we could still hang out. Seth reminded her we had early morning rehearsals and he'd be here to pick me up. No more Jeepers Kreepers. But I hated the thought of having him drive all the way down here to pick me up when I could ride with Tucker but he insisted to get me and Alex.

When Momma closed the door behind her, he grabbed me and pulled me in his arms before I could even ask.

Seth whispered in my hair, "Thank you for tonight."

"Thank me? I didn't do anything but love you and eat. The food was delicious. Thank you."

He laughed. "How did I do? As far as dates go?"

I snuggled close to him, yawning. "On a scale from one to ten, a kazillion and two."

He pulled me back to stare into my eyes. "Was it that good?"

I sighed and pulled his face close to mine. "My first kiss was that good."

And I kissed him full on the lips. He was mine.

When we broke away, he whispered, "It's so difficult for me to believe that you have never went out before or had a boyfriend? You are so beautiful and so everything."

I reminded him. "Well, I did go out with Colin."

"Is that what you call it? Bree told me how you would have rather died than to be dragged along with them."

I grimaced even though he wasn't all that bad. "I guess I over-reacted. How is he anyway?"

He shrugged. "He's off to Massachusetts in a couple of days for summer school. Of course, he was accepted to MIT. It was hilarious that he thought he didn't have a chance. That's kinda like me. It's hilarious."

I couldn't follow him again. "What is?"

He pulled me close to him. "I thought I would never have a chance to have a relationship, much less have a beautiful angel kiss me like this."

I whispered, "Like this?"

And we kissed again. How could I have found him? God truly had answered a prayer I never even knew that I had asked. God knew what I was missing in my life and filled in the lost pieces by bringing me Seth. By bringing Bree into Tucker's life to keep him here with me, too. God bless the MacKenzie clan. One and all. Even Colin.

It was so hard to watch Seth get in his car and drive away. But instead of going in, I hollered through the door, "I'm going to

Tucker's." Momma was still in the den with the television off. I was sure that she heard us.

She cried out, "That's fine, dear."

When I heard her voice, I knew that Tucker would have to wait. He wasn't going anywhere, thank God. Momma was on the couch. Her fingers were shaking as she blew into a Kleenex.

I sat beside her. "What's wrong? Did something happen? One of those movies again?"

She blew hard. "My baby is growing up. When did you fall in love with him? Tell me everything."

So, I did. We stayed up until two o'clock talking about everything. Momma and I had our first heart-to-heart when my heart was full, and it made it so wonderful to share it with her. To share how wonderful Seth was for me. Before we went off to bed, the question she had been waiting to ask me couldn't wait any longer.

She said, "How can you do it?"

"What?"

"How can you kiss him with his face like that?"

Momma still didn't understand. And honestly, if no other person in the world other than Seth's family understood it, I didn't care not one bit. All I knew is that when I kissed him my world was on fire and alive and wonderful and new. There was no way that Momma's doubts or any stranger's looks would stop me from loving him. It would have to be God Himself to tear us apart. And this was day two.

"Momma, it's not what you look like it's who you are inside."

She chuckled. "That's an old one, and one that I've always heard, but when it's there staring you in the face it's always a different story. I know you, Jazzline. Once you get your mind set on something, you stick with it. Look at you and your church mess. You never gave up on God. Even when he clearly didn't answer prayers."

"Momma, He does answer prayers. It just might not be the way we think it should be. There is a greater purpose to all of this. Even with my relationship with Seth. I know it might sound crazy, especially because he's my first boyfriend, but I know for sure he'll be my last."

"That's so ridiculous. You're young, Jazzline. I did this same mess with your father and look where it got me."

Jazzline wanted to say that no matter how much everything went wrong with her parents, at least they got her and Alex because of their love, but she didn't go there. There was no point.

"I know it's right. I'm not going to question it and follow my heart on this one. Completely."

She sighed. "I'm trying to be honest with you. I don't understand, but I guess it's not up to me."

"I'm sure of this. God gave me Seth MacKenzie, and I'm thankful."

This would be the last conversation we'd have like this. I was sure.

As I tossed and turned the rest of the night my mind was filled with images of him holding me, kissing me and the overwhelming urge to need to see him again to make sure it had all happened. Life was more than me alone. I knew that now. What a way to step into being a woman, with life right around the corner for all of us. With Seth by my side, I could actually look forward to my future. Whatever it would be.

CHAPTER 9

Against All Odds

Alex made sure I was up before my alarm clock chimed. I had about two hours of total sleep, but I felt so energized when Alex jumped on my bed. I was ready in a few minutes, pacing with him up and down the sidewalk.

"What has you so wired this morning? Ready to watch our rehearsals?"

"Not really, but I'm ready for Medieval Journey. Momma said it was okay."

I ruffled his hair and smoothed down his T-shirt that had apparently not been folded in his drawer. He was a stuffer. "Did you behave? Tell the truth."

Tucker banged the screen door. "Hey, Mooch. Hey, Smooch."

I laughed. "Hey, yourself Whip Stick."

He tickled me in the side. "Oh, you think you're funny."

I hugged him. "Not as funny looking as you are right now. What are you going to do when you have to sing with me today?"

"Oh, it's that kind of day? The one to show off my brilliance? Just go with the flow, Jazz. I've got it covered. Bree is my song. I'll have some inspiration on the sidelines." He put his hand over his heart and danced in a circle.

Alex went towards the Jeep, and I called out, "Wait, Seth is coming for us."

Tucker frowned. "Why would he drive all the way out here?"

Alex started sticking his tongue out and moving his head. "Jazz is in love. Jazz is in love."

I pointed my finger at him. "Tonight, at five thirty you will shuck oysters."

Tucker twisted Alex in the air and started shaking him out for loose change. "What's going on tonight?"

Alex squealed, "Medieval Journey, baby!"

Tucker jumped up and down in the same fashion as Alex earlier. "I wanna go. Please, Mommy."

Just then, I heard the sound of Seth's car revving down the quiet street. The bagpipe music was playing again, this time with him and Bree singing along in perfect harmony to some foreign band. Tucker dropped Alex like a sack of potatoes and ran up to Bree, lifting her out of the car without even fully opening the door. He was such a big goofball. But he didn't know that she was coming and there again, another few stolen moments were so precious with a MacKenzie. Only we would know how much. How wonderful it was to share in this together.

She kissed Tucker, then Alex, who was blushing, then bee-lined straight to me and gave me the biggest hug. "I heard. And I'm so happy for the two of you. I knew it from the minute I saw you at the house that very first night. Do you remember that moment? Oh, I do, and it has burned in my heart ever since. I can release it now. You are my brother's soul mate. There. I said it."

I hugged her back, wishing I could pry out every bit of knowledge she had about us. Knowing he had gone home talking about me made my face turn beet red. Did he tell them we kissed? Alex was already in the backseat taking his new place in our lives. Seth was waiting for me by my door with his arm outstretched to me.

He kissed me. "Good morning, baby."

I smiled up at him without his mask with the sun playing tag with his eyes, making them glow again.

"Hi."

That was all I could say as I slid into the car and flipped through the script. I brought along my highlighter and began to mark my lines.

As we pulled out behind Bree and Tucker, he saw my enthusiasm for the script. "You'll be off-book in no time."

I asked, "Off-book?"

He explained how I'd learn my lines easy because we'd go over them so much in rehearsal, I had the song set on download. Not to mention there was him and Bree who knew every line. That would come in handy if I were on stage and panicked. At least I could depend on them to mouth them to me.

Rehearsals were just like he said. We stayed all morning in little circles on the stage, going over Act I over and over. Then, we read over lyrics. I could remember the songs quicker than the lines and was relieved to see I sang my way through most of the production. I was feeling comfortable with myself by the end of the day. That would change when the auditorium filled. But I let that thought drift far out to sea and kept trying.

There was something unique about being up on the stage and around everyone with the same focus and determination, the same passions. Tucker's was misplaced, but it was still there. Ms. Dot was the driving force creating an atmosphere almost dream-like in her mannerisms and tones, her words of encouragement and strange stage vocalizations. Whatever it was, the combination of it, I felt like I belonged around a whole group of strangers and nobody seemed to mind I was plain old me. It was special. I felt enough. How I needed this for so long. Never knew I could find it with drama kids.

~

SETH DROPPED US OFF AT CHICA'S, AND I KNEW THAT I would report for duty again. If I couldn't give her the lunch schedule, I could at least help when I could. Seth had to help his brother Colin pack anyway. He would leave tomorrow and had a lot of equipment that needed shipping. I assumed it was boxes of wires and computer chips and memory sticks, or whatever computer people have. Alex kept asking me every five minutes, then three minutes, then about what it seemed every second - what time was it? Until it got to the point where I took off my watch and let him wear it.

He didn't care that it was a tiny gold band with a red frame. In his early morning wake up he forgot his Superman watch. I watched him huddled up in our family booth with his knees tucked under his chin, staring at the hands of the clock. His goal was to make it pass. And I wanted it to go by fast, but not to eat a big old chicken chunk and see the falcons fly. It was to be with Seth again.

When he came to pick us up, he had Bree with him again. "I hope you don't mind that Bree wanted to come with Tucker. We've never been, and supposedly this is Tucker's favorite place in the world."

He exaggerated it, and I laughed.

I kissed him. "Alex's, too. You'll see. You've already seen my favorite place in the world. Can we go there once the chivalry and clink-clanking is over?"

He winked. "How about if I take you to mine this time?"

I hugged him, smelling his cologne and it made me dizzy for him. "As long as you're there, it'll be my favorite place in the world." I heard Alex gag and hold his stomach. "Okay, okay, Alex. Get in and let's go."

Medieval Journey was crowded, but we still got a front row seat, met the King and got Alex, Tucker, and Bree's pictures made with the court. Seth refused his picture and was already dealing with the stares well, but I was having a harder time. Why couldn't people live their own lives?

Bree and I stood looking through t-shirts trying to find Alex's size, so I could get him one as a surprise when Seth came up to me with a helmet covering his face.

His voice was muffled, "Do you like me better like this? I'll buy it."

I pulled the helmet off his head, carrying pieces of his long hair with it and he winced. "Sorry, but no way. Remember, I don't care. Let's do this for Alex. It's not all about you, you know."

Bree laughed. "Oh, oh, oh. Who just got slammed?"

He smiled at me. He appeared the least bit worried about what anybody else thought either from the look in his eyes. "I was buying it for Alex, silly."

"Oh."

Alex came up with Tucker and flipped when he got the helmet and shield from Seth. I had a funny thought cross my mind of how he might be if we had a child together. Would he be dark or fair? Would he be calm, like both of us together? Then, I put my nonsense thoughts aside and remembered that I was only seventeen and we went on inside the dark arena to cheer for the blue knight.

Bree and Seth were so into the actual storyline, and I had to remind myself that they were drama personified. I could hear Seth telling Bree how he would have used that move or done something during the battle scenes. They were critiquing the show. This would now become their most favorite place, too, with the costumes and set designs and prop changes and all that technical stuff I was learning about.

Bree stood up and cheered when the roses were being flung through the air and one fell right in Bree's hand like magic. She squealed as if she were surprised. Bree had that kind of life where everything seemed to fall perfectly in place. Maybe if I hung out with her enough, my luck would change. It had already improved by a country mile.

Luke was waiting for us when we got home, and once Alex was inside, Seth and I were off again. This time to his favorite place in the world. What was so funny was that we were driving up the road to his house. His mom and dad were in the family room watching a film that his mother finished print on and were critiquing the lines. I stopped when I heard Tucker's voice blaring out of the screen. Seth told me he'd been ever so willing to play the serial killer role, which had his Dad suspicious since because apparently, he wasn't bad at it. Tucker and I loved scary movies our whole life, and now that their mom was writing a suspense/thriller, it made it cool to be watching how her mind worked and played out on the homemade video.

We went up to his room, and he closed the door. "Why did you bring me here? I thought we were going to your favorite place?"

He whispered as he used a remote control to play a soft instrumental piece. "You don't know? This is my favorite place because this was the first place you told me you loved me."

His kiss was new to me even though I had one the night before and dreamed of it since. Each sensation made me feel the love for him all over again, and my body shivered with emotion.

"Are you cold?" His muscular arms wrapped around me and cuddled me close to him.

"No, I'm so happy with you. I've never felt this way. This happy."

"Not even when you went to the fair?"

I sighed, kissing him on the cheek. "The MacKenzie Park is so much more fun for me. No lines or crowds or waits, just you and me. Here would be our theme song." I began to sing to him and he spun me around.

He sat down on the edge of the bed, pulling me with him. "I want you to see something."

With the push of a switch on his remote, the ceiling began to melt away, parting in two sections to reveal a crystal-clear glass ceiling above my head. He leaned back on the bed and pulled me up to his pillows he shoved up under my head and adjusted for me. I snuggled on his arm anyway, so all the fuss was of no use.

"This is amazing. Now I see why you have it all black in here."

"Did you think I was like the phantom of St. James? Living in a cave? Jazzline, you watch too many movies."

I kissed his cheek. "I didn't know. It's kind of weird."

"Say it again."

"You're weird."

He turned sideways to me then, his scarred cheek hidden in the bedcovers. "No, not that. Jazzline, tell me you love me."

I touched his face and smoothed back his hair that had fallen over his nose. "I love you, Seth MacKenzie."

"I love you, too."

And there it was. The explosion of every thought I had contained my whole life, all rippling around me like a waterfall. All thoughts of isolation and abandonment, of not being good enough. Of not being heard. And he heard me. And he loved me. He told me he loved me. And what mattered more to me than anything was that he wanted me just the way I was. Without a game or an agenda. Just me, even if it meant tag-along Alex to come for the ride, too. That made me love him even more.

Every now and then, he would point up at God's sky and show me a constellation or tell me a myth. He showed me his star that his brother and sister named for him. Then, he told me how he wanted to be an astronomer and study physics at either the College of Charleston or UNC-Chapel Hill. His father wanted him to go to a big ivy-league school, Yale, his alma mater, but he didn't want to be that far from home or his doctors.

He asked what my plans were, and I had none. I'd never even thought about my future so wrapped up in the thought of Tucker not being in it I shut down to all that talk. But now I was one year away, and I knew that it would be here tomorrow as fast as my life had passed me by to seventeen. I wished that I had a palm-reader to give me some insight. Then, I knew exactly what I needed, a Bible.

He pulled one out of his desk drawer, and I opened it. It fell to John 6:27, " Do not labor for the food which perishes, but for the food which endures to everlasting life, which the Son of Man will give you, because God the Father has set His seal on him."

I couldn't believe how God could answer me when I asked. *Don't labor for food which perishes.* I placed the Bible on Seth's lap and asked him to read Jesus' words.

Seth handed me the Bible back, and I held it close to my heart. "What did that mean?"

I turned to him. "Don't you get it. Momma thinks I'm going to chef school and live with my daddy in Charlotte. She thinks I want to take over Chica's but honestly, Seth, I don't want that for my life. I really don't. And I don't want to live with my dad. It's not like we have a stellar relationship or anything. I barely know him."

I could feel the tears wanting to fall from the pressure building up within me. It had been coming for so long.

He pulled me close to him and being there made me feel like everything somehow was going to work out, even if I couldn't see it now.

Seth asked, "Why can't you just be honest with her?"

"You need to know how I am. You need to know why I can't."

And then I began to tell him I didn't go there with people, with confrontation and possibilities of arguments. It wasn't worth the risk. He wouldn't understand that about me, yet I knew that it was turning out to be a really serious problem for me. When I was younger, it didn't matter much. What decisions or input could I give Momma that would change my life? Converses or Vans? I didn't find it necessary to open up. But now, I was feeling myself shrinking away further and further and backing myself in a corner I'd have to fight out of or suffer.

"But you aren't like that to me at all. I don't understand why you say that when you pushed me and told me all your feelings from the beginning. How can you be like this when you aren't with me?"

I kissed him. "I don't know. Maybe because you're like the

missing part of me. Maybe with you now I can be strong, and you can help me find my voice."

I tried to find the words to really paint the bleak picture of my life. I told him how I never talked at school or with anyone other than Tucker. Only teachers, and if asked a question. And I was sure I'd done it to myself all these years, and I didn't even know why. He frowned as he lay back with his arms crossed over his chest, holding my hands, twirling my costume ring with his finger.

But the more I stared up at the night sky and felt the peace wash all over me the more I began to find a place within myself that needed answers to those unspoken questions I'd been harboring for years. I opened myself up to it once again. Why was I so stifled and silent? What started it all for me and made me who I was today? That girl who didn't know how to reach out, who couldn't find her own voice? I didn't want to hide behind Seth like I'd done with Tucker so many years. I wanted to stand beside him on solid ground.

Then, the image popped into my mind like I could reach out and touch it there in front of me, flashing lyrics of an old country song, "D-I-V-O-R-C-E became final today."

Seth was silent with me lost in his own thoughts. When I started to sing, it startled him. "What? Where in the world do you get these songs you sing? They come from nowhere!"

All of the years came closing in on me at once. The cheating. The yelling. The name-calling and the choosing. Alex wanting Daddy, me wanting to stay by Tucker so I chose Momma. The realization of it all hit me so hard that there was no way I could think in complete sentences or even try to describe it all to Seth, whose family was so close, so dependent upon each other. They were a clan. We were just driftwood washed up on the shore. The remnants of a loveless marriage.

I'd chosen to wash away like a message bottled up yet never moving out to sea, never making it over the break. I'd find myself right on the same sand, in my same spot, then taken back out again at high tide having no control. With the same message. With the same story. Until now. My glass shattered against the rocks, and it took me under the current, swelling and falling, crashing and floating.

But somehow not drowning.

Seth looked over at the clock by the bedside table and broke our revealing silence. "I know you technically don't have a curfew but does twelve o'clock alarm you any?"

I shot up. "Midnight already? Are you serious? No!"

I didn't want this to end. I didn't want to leave his favorite spot. What deep realizations I'd discovered by being with Seth and letting God lead me.

He got off the bed pulling me up along with him. His parents had long been asleep, and I wondered if they thought we were being intimate in the room behind closed doors with no lights. I hoped that they would know that I wouldn't do that. That I would remain pure until marriage. I'd never had another guy around to breach the three-letter word subject with until now. But what would Seth's reaction to that be?

I told Seth what I was worried about and he shrugged. "What was it you told me? You didn't care what others thought about you? You and I know what we do. God knows. Don't be concerned about anybody else. I believe the same way you do. We will wait."

His parents didn't come out with flashlights or alarm systems blaring. We slipped out, backed down the drive and made it back to my house with no pointing fingers or raised eyebrows.

The house was quiet, and there was nothing but a light waiting for me in the kitchen.

I still didn't want to let him go, but I knew that we were stepping over some kind of normal boundary, pushing ourselves to the point of exhaustion. "We've got to stop doing this, you know. I need my beauty sleep. I'm going to fall over tomorrow.

He laughed. "Maybe it'll be a faint scene, and you will be right on cue. Ms. Dot loves a believable faint. You should have no problem with that."

I kissed him one last time. "As long as you are there to catch me."

He breathed into my hair, crushing me against him, my tiny frame enveloped by his huge arms. "I'll always be here for you, Jazzline."

And I believed it. I closed the door and leaned up against the frame and felt the tears want to well up again. I wondered if Seth and I would ever make it? Was this just a summer of love? Was this my time then he would leave me, too? Would we be another stupid statistic? I prayed as I turned off the light for us to be the ones that make it. God could see to it.

CHAPTER 10

Heaven

The professional set crew arrived from Myrtle Beach for the weekend transformation of the theater. That meant no rehearsals since they would make the stage come alive with props and backdrops. Ms. Dot shooed us away like flies saying we would only be in the way but assigned notecard schedule reminders that she wrote out by hand. I felt like we should be on Broadway. Belonging was so sharp here. I knew I was meant for the stage. And it came naturally for me, contrary to what I would have ever believed.

"Why the long face? You aren't getting rid of me that easy. I told you I'd help you with your lines and Bree is intent on working on the songs tomorrow morning. Bright and early. I'll be there."

He took my hand in his as we entered Chica's.

"But what about tonight?"

Momma heard and gave me the aren't you going to work look.

He said, "Can I steal her away from you again, Ms. Chicand?"

"You can have her. And Alex, too."

Alex was out of earshot and by the look on Seth's face; I knew that he would want me alone. I could feel it. Maybe momma could, too.

"Okay, I'll take Alex. You spend way too much time with him anyway, Jazzline."

"Please promise me you'll step out and check on him now and then. Make sure Luke knows."

Momma laughed before disappearing again. "Don't worry about a thing, and tonight try to make it home by one."

That was a more than reasonable curfew, and I was so appreciative that Momma respected me enough to give me that freedom. Especially compared to Bree's ten o'clock hour.

Seth kissed me as I tried on my black apron over my new clothes. He'd commented on my wardrobe again today, and I got some wisecracks from Tucker over it, but I did feel good in real girl clothes. Wearing Tucker's surf shop shirts weren't the latest fashions I was sure, and I started to feel a little bit beautiful beside Seth. The clothes were an added bonus.

He kissed me. "I'll pick you up at your house around four. Is that okay?"

I wanted to tell him to pick me up now and run me out of the door like a rescue attempt from heavy tray abuse, but I couldn't. Three would be long enough for me to do my part for the family, smile until my face hurt, then manage a quick trip home to shower and change.

Today was busy. When the doors closed for the daily midafternoon break between lunch and dinner, momma was relieved. She leaned her arm out of our old Volvo station wagon and popped her hand on the mirror as Bon Jovi blared from the speakers.

"What are you going to do when school starts back?"

"Not stay up late."

"Good answer. Wanted to make sure you knew that it was summer time zones. Is this a summer thing?"

I was hopeful it would last forever. Certain. "No. It's not."

It was without explanation or details. She didn't need to know how I'd run away with him to Charleston or Chapel Hill when he went off to college next year, if he asked me. His dad was already encouraging him to apply for early decision, and I might go do the same thing. At least I now had community theater to add to my college applications.

"What are his plans with you? I don't know about people like that?"

I couldn't handle an argument. The words she and Luke spouted at me last night were hurtful enough. But I could feel the heat rising and my fingers starting to curl and ball. I breathed. The words I wanted to say released from my brain at my exhale, and it sounded like a whooshing wind.

I managed to only reply, "Like what?"

"You know rich ones like that? If they're that rich, they think they can get whatever they want. And it looks like he wants you, and it doesn't matter what it costs for you, he'll take you."

"What it'll cost me? I'm gaining here."

"Have you ever considered what it'll cost you to be with him? To live your life with people teasing and pointing? You'll be an outcast right along with him. People can be downright mean, Jazzline. It will cost you a normal life. And for what?"

This must have been what Seth was always afraid of. That's why he was hidden away with his family, living his closed-up life. If she worried about me being an outcast, she could have started this talk six years ago, not today.

It was so hard to look at myself in the mirror when I was trying to get ready for Seth to pick me up. All I could see were her words on me. Would he know what she said? He could read me so well it was dangerous. Makeup couldn't hide the hurt I was feeling at Momma's lack of acceptance of him. Luke was filling a little sick, so he had to come home during lunch hour. Alex was to stay home and tend to him, fetch him food and drinks and medicine. Alex playing nurse would be as useless as a doll. We still had to keep Bree under house arrest one more night until the MacKenzie's got back from MIT. But the house was big enough for us to disappear and never be found again. That was what I wanted.

When he pulled up, I could hear Bree's laughter through my window. She was already heading over to Tucker's. It was the singsong voice of an angel and the burly sounds of my man so close to me. Momma picked me out a yellow sundress that went down to my ankles with a pair of strappy sandals to wear tonight. It was perfect.

Momma was holding him hostage, questioning him about his grades, his senior year course schedule, and his college plans all in one swoop of her talons but he answered every line with ease. His confidence in his future took me back. When would I know? When could I decide how to tell her that I didn't? He stopped in mid-sentence. His eyes turned to a burnt gold.

Momma smiled, taking credit. "I knew that would be perfect on you."

He didn't speak, and neither did I as we left the house. I tried to smile back at Momma, but my lip was quivering. We were just going back to his house. My stomach swirled, and I knew the old feeling and what could happen. I prayed and the feeling of peace washed over my body, sickness leaving me at once. I wouldn't get sick in his car. I wouldn't get sick and be weak anymore. God could give me the strength I needed to face each situation new.

"You're beautiful in that dress."

I wanted him to hold my hand but he was gripping the steering wheel, looking like an awkward fifteen-year-old getting his permit.

"You don't know, do you? You don't know. That's what makes it even more appealing."

"What?"

"You're the most beautiful girl I've ever seen in my life, Jazzline. And I can't believe that you're really mine."

"You don't know a lot of girls, then."

"I've had a few."

"Go on. I'd like to know the dating secrets of Seth MacKenzie. What were you up to before you met me?"

I wanted to know, but I didn't at the same time. I wanted him to say I was the first girl he'd ever kissed. How it was with me. I wanted to be his only girlfriend. His first love.

When we got up to his cave, we snuggled up, and he switched on an old movie classic, Shop Around the Corner. Instead of paying attention to the movie, I wanted to know more about his past. He told me about dating girls and double dating with Colin when he was younger. The thought of that made me laugh. He continued, grinning at me. But when he was fifteen, the Lupus was discovered, and he fell into a dark hole. Now, he'd spent years trying to learn how to move without thinking of them or other people's reactions. He said it was the right time for God to send me into his life.

I kissed him on his cheek, and this time he didn't flinch. "God's timing is never wrong."

I reached for his hand and could feel the heat off him. He was sweating. "Are you sure you're okay?"

He smiled. "I'm alright. I have days."

In the middle of our moment, without explanation, the doubt bird started to peck in my head again. My momma's words hit me. Was this a summer thing? Was this real?

He pulled back to look at me as if he could sense the shift. "You're the one that's now acting all weird."

I asked, "What's this between us?"

He cradled my head against his chest, and I could feel the warmth of his body against my cheek. "I've never loved anyone before I met you. I'm sure that is what is between us."

"But how can you be sure it will last?"

I wanted to know it all, the ending of us before we could even get past the beginning. But life didn't work out that way, and I would have to learn to trust in this. Love was hurting me from the inside out, and I hated that her words stirred the doubt. Momma could cook up some internal drama, and she wasn't even around. Five-star rating.

"I know you are hesitant because of your parent's divorce. I would never cheat on you. I would never leave you. I promise you

I'll never hurt you if I can help it. I can give you all I have and know that it would never be enough to explain how I feel about you."

Promises were made and broken every day. Just what if this was all a dream? But it felt so real to me, so consuming. "This is so much for me. I'm sorry that I'm doing this."

The doubts could eat away at me and tear us apart. I could go back into my old mode and shut down. Shut him out and pretend like I never knew the feeling I had with him.

I faced him. "I know we're young. I know people will talk. But I don't care. I love you so much, Seth."

"People meaning your momma?"

"How did you know?"

"I just figured. She'll come around. Eventually. Maybe not now."

"Maybe when I'm fifty?"

"Maybe so. Promise me you won't fight her about me. I don't want to be the cause of any conflict."

"But I will stand up for what I know is true. There's going to be a change a'coming with Jazzline Chicand. You'll see, and so will she. The Lord will help me fight my battles anyway. I'm covered in that department."

We turned our attention back to the movie. We didn't talk for the longest time, and it was such a comfort not having to think of the right words to say. Seth was mine, and he knew it. I knew that it was more than a summer thing. It was forever, and the doubts disappeared with his lips on mine. The fear of being too close was taken over by the fear of not being close enough.

The sound of a phantom ring tone broke our silence, and Seth grimaced. "Bree put this on my phone. She's obsessed. What?"

He acted annoyed but I could see the smile on his lips.

He turned his phone off. "Where were we?"

"What was that about?"

"She's ready for us to go to the theater. She has a surprise for you and Tucker." By the hesitation in his voice, I was sure he didn't want us to go.

"I love surprises."

He pushed himself up and carried me along with him. He closed the ceiling as if he already suspected that this would take a while.

"If we must."

Bree was waiting at the door to the theater. Tucker was smiling at me as I walked up, and I smoothed down my hair, looking like a mess. He did, too. His face was glowing red.

Bree was luminous as she smiled at us, poised with her delicate fingers twisting the doorknob holding the suspense as long as she could. The theater had been turned into some kind of dress rehearsal for some Scottish play. Seth went over to one costume and touched the hem of the skirt.

"What's all this stuff?"

I tried to pick up a sword off the table, but I couldn't even lift it. Seth came over and grinned at me and with one hand picked it up and held it in the air. Tucker went straight over, and they talked broadswords and claymores. I ducked out of the way and went to stand beside Bree who was twirling around a dancing costume.

"Next weekend is our Scottish Festival at Southdale. All of our family is coming from Scotland to spend the next month with us. My cousin Cat is coming. Oh, you'll love her. And Alasdair and Donell and Devon, the twins. Alasdair is close to Alex's age, and they'll get along fine. Then, Douglas. I can't wait for you to meet my Aunt Shea and then Uncle Colin, too. Don't confuse the Colin names. My brother was named after my uncle."

I laughed. "Wow. Okay, then. Let me try to remember all you said and see how that turns out."

Seth came over and led me to the recliner seats. He looked as if he could rip them apart because the armrest was in the way from our bodies touching. He then stood up and grabbed a blanket to throw on the floor, and we fell on it. He made sure that I was as close to him as possible. If we had to endure whatever Bree had planned, we could at least do it holding each other.

He whispered as Bree turned on the video and cut out the lights, "I'm a little nervous for you to see this."

"Why?" The credits started to play, and it was yet again another home movie made by Mrs. MacKenzie, her children willing yet again to be her stars. But this time Seth was there with his family, maybe a little shorter, not as big as the man beside me.

He yelled, "Bree, turn it off."

Bree's eyes twinkled. "Why? She has to see you now, or she won't be able to handle next weekend."

Plans I didn't know about. "What's going on next weekend?"

"You have to go with us to the Highland Games. And you might as well know he'll be wearing a kilt and fighting and feeling weird around you because of all the violence."

"Did you say violence? Like fighting? For real?"

Bree nodded, pointing to his green tartan plaid kilt pressed in a row with one more to match beside his. "Wait, I thought your brother Colin was at MIT."

Bree smiled. "No, Colin hates he'll miss the family, but he had no choice with classes starting on Monday. The other kilt is for Tucker."

I saw the look of terror in his eyes. I thought that must have been the way I looked when they first told me I'd had the lead in the play.

"Even though I haven't seen the fellas in ages, Jazz, if you tell them..."

We all laughed.

The rest of the film highlighted Seth's skill with the broadsword, but the fighting seemed a little vicious.

"Can you please explain to me why so brutal? Is that a competition or a play?"

Seth said, "It's no play. It's what I do."

"You fight with swords? Who does this?"

Bree said, "They fight because they must, Jazzline. We must always be in the ready."

Tucker said, "Did you know Bree was a black belt?"

"Yeah, I heard. Don't get on my bad side, Bree."

She smiled. "Never, Jazzline. You are my future sister-in-law. Seth has already seen..."

"Seen what?"

Seth's voice rose, and he glared at Bree. Something just happened between them, and I couldn't read it. "Seen to it. That's all. Go ahead and start it back. The caber toss is more Jazzline's speed. Fast forward the fighting."

There was a take of Bree's dance where she'd won first place in the solo division. His parents were laughing and singing around a campfire. Green tartans were everywhere. The MacKenzie colors, I found out. I also found out that each year there was a tradition they called the exchange. The look Seth gave Bree sent a chill down my spine. He was serious. He wanted her to hush, but she kept on going. She told me that Seth's exchange was up. He was to go and his cousin Douglas was to come to stay here at Pawley's Island.

My hand caught my throat as if I could stifle the sound that escaped my lips. "You're leaving senior year?"

Bree bit her lip and looked apologetically at Seth.

"You just promised me, swore you would never leave me and you're leaving?" Panic, fear, my heart was pounding, and I felt the dark close in.

CHAPTER 11

Time After Time

Seth glared at Bree. "It's not like that. My father knows."

I whispered, "Knows what?"

He tried my hand this time, but I pushed him away, feeling like he'd already left me.

"He knows that I love you, and I am not going away. Instead of the exchange this year, Douglas is coming here to stay with us. I'm not going anywhere."

"Don't scare me like that."

"Bree didn't have time to finish the story." He looked to Tucker. "Don't worry, she's cleared herself, too. No more school exchanges for the MacKenzie's. We won't leave US soil without the two of you. But you need to know that it is our duty to fly there next summer for a month to visit my father's people. We go every other year, they come here the off years. It's always been so. So, get your passports for the trip next year."

"Tucker, baby, go try on your kilt for Jazz."

"You mean you already tried it on?"

Bree clapped. "He did, and he looked so dashing. It looks like he just stepped out of our castle."

Maybe Luke was right. Maybe they did have a castle in Scotland nestled away somewhere by the sea.

Tucker stood up and went towards the door. "Woman, you promised me some grub. Let's go round some up, pretty lady."

Instead of following them, Seth pulled me back and led me over to the wall of costumes. Dresses of every kind were hanging, full skirts, long skirts, short skirts, all pressed and waiting. If this weren't so close a part of his life, his heritage, and with his father and mother, then I would have thought it a little strange.

"I want you to do something for me."

I sighed, hoping he'd say to kiss him. "What?"

"I want you to wear this." He held out a long skirt, plaid tartan with a puffy white blouse and matching vest. "I know you might think it's ridiculous. But I've never asked a girl to the games or to meet my family, and it would mean so much to me if you could come with me. To see what we love and to be by my side."

"Yes," was all I could say.

He handed me the dress to carry with me. We walked out to meet Tucker and Bree who were feeding each other chips. Seth said, "That's a little extreme. Isn't it supposed to be like strawberries or chocolate?"

Bree's eyes twinkled. "We've done that, too."

Seth growled. "Sissy, you better watch it. Let's remember your age here."

Tucker's tone grew serious, "I know, Seth. I know."

Seth's said, "It's not you that I'm worried about. It's Bree."

I chided. "It's always the women. What's up with that? I know Tucker."

"Hey, he's been a perfect gentleman. Change of subject. Let's go over the agenda for tomorrow morning."

Bree waved the paper in front of my face. She'd gone to the extreme of typing out a weekend agenda and how our rehearsal schedule would go.

"Are you the new Ms. Dot?" I laughed when I read her hour-by-hour plans. Much stricter than our darling director.

She twirled around. "One day I hope to be." She told us

about attending college for theater and hoped to be a director one day.

Their parents announced at the gate. "We're home, kids."

Seth spun in surprise, looking around at the disarray in the kitchen and Bree and him had it perfect in the minutes they took to drive down the long driveway and make their way to the family room, where Bree sat down on the floor crossing her legs with her hand in her lap so delicate and dancer-like. Seth greeted his parents and grabbed their suitcase to carry it for them to their bedroom. We heard all about the trip and Colin's new apartment by campus. As soon as Bree had some airway, she burst out with the details of her working weekend and her mother laughed.

"I see I've got a little protégé. You've never quite taken rehearsals this intense before. Other than already knowing your parts, and everyone else's for that matter."

Bree pointed to me and Tucker. "But I want them to be perfect."

I said, "That's a lot of pressure, Bree. I don't know about perfect."

Seth put his arm around me and his mother smiled.

Tucker reached for Bree's hand. "Well, if keeping us hostage here all weekend will do it, then I'm up for some rehearsals. When do we start?"

Bree turned to her Momma and asked, "Can you help us?"

She was tired, and I was sure she could have found better things to do than run lines with us for the weekend, but she hugged Bree and said, "I'll help you, dear. Whatever I can do."

Mrs. MacKenzie said, "You bring out the best in my daughter, I see."

Tucker smiled. "It's the other way around, Mrs. MacKenzie."

And he was so true. I'd never seen Tucker so happy in his life. It was so cute to see how he looked at her when she didn't know he was. Then, I turned to Seth, and he was looking at me the same way, and I grinned. His eyebrows raised, and I smiled all the more at him.

Her mother pointed to the clock. "Sorry, Tucker but lights out for Bree."

She whined, "But we're talking about rehearsals."

His mother came over and kissed my cheek and patted Tucker on the arm. The night was over. My dress was hanging over the chair, and Seth grabbed it as we left out of the room.

Tucker laughed. "You've got you one of the green things, too?"

Seth said, "Her legs will look a lot better than yours, I'm sure."

Bree giggled. "I don't think so."

Her mother swatted her. "Brianna Rain MacKenzie. How dare you speak like that?"

I stifled a laugh, and when we made it outside, I couldn't help but let it out once more at the thought of my Tucker in that kilt. "Where is it?"

Bree grinned. "He's not taking it with him. I'm carrying it with us on the trip, so he doesn't accidentally leave it behind for the weekend."

I smiled. "You know him all too well. You make it sound like it's an overnight trip."

She frowned. "Didn't Seth tell you? We'll be leaving Friday and won't be home until Sunday night."

Alex. I couldn't leave him behind. Three days were years in a kid's life. "Alex. My momma."

"I'll speak to her this evening. My parents would like to meet her. Tucker already got the green light, and his mother is coming over tomorrow to meet us all."

"I don't know if a meeting with my mom is a good idea."

I couldn't say I didn't want Momma anywhere near their family. What if she would say what she felt? What if it would be over between us because of her negative, closed up mind? His parents wouldn't want me to be with Seth if Momma was like that. Unnecessary drama.

I didn't talk on the way home and what turned out to be such a wonderful evening went straight to the dumpsters. Seth blared Cyndi Lauper, Time After Time, singing soft.

I held back tears. "Seth, my momma..." I still couldn't find the words to tell him.

He knew without me having to go there, and my heart hurt.

"Jazzline, I don't care if your mother loves me. Just you."

But it would have been so much easier if she approved, and he knew it. Asking her to let me go for a weekend trip was pointless. She needed me to watch after Alex because she had to work. Being the owner-chef was an all-out commitment. She gave her life to Chica's and left me to run the minor details. She wouldn't understand that because she only saw what she loved.

The house was quiet when we walked in. Momma frowned, looking up from one of her collections of romance novels. "What's wrong?"

Seth asked could he speak with Momma alone. They stepped outside to our little patio, and I watched as the sliding glass door separated us. I paced the floor, walking back and forth across the carpet, sitting down on the couch and getting back up again. He said that he'd talk to her earlier, but I thought that meant us together. It was probably better this way anyway. I would be no good to him. I didn't know how to fight.

After what seemed like an eternity, she opened the sliding doors and came over to me. Her face was tired. She caught what Luke had and whatever it was, it looked nasty.

"I'm feeling too bad to discuss anything more. Just talk with Seth about it. I'm sure he can fill you in. I'm not hugging you goodnight because I don't want you to catch this. Best if you stay away from me, Luke, and Alex."

"Alex?"

"Yeah, apparently his nursing led to him catching it, too. It feels like the flu or something. Summer colds are the worst."

"I'm so sorry."

She looked at me, then Seth and said, "I'm sorry, too."

As soon as she walked out of the room, he grabbed my hand and led me out the door, back into his car. He turned down our beach access road and we were back. My second favorite place in the world.

I remembered the first night on the beach with him. My first kiss. We had kissed a thousand times since that night, but I wanted him again. I pulled his face down to mine and kissed him. Whatever it was between them he would have to know that it would change nothing for me.

"Jazzline, I can't."

Crash. Out again. The sound was not soothing anymore. It was loud and intrusive. Hurtful. "Can't?" My heart had stopped, and I fell forward, clutching my stomach.

"I can't take advantage of you." He whispered over the waves, but I heard him.

"What?" Those words had to be Momma talking.

"When you kiss me, I forget everything. The consequences of this." He pulled me closer to him anyway, so this wasn't a breakup conversation, thank God.

"Is my momma getting to you, too." I couldn't finish it.

"Your momma is very heated. She can get a little emotional. You don't take after her, I'm sure. But don't worry about any of that right now. Kiss me so I can forget."

And I did. But it must not have been working because after a few more minutes he started to tell me their conversation. Seth said that it was better she was honest with him now than a year down the road. I wondered what a year would mean for us, but I tried not to think about that. Momma agreed to meet his parents, but they'd got to Chica's after lunch rush for a cup of coffee. I could only imagine Momma wanting to meet them on her turf. That would be her safest vantage point.

"I'm so sorry."

He shrugged. "Don't be sorry, Jazzline. You didn't do it. You don't feel this way. I still don't understand it myself. How you could stand me?"

"I can't stand being away from you. Thinking about the weekend already makes me so sad."

He frowned. "Why? I thought you said you'd go."

"Yeah, but I know what Momma said."

"She said you can go as long as you would promise to stay with Bree and Momma. Tucker is forced to be with me."

That came at such a shock. "For the first time in my life, I'm jealous of Tucker Lane."

"I've been jealous of him from the beginning."

"Why?"

I couldn't imagine anything that Seth would want of Tucker's. If he got dreadlocks, I'd rub them out myself. He had better not say his face or body. He was even bigger than Tucker was. I couldn't stand to hear the comparison and know that Seth wanted that. I wanted him to love himself how I did.

"He's known you his whole life."

He kissed me again, long, and I was breathless.

I wanted to say it. It was right there and instead of holding it back, I let it out. "Tucker may have known me my whole life, but you can love me for the rest of yours."

The conversations were over. Kissing and holding took priority. Seth was no more bothered by my momma, and neither was I. Her attitude would soften. She would see how good he was for me, and she would let it go.

ALEX WAS STILL ASLEEP WHEN SETH CAME TO PICK ME back up for our rehearsals. I felt exhausted, and it was from the lack of sleep or the tossing and turning of the thoughts I had of him and Momma pacing back and forth on that patio. It seemed like something more occurred there that I wasn't aware of.

Bree handed me an agenda and asked me to review it on the way back to their house. I let the paper sit in my lap as I stared at Seth. "How do you fight?"

He laughed. "You want me to teach you a right hook? I've got a mean one, they've told me."

I pictured myself trying to beat somebody up and smiled. "No, not physically fight. I mean, how do you fight with words and win?"

He shrugged. "It takes thought. You choose your words. You realize going in that half the battle is awareness, and you're not always going to be right. You pick it apart like a chess game. I think listening is the most important part of winning. If you'd only listen to what the other person says or doesn't say, you can find the response you need."

I frowned. "Never was good at playing games."

"No, I didn't mean to make it sound so much as a game. It's an art form. Your momma has it down pat, but I was better. Not that I manipulated her, but I got what I wanted. I got you to come with me to Southdale. So, I won round one. I'm sure she'll be more careful about round two. Let's hope that was our first and last encounter with boxing gloves raised."

I thought about what his boxing match would have looked like with his father over the Scotland family exchange program. "How did it go with your dad about you staying here for senior year?"

He squirmed in his leather seat. "You don't want to know the details of that one. That one is still stinging a little. We went twelve rounds on that fight. But I'm here, aren't I? So, it was worth it."

"Would you have left?"

"If it wasn't for you, the answer is yes. I have a connection to that place I can't explain. Like my feet hit the ground, and I feel the pulse of the earth."

Bree mentioned that we'd be going with them to Scotland next summer, and the thought of leaving Alex behind for a whole month was too much. What would I do when I went off to college? I wondered what rights I'd have and could I take him from Momma and keep him with me? I was sure I could make it legal.

"But in senior year? Wouldn't you have missed everything that goes with that?"

"I could've completed some research I've been working on with my brother, Colin. I would've been with my family there, too. I don't have that many friends other than my football teammates. I have you, and I can't forget Alex and Tucker. Douglas will like it here. He's been when he was younger. It'll all work out for the good."

He turned the 80's station up, and I couldn't help but sing along to Every Rose Has Its Thorn by Poison. He was learning my music, too, and it made my heart glad.

His mother was setting up the theater room when we arrived. She had makeshift stage settings marked to give us familiarity with the stage directions at First Take. Ms. Dot would have been pleased to see that with Bree's genius planning I was to have Act I and II down, memorized and off-book by Monday. Mrs. MacKenzie also had the piano moved in to complete our rehearsals. Bree and I did our Angel of Song duet. Her voice was innocent, sounding like an angel herself. Mrs. MacKenzie pushed a call button and asked Mr. MacKenzie to come down.

Seth asked, "What is it? I thought dad was working on a last-minute golf project before going to the club."

Seth's father designed elite golf courses, from Scotland, across the world, to South Carolina. That is how they came to the US when he was a kid. His father did the same.

"I want him to hear this next one."

I looked down at the list, and it was Seth's turn. I'd never heard him sing but once, a short burst of Time After Time. His momma kicked him off the piano bench, and he came over to stand by me.

Bree asked, "You've heard this one right, The Phantom?"

I'd heard it. Since he'd made me the soundtrack, I'd been studying it all week, every spare chance I had. Alex was even turning out to be an impressive singing partner. I didn't let Bree in on the secret I'd already learned all of the lyrics. She would need to feel special. Like her weekend meant something for me. So, I asked her for the sheet music anyway.

She patted me on the hand, twisting the ring on my finger. "You'll get the hang of all this stuff, I promise."

I smiled at her and then my composure changed when the big frame of Mr. MacKenzie barreled through the door. He announced, "I'm here. Where's the bloody fire?"

"About to explode in this room. Come in and sit down, sweetheart. Seth and Jazzline are getting ready to sing for the first time."

He didn't respond but his eyebrows rose in the same fashion as Seth's. Their mannerisms were so alike. Mr. MacKenzie was an intimidating looking man, fiercely handsome. And I knew that Seth would look the same when he was older, with salt and pepper hair cut short. Seth's hair was long, with dark curls down past his shoulders. His eyes turned burnt copper as he stared down at me, and I bit my lip.

He could sense my fear. "Don't be afraid to sing in front of my family. Think of it as a real performance."

"You're supposed to be helping here."

Seth's mother frowned. "What's wrong, dear? Are you not ready?"

Bree sighed. "She's getting stage fright again. Look at how pale her face turned. Just start the music, and she'll snap out of it and be fine."

And the music started, and I stared at Seth, refusing him to look away from me. His eyes were pushing me on. And when I began to sing, it turned into something more than me. It turned into Christy, and I allowed the character to take over. Seth's voice was pure and strong, beautiful and tender. His voice was the most beautiful sound I'd ever heard in my life, and I felt it hard to continue with him. My heart was about to explode out of my chest.

When the lyrics were mine to sing, I turned away. The

repeating of the words "never will I know this love again" felt as if they were ripping out my heart. At least in our adapted version, I ended up loving the Phantom.

When the song was over, Ms. MacKenzie's hands were still on the keys. Mr. MacKenzie leaned back in one of the recliner seats, his eyes closed. Was he sleeping? If I had that effect on everybody that night, then I'd be okay. I could deal with snores better than boos. His head raised, and his eyes were brimming with tears.

Bree was standing by with her mouth gaped open. Seth reached out and touched my hand. Mrs. MacKenzie stood up and came between us. "I've been to many a musical in my day. You know this is true, Seth. I've never in my life felt the love and emotion I felt from the two of you when you sang to each other. It was timeless. Ms. Dot doesn't know this, does she?"

Seth whispered, "No, Momma. She's heard Jazzline sing, though, and that's enough."

She pulled her cell phone out of her pocket. "I've got to call her right now."

She turned and went to sit beside Mr. MacKenzie leaning into his arm and whispered to him as she waited for Ms. Dot to pick up. I could hear the excited rise and fall of her voice as she told Ms. Dot about her discovery during practice.

I asked Seth, "Was it that good?"

He laughed, and it echoed around the room, much like his voice had just done seconds ago. "Good? Jazzline. It was perfect."

Bree stepped forward. "You were amazing, Jazzline. Seth, you weren't so bad yourself." She elbowed him in the side, then, turned back to me. "You've never even taken any lessons?"

I shook my head. "No."

His momma jumped in then. "Natural talent, this girl has it. You're going to be a star, Jazzline. A bright and shining star, and Ms. Dot will be thrilled to say she discovered you in our tiny little theater at Pawley's Island, South Carolina when she will one day be interviewed by a Tony Awards journalist."

Seth pulled me away from Bree and their momma's excitement over my singing voice. "I'm stealing away my star for a few minutes break. Is that okay?"

Bree interjected as if she was the boss, and she began checking off her agenda. "Yeah, it's Rao's turn to go over his singing parts. I can work on them without Christy."

As soon as we hit the hallway, he picked me up, pulled me into his arms, and carried me two steps at a time up to his bedroom. He pulled me close and kissed me with an urgency that made my mind reel.

He buried his face in my hair and I giggled. "If this is what I get for singing with you then let's plan this more often."

"I love you, Jazzline." His voice was sweet. "I can't believe that you are mine, but I swear to you right here and now, I'll never hurt you."

Something changed in his voice. It felt urgent.

I asked, "What's wrong?"

"Nothing. I've completely lost my heart to you. I'm thankful to God that he gave me you, and I am overwhelmed knowing I will love you for the rest of our lives. No matter how short that may be."

I sighed. "God has blessed us so much, Seth. Out of all the people in the world that could have loved me, it had to be you."

Bree knocked on the door. "Okay, you two. That's enough. Jazzline, come on and sing with Tucker now. I'm on a time schedule here, darlings."

She drawled out that last line, and we couldn't help but laugh. Seth growled at her but followed her all the same. I tried to smooth down my hair.

With his hand resting at the small of my back, it was hard to concentrate on the next song. Even though I knew every line, this time I had to follow the lyrics sheet. One, I was still feeling the love that passed between Seth and me in our song, not to mention our kiss, but having to sing with Tucker was at the point of being ridiculous, and I was trying my best to make it real for Bree's sake. She depended on it.

114

It was easier when he turned to look at Bree. That gave me the opportunity to sing my line to him. After our song was over, I hugged Tucker. He wasn't bad but he wasn't good either, but I couldn't tell him that. He was, after all, just a surfer trying to impress a lady. His lady thought he was wonderful, and she kissed him on the cheek. Her father coughed, and she distanced herself again from Tucker.

His mother sighed. "Okay, you stage lovebirds. Look at each other while you're singing. Tucker, Bree won't be right there in front of you. Jazzline, make that sound believable. Like you did with Seth."

Bree frowned. "What if I stand stage left, right behind the curtain so he can see me? He can sing to me, and no one will know the difference."

Seth was still holding on to me. His voice was low. "I don't have to be standing there to know that she's singing for me."

His mother and Bree let out a stream of ahhs and Bree agreed with him that she was being too melodramatic. With that settled, we went on about our day, one song after the next until my voice started to hurt. Then, Seth announced it was time to go.

Bree explained she would stay behind and coach Tucker on body language. I giggled at that, and when Mr. MacKenzie stood up, he said, "Not alone in this house you aren't. Young lady, you're going with us."

"Where are we going?"

I was sure Bree had us going to some underground theater tunnels or getting us caught in a cage rigged down on the inlet side of their property.

Seth's face grimaced more than a smile. "My parents are going to Chica's remember. It's close to two."

"Oh, that's right. I forgot."

Momma was still feeling sick, but she went to work regardless of how she felt. I was sure she didn't feel like another confrontation today. Maybe it was good for them to meet her at Chica's with a cold. Her defenses would be down with a decongestant swirling around in her head.

His mother turned to me as if she read my thoughts and said, "You don't have to go, Seth. We can handle Jazzline's mother. I promise you, dear."

I sighed. "I don't know what she'll say."

His father chuckled that deep hearty laugh I recognized from Seth. Even though he was making light the whole meet the momma ordeal, I couldn't look at them. I didn't know how much he'd told his family about their boxing match last night. I still wished I had the complete play by play.

Mr. MacKenzie patted me on the arm. "Don't worry, love. We need to meet her, and your father, too, when he comes into town for the play. It's the proper thing to do in this situation."

I wanted to ask him what situation he was referring to. The one where I'd be spending a weekend with them in some outdoor tents camping or the one where their children were in love with each other and would probably get married when I turned eighteen. It was there between us even though I hadn't received a formal proposal. I knew that I would. Just in case, mine was on countdown status, one month and eighteen days.

I didn't understand it, but I heard Mrs. MacKenzie gasp and watched as she clinched Mr. MacKenzie's arm.

Seth's eyes narrowed as he watched his mom's face change, and he said in a low voice, "Momma, that's enough now."

Something just happened, and for the life of me, I didn't understand it.

Mr. MacKenzie told Bree that she could stay as long as we were here. He gave Seth that look. The glaring one that spoke volumes. Like you'd better not get too far from her.

Bree had another plan. "Can we go swimming, Daddy? The acoustics are good in there and we can sing in the pool and relax at the same time. I think it might be good for Tucker's voice."

"Okay, Bree. Whatever."

Nobody could say no to her, either. These MacKenzie kids had it down. I needed to take notes.

Bree and Tucker flew through the house to get away from us, and be alone. I didn't feel like swimming. Besides, I didn't have anything to change into. Tucker had a bathing suit in the pool house. Bree made sure she had what she needed for him here. I wondered if she had him stashed away a toothbrush somewhere.

Seth said, "What would you like to do?"

I knew he couldn't walk on the beach in the daytime. His How to Deal book was letting me in on the side effects that over-exposure to the sun could have on his type of Lupus. How ironic that my favorite times in my life were spent at the beach at nightfall? I wouldn't miss the sun. I had Tucker to shine for me.

The only thing left for me to escape the thoughts of Chica's coffee meeting and the fears that were mounting was to do one thing. "Will you sing me to sleep?"

"I'm sorry I've been keeping you up so late. Do you want to stop our late nights?"

"No. I feel like I could crash."

He didn't realize that even after he had left me to sleep in my bed, I couldn't for the thoughts that overtook me. He put his arm around my waist and helped me up the stairs. Maybe he could feel that I was about to fall over with worry and exhaustion.

"Kiss me and tell me what you want me to sing. I haven't been studying your 80s music long enough to get one in my head yet. Something about that Time After Time song makes it my favorite so far."

He pulled his pillows out of the king-sized down comforter. I felt my face dive into it to take in the scent of him, then turned against his chest, feeling him. That was better.

I murmured, already feeling my eyes heavy and closing. "Anything you want."

I would never forget the way his voice spoke to my soul as he crooned me a song in Gaelic. I didn't know what he was saying, but I was sure it was a love song just for me. I tried to imagine its meaning as I fell asleep to the sound of his voice and the rhythm of his heartbeat.

I woke with a start. It was four. They had to be back by now. They would hand the verdict out. Seth had fallen asleep. His hair falling over the side of his face. It was like a shield for him, and I wondered if that was why he wore it long, like a phantom mask. I smoothed his dark curls back and tucked the thick strands behind his ear. His scars were deep, raw red, and seemed as if they would hurt to my touch. But he didn't move as I caressed his cheek.

I found my lips on his and they were so warm still. He was my man. "Baby, it's time to get ..."

I couldn't finish my sentence because he was up, throwing me back against the bed with his eyes wild and sweat popping up on his forehead. He had my arms pinned down to the bed, and it was painful.

"Wake up, Seth."

He was having a nightmare, and I was being taken down with him.

He shook it off, and then refocused. I could see his eyes coming back to me, and it appeared as if they shifted colors from darkness to light right before me. His grip loosened on my arms but I knew there would be bruises there. He shifted his weight off me, and I breathed. The fear creeping away back into its hole.

He sat up, and turned his back to me. "I'm so sorry, Jazzline. I didn't mean to hurt you. Anything but this. Not this."

I got up to sit beside him, holding my arms and rubbing them to get the feeling back in them again. "It's okay. What were you dreaming?"

The bed was slightly shaking from the involuntary movements that his body was making. Whatever it was, it had rocked him. He couldn't find his voice, and I understood. I just sat there with him as his shoulders slightly shook, his fingers grasping his hair that had covered his face. He seemed like he was being tortured and tears were falling from a pain I could not see.

He turned to me then and took me in his arms. "I'm sorry."

When I stood up, he didn't.

He seemed like he couldn't. "Could you give me a minute?"

He pointed to the door, and I realized that he needed to be alone. I left him there to go find Bree and Tucker. I needed to see a smiling face and needed to separate myself from him because it was almost like I could feel his hurt, and I didn't even know why he was. Before I could find them, I ran into Seth's parents. They walked in, and his momma seemed her calm and elegant self. There were no scratches or bald spots from a cat fight, so I had to assume that everything went well, or at least civilized.

I didn't know that Seth had approached me from behind, and I jumped when he put his hand on my shoulder. His voice was strained, "How did it go?"

Mr. MacKenzie gave him a look then went off to the family room to turn on a Braves baseball game. Mrs. MacKenzie sighed. The sigh. That meant trouble.

"It went fine, dear." But her lips were pursed and tight. Her nerves were frazzled.

It was my turn to feel like I was living in a nightmare. "I'm so sorry you had to meet her. She is a nice woman. Really."

It was tough having to defend your own mother.

She grinned. "It wasn't that. She was nice."

Seth was quiet and followed his mother down the hall until she made her way into the kitchen. She spoke with the chef about preparing for Tucker's mother to attend in a few hours. I didn't want to be around for that one, either. I was sure that whatever awkwardness that Ms. Lane felt, she would mask it and be a normal woman in awe of this place and his family. Tucker would survive the future-in-law fiasco. Would I?

Seth whispered, "Do we have her blessing?"

His momma patted him on the arm, "Of course we do, dear. I knew that we would in the first place. Leave me now to Ms. Lane. Both of you run before Bree finds you with a revised schedule."

Seth grabbed me by the hand and took me back to the theater. "Good idea. I thought we would try to avoid Bree, too."

He frowned and I could tell that he was still harboring the dream. "They're not in here. They're still at the pool. I want to sing."

He handed me the sheet music, and we practiced together. Without an audience, it was much better. I could sing and not worry about an eye or a thought, a critique or criticism. I knew that Seth loved my voice. There was no turning back with the play. My heart was in it now, and it trapped me in its spell. There was no turning back with Seth, either. He had consumed me like a raging fire, and before we could finish the song, I sat beside him on the piano bench and reminded him how much that there were no second thoughts. I'd decided.

Tucker and Bree bounded in. She handed Seth a flyer. "Momma said that you and Seth ought to go to this tonight. They're having a concert at Brookgreen Gardens. She picked one up at Chica's and thought you might like it."

I'd seen it posted at the front of the restaurant to advertise for the summer concert series. I'd rather be there than interrupting dinner with Ms. Lane and Bree's family.

Bree smiled when she saw the sheet music from the second act. "You've been practicing. Was that song as good as the first one this morning?"

Seth answered her because he knew that I hadn't found my voice. "Better."

Mrs. MacKenzie leaned against the doorframe. She eyed her children with such love. "Seth, it's almost time for dinner. We've made you and Jazzline a picnic basket to take to the concert tonight if you would like to attend. You could stay if you'd..."

"No. The concert sounds great. Thank you."

He kissed her on the cheek, and she patted my arm as we left out of the theater.

When we were in the car, I turned to Seth. "What did my momma say?"

He shrugged. "I wasn't there."

"What is this blessing stuff your dad was talking about?"

He wouldn't look at me. His voice was tight, and his eyes still looked wounded from the leftovers of the nightmare. Why wouldn't he talk to me? I thought I was the one having that problem.

I called home, and Alex answered. "Are you okay? Do you need anything?"

He said that he was feeling better, but he needed to be close to the bathroom just in case. He wanted ice cream, and I promised to bring him some by, looking at Seth, and he nodded. We grabbed a carton and stopped by before the concert to check on him. Alex and Luke were watching TV on the couch covered in blankets, yet it felt like it was ninety degrees in the house.

I'd brought enough ice cream for both of them.

Alex tried to jump when he saw the container in my hand, but he held his stomach. "You saved my life."

I heard a sound escape Seth's lip, and when I turned to him, he was already standing at the entryway ready to escape. I was sure that he didn't want to be near my family with this virus or flu or whatever they had. I hadn't gotten to that chapter of the book yet, but I figured by his reaction his immune system was more fragile.

"Is Alex behaving himself?"

Luke grinned, and then coughed out a lung. "Don't go worrying about Alex, Jazzline. You're too wrapped around him. He's perfectly fine. Well, he's perfectly sick. Go have fun, and live the teenage glory days. Sometimes I wish I had them back."

I blew Alex a kiss and Seth was in such a hurry to leave he already had the car running. So, I called Momma at the restaurant to check in on her. It was more than that. I couldn't lie. I wanted to see what her reaction would be to me on the phone after today. To gather some clues of what might have happened.

She was breathless but it was seven o'clock frantic hour. I told her I dropped off reinforcements for Alex and Luke and then waited for her to say something, anything. When nothing came from her end, I had to ask, "What happened today with Mr. and Mrs. MacKenzie?"

"I don't want to go into that right now over the telephone. They're nice people."

I smiled thinking of how that was the same remark that Mrs. MacKenzie made when she was asked.

"They are very nice people, Momma. They've accepted me for me."

I wanted to add just the way I am without demands or pressure or expectations, but I could never say all of that.

"It seems they have."

I heard her call out an order again and told them they had better pick up the slack or she'd throw them in the deep fryer, and I knew that I needed to get off the phone, but I wanted more information.

"I'll talk with you later, Jazzline."

"Okay, Momma. Bye."

And she hung up. Clink. No, love you, no be careful, or do something wild for once in your life. It was just clink.

Seth was still trying to mask his emotions.

"What's happening here?"

We pulled up into the beautiful drive of Brookgreen Gardens. I loved walking here. The combination of poetry, art, and flowers made me happy that places like this still existed in the world. When everything on the outside of the gate felt crazy.

"Seth, I'm talking to you. What are you hiding from me?" I knew that it had to be something.

He didn't answer but paid the entry fee, and we were off again pulling up into the parking lot. He opened the door for me, grabbed the basket, then my hand as we strolled down to the picnic area by the Jessamine Pond. It was so beautiful at night, and they had extended hours in the summer months to beat the heat and draw in more crowds.

It should have been peaceful and serene sitting under the stars, but something was looming over us like a shroud and I couldn't figure out for the life of me what was going on. We ate in silence, then cleared everything away. Seth grabbed my hand and we began to walk down the lit garden paths.

He whispered, "If you knew something about me, I wonder what would you do?"

"I don't know. It's according to what I knew."

"How does it feel to you to take care of Alex?"

He asked me but I was sure that he already knew the attachment that I had to my baby brother was more than just a big sister role. That I felt more maternal to him than Momma. I told him how next year when I went away to college, I didn't know how I'd survive without Alex.

"You know that it'll happen, and you'll have to move on."

He spoke it aloud, and I hated it. It swirled around me like a fog, and I wanted to scream at him. I couldn't say don't push this conversation on me.

"I can't pack him in one of my suitcases and carry him along with us?"

I was trying to joke the situation but, in all honesty, I meant it. Then, I realized I talked about our future, the us in my sentence as if he had known I was planning on following him anywhere.

He squeezed my hand. "I wish it were that simple, but you know it's not."

"Nothing ever is."

My mind tried to picture a life that would include Alex, Seth, and me. Living in an apartment. I'd take classes while he was at school. Cooking dinners together. Taking walks in a park like this. Going to the movies. Helping him with homework. But he was not my child. He would be left behind.

"I know you want him, Jazzline. But you know that things change. Lives change."

"You're proof of that. But Alex needs me."

I couldn't tell him how much Alex or Tucker meant to me. It was easier now with knowing Tucker was to stay in Murrell's Inlet because of Bree. But, then, what if Seth moved away to

Charleston or Chapel Hill or Scotland? There I was again, caught in the middle. Custody was bad enough. This was actually worse. Alex and Tucker vs. Seth. The only thing was I'd already decided, but it didn't make my heart heal any quicker at the thought of only seeing them once in a while, or on holidays, not every day like I'd grown to know almost my whole life. My life was changing. It sounded simple enough, but it was the most frightening feeling of my life.

Until we saw Alice Flagg.

CHAPTER 12

Invisible Touch

Seth whispered, "Did you see that?"

He pointed by the pond and I saw a crane resting on a rock by the edge. It was too dark for my eyes to make out anything else.

His voice was urgent, "Look, over there."

Seth dropped my hand and started walking in front of me, stepping past the path and down the embankment by the water's edge.

I heard him speaking, but I didn't hear a response or see anyone there. Fear grew goosebumps on the nape of my neck. I was compelled to move closer to see what Seth was doing. Mainly because I was too scared to be alone even though I was still standing on the lit path.

I called out, "Seth? Please, Seth."

He kneeled down by the edge, his hands skimming the top of the water. He was talking but not to me. "I know. I love her, so I know. No. That doesn't matter to me. I love her no matter her station. I will. Soon. In a couple of months. Now? Before then? Yes, I will."

I couldn't break this, whatever it was. The sensation was raw and unnerving. But when Seth turned to me, I could see the look in his eyes. He was calm. I was far from it. He moved slightly, shifting his knees so he wouldn't fall head first into the pond, and I caught my breath. I could see the white dress, a flowing white gown, the pale skin, dark hair. A deep feeling of sadness came from the apparition that was more than death itself. It was pain in death. Loneliness. Emptiness. My heart hurt for her.

"She wants something."

I knew what it was as I approached them. I knew what she was and who she was. Even though I'd always heard the stories, I thought that was all they were. Silly ghost stories of our community to draw paranormal hunters for a spike in tourism. But I was seeing, and I was hearing his one-sided conversation. Yet, I still couldn't believe. Once, Tucker walked around her gravestone thirteen times with Alex counting him down. They waited impatiently as I sat in the Jeep feeling completely freaked out. But now I would have given anything to be in the confines of a steel automobile. Not this.

He grabbed my left hand, and I could feel the sweat on him. He was shaking a little as he slid the ring of off my finger. His voice was soft, "I promise to replace it soon enough. With something real and everlasting."

I couldn't move. I couldn't respond. I sat frozen in fear as he walked back up to Alice Flagg, or what was left of her. His body was blocking my view, but I didn't care. It was better for me to stand safely behind him. I didn't see, but I could hear. I could hear his side and only guess what she was saying to him.

"Yes. She's beautiful. I know. Yes. I will. Soon. Forever."

Then, she was gone. I didn't hear a sound. Seth turned to me then, and his eyes were clear. They were not as troubled as before. They were not scared yet he sat face to face with a legend. He grabbed my hand, and I could feel his finger press in the place that once held my ring. I'd not taken it off since Seth had placed it on my ring finger. Now, my finger felt the ache of the missing weight.

"Was that real?"

We walked steady, but I wanted to run.

"I know her. She kinda goes to my church." He spoke it with a sheepish grin.

"Did you lose your mind? Did you just see her and talk to her?" Even though I was there, I still couldn't believe.

"Yes. She wanted your ring. It was nothing more than that. You know the story, right?"

He sat down on a bench beside a magnificent sculpture of Wind on the Water, and it made me shiver thinking that Alice might be waiting for us here.

"I've heard it. We went to All Saint's Church where her grave is but nothing happened when Tucker walked it."

Then it made sense with what he meant by her going to his church. He was Episcopalian. Very funny.

He told me that he loved folklore and legends. Especially the ones that were tied to our local area. He said he'd researched them out of pure interest. He said the Scottish folklore and ghost stories were his favorites, and he'd spent his year in Scotland tracing down ghosts.

"Do you know about Alice?"

"Just that she couldn't marry the man that she loved."

I took in a sharp breath. Was their conversation about us back there? I heard him say that station didn't matter.

"She couldn't wear her engagement ring, in fear of her mother and brother. She died so young, of Typhoid Fever and could never marry her true love. When she was buried, the chain went missing. Her ring was gone. Now, she's looking for her ring. Or, like tonight, a ring that symbolizes the love that she felt for her man. She said she felt that from you. From me. Confirmation even from the grave."

"I don't believe in ghosts." I was having a hard-enough time understanding reality.

He whispered into my hair, holding my hands in his. "Sometimes when you come face to face to life or to death, the only thing you can do is believe."

He took me back to the car, and we left the gardens. We went to my beach, and he held me until the tide was pushing against our toes. He held me as the moon hid behind the clouds and left us in an unimaginable dark but I felt the warmth from him and the strength resonating from his very being.

I believed there was truly more than me out there crashing against the waves. That God was looking down on me and Seth and He had given us His blessing. No matter how my life would change, I must accept that it would, one way or the other. And as I leaned up against Seth's chest and felt the rise and fall of us together, one soul, one spirit, the moon breaking free again and God whispering to me in the sound of His Ocean, I knew that it would somehow be okay. Even on nights when ghosts roamed free.

CHAPTER 13

Hello

Being in church on Sunday morning had been a constant for me since I was a little girl. But even there, I found an absence of family to be glaring. Whole families would fill up pews. Whole families were committed. When my family commitment was torn apart, Momma refused to step back in church. She was the one cheated on. She didn't do anything wrong, but somehow, she lost faith in the system.

God was what I could hold on to when everything was falling apart. And Tucker, and Alex, and now Seth. He squeezed my hand when Reverend Harvey read the scripture from James 1:6, " But let him ask in faith, with no doubting, for he who doubts is like a wave of the sea driven and tossed by the wind."

I had spent years doubting. Did God love me enough? More than enough. Did I deserve to have a relationship with someone? Yes. God would want me to find joy. Would I be able to use my voice? It was my choice now. I would no longer be slammed by waves crashing up against me. I was determined to see my life for what it could be with me in control, with God at the helm.

We sang, *Trust and Obey*.

Seth and Bree's voices rose above the crowd, and a few heads turned. We'd already had the complete stare down from every nosy person in the room, which meant practically every member, visitor, and choir singer. Especially them, because they had a front row seat to gawk at Seth and me. I could only imagine the thoughts. But when we closed our eyes to pray at the beginning of service, I reminded myself why we were here. It wasn't for those other people. It was to share my place with Seth. God was here, I was sure. But he was everywhere. Maybe it was better to start going to Seth's church. My Spirit whispered yes, as soon as I had the thought.

After service, Reverend Harvey held out his hand and shook Seth's vigorously. "Well, hello young man. I've been waiting on Jazzline to bring a suitor to church."

He was old. He used suitor in a sentence and kept talking.

Other members were piling behind me to get a chance to shake Reverend Harvey's hand and wish him a good week or comment on the service or how his wife was doing after surgery.

He nodded at us. "Stay and meet me in my office for a chat."

We walked around the back of the church, and I stopped before we went inside. "You know this means a lot to me."

He smiled. "I know. That's why I'm here."

Tucker didn't introduce Bree to Reverend Harvey. They were out of the church at the last hymn. Since I could count, we'd gone through four preachers. This one was my favorite.

He led us into his office and sat back, sipping a glass of water. "Ah, so. Jazzline, who do we have here?"

Seth stepped forward. "Seth MacKenzie, sir. It is a pleasure to meet you."

Reverend Harvey smiled. "You, too. I see that Jazzline smiled through service today and your voice, it was amazing. Will you be joining our choir? We need some male voices. No offense to the ladies, but we could use you."

I told Reverend Harvey that Seth's family were members of All Saints, and I felt it best we attend there. It flowed through me, and I knew the decision was the right one. Seth squeezed my hand and looked a little shocked. Even though it would be hard for me to leave my church, my comfort and routine, I knew that church was also important to their family. I knew that compromise went hand in hand with commitment, and I would do whatever I could to make this work.

Reverend Harvey smiled at us, approval clearly on his face. "Young love. Remember to keep Christ in your relationship. Pray. Believe. This is really good for you, Jazzline. The Holy Spirit tells me so."

"I know. I agree. Thanks again for meeting with us."

I told him about our play at First Take, and he said that he would mark it on his calendar to attend. Hopefully, his wife would be able to come, too. She loved music. When Seth went before me through the door, I turned to Reverend Harvey and whispered, "Is Alice Flagg real?"

"So, you've been holding out on me? You saw her, too?"

Seth's hand was on the doorframe. His body was rigid. It was like he was waiting. Waiting for something. I wished that I could've seen his expression, but I wasn't going to twirl him around.

I said, "Yes, I saw her. She took my ring."

He smiled. "Once, when my Jessica and I were walking down the Marshwalk after dinner we thought we caught a glimpse of her. She was smiling at my Jessica, but who wouldn't, that pretty lady." He always referred to his wife as, my Jessica, so endearing. Would I someday be, my Jazz?

"Are there really things like the supernatural existing with us? Things that can't be explained?"

That was when I heard the sigh released from Seth. It was as if he were holding his breath this whole time waiting for me to ask it because he didn't have the courage to.

Reverend Harvey turned thoughtful. I could see him turn back to preacher mode and his Biblical index began to unfold in his mind. He told me to look up what happened to Samuel when Saul used a seer to call him back from the dead in the Old Testament. He spoke about clear examples of angels and demons.

"The question has fascinated people for ages on ages of time. Sometimes there are mysteries that cannot be explained. Sometimes we're faced with challenges. Pray to God for guidance in any situation, but don't get caught up with playing around with spirits because you may not know what you allow in. Where there are angels unaware, a the Bible tells us, there could also be evil spirits lurking to kill and destroy."

Seth shuddered. "That, I know is true."

I knew I'd seen something, and my ring was gone as proof. Even though it was just a stage prop, I missed it.

As we were heading back to his house for Sunday lunch, I noticed that he hadn't spoken since we'd left church. His mood seemed dark and brooding.

"Are you okay?"

I knew he was close enough to touch her. Maybe he was more frightened than he appeared to be last night.

"Seth? Did you tell anybody about what happened?"

I didn't. They wouldn't have believed me anyway. Tucker might have. But I didn't want to talk about it with anyone else.

"Bree."

His voice was strained. Since yesterday, he had acted so differently. And then, after last night, he seemed to disappear.

I whispered, "I need you, Seth. Come back."

He knew what I meant and I heard him sigh. "I'm sorry, Jazzline. I love you. The sermon was nice. My church is a little more formal than yours but it's pretty much the same. I'm sure that you'll feel right at home. Thank you for that, by the way. It would mean a lot to my parents, too."

I was faced with the harsh realization last night that life can change. I could change with it. The world would still turn, and I would not break.

"Is it fine that Alex attend church with us with your family, too?"

"Of course, he can come, Jazzline. I want you to know that I take responsibility for Alex, too. I promise to always look out for him the best way that I can."

"What is it, Seth?"

There was a deep concern, something more than I could not read crossed his face.

He said, "Just let's make sure that Alex always rides with us, okay? I'd like to use that time to spend time with him and get to know him better."

It sounded odd the way he put it, but I knew that he was referring to Alex riding with Tucker. Maybe Bree and Tucker had said something about Alex interfering with their little love drives. I hoped that they weren't hitting any dirt roads.

"Do you know how much Alex looks up to you?"

"I take it seriously, I truly do. I want to show him what it's like to live a strong, Christian life as a young man. So, one day when it's his turn he can fend for himself and do okay."

I squeezed his hand. "With you around, he'll do more than okay."

His family was so colorful. They were filled with stories at the dinner table, and I laughed until I cried, picturing Seth as a child. His mother painted vivid portraits of her children for me and Tucker as we ate our dessert. When we were promised baby photo albums that was when Seth held out his hand to signal enough.

"I want to spend some time with Jazzline at the beach, if that's okay with everyone?"

His father stood up. "I'd like to spend some time with Jazzline first, if I may?"

Seth's eyes rose quizzically, and his father's eyes matched his gaze. They had this unspoken language among them, all of them. It made me think they could speak to one another without having to say a word. That was what being a tightly knitted family with such a rich tapestry would do for you. My family felt like a store-bought comforter that faded in the wash.

His father took my hand and escorted me out of the dining room into a study. It was bigger even than our public library. Religious books spanned one side of the entire wall, from commentaries, biographies, to religious relics, all kinds of titles. I'd always been interested in biblical archeology, and I saw that he was, too. I stopped to study the section and then saw a glass case that held what looked to be an emblem of a fish-with a cross. It was a broken piece of pottery but the symbol still remained.

He stood beside me, looming there with his massive build and dark eyes. "I found that in Jerusalem on an excavation about twenty years ago. It's my prized material possession."

He told me about the early Jewish Christian symbol that was believed to be a representation of bridging two worlds and beliefs into one.

"This reminds me of you."

I was so confused. How did I remind him of a piece of pottery from antiquity?

"You mean, broken?"

He asked me to sit with him on the leather couch. It was hard to read his expression. His eyes were so dark, and his face so ruddy. He seemed not of this world.

"No, dear. That's not what I meant at all. I don't see you as broken. I see you as a bridge for my son to find his life back. I see you as a gateway between Scotland and America. Two people will be one. You've made an impression on all of us. I hope you know that."

I'd never thought of myself being solid and strong enough to be able to support anyone, let alone be their bridge. My foundation felt so weak and crumbling. But for him to think that about me and put it that way, maybe I could believe it, too.

"I love your son, Mr. MacKenzie, and I hope that we get married soon."

My hand flew to my mouth and my face turned red. I couldn't

believe that I spoke it in front of him. I couldn't keep my thoughts hidden.

He laughed. "We know you do, dear, or we wouldn't be giving you this."

He took out a red velvet box from a drawer of an ornate antique armoire. "When I was to be married to Maura, it was her first present from my father. Maura wore it, and now it is to be passed on. It's to be passed to my son's future wife as a token of acceptance into our family. It would honor me if you would wear it always. When I say always, please always wear it close. Never take it off when you are in the presence of our family. There are reasons I can't explain as of yet, but it will all make sense in God's timing."

He opened the box for me and with clumsy large fingers; he took out the delicate butterfly hair clip made from abalone shells embossed with emeralds and rubies for the wings. He went to try to fasten it in my hair then pulled back his hand. "Will you accept our gift?"

My eyes filled with tears. They accepted me. They loved me.

"I can't believe that you would want me."

He frowned, clearly, my words were not expected and then I realized what I said. I tried to back pedal, and I felt my face flush. "I didn't mean it like that. I mean, I can't believe that Seth loves me. I can't believe that your family is so nice to me and that you would want me around. I've really nothing to offer. There I go again. I can't stop myself."

He put my hand over the clip and pressed firmly. "I bring out the secret thoughts of people, Jazzline. Put aside your doubts. We have spiritual confirmation that you're for our son. You're a wonderful girl."

I shrugged, feeling stupid that my self-conscious behavior was rearing its ugly head when he was truly giving me a moment to remember. "I've never let anybody see before. I've never talked before. And now, around Seth, and all of you, I can't seem to stop."

His eyes twinkled. "Us MacKenzie's have a way about that. Once you get to know us you can't help yourself." He chuckled at his little joke.

"I truly love the clip. I'll always wear it."

I could feel the cold in my hands. I knew it was real. He used the word future wife as if he already knew my thoughts and my heart. Maybe Seth had spoken with him about his feelings. Maybe that was what they meant by blessings. Had they talked to my momma, too? My thoughts swirled with so many what ifs. Maybe this was real after all. Maybe I wasn't still walking in a dream.

Seth was waiting for me outside the door, and he grabbed my hand. His eyes searched my face for any signs of what we'd discussed. When he noticed the clip fastened in my hair, his eyes lit up, and he turned to his father and wrapped his arms around him fully. I wouldn't think many people could do that. Seth lifted him up slightly off the ground and whispered something that made his father laugh. He came back to me and put his hand firmly around my waist, and almost picked me up as we walked down the hallway.

His mother smiled at me when we made our way back through to the family room. She had the knowing look of what had happened. It might have been her idea. Bree kept shifting uncomfortably at her mother's feet. When Seth announced we were going down to the beach, I saw Bree search for her momma's face for approval to flee, but her eyes said no. Poor Bree. Poor Tucker.

He pulled a blanket out of the outside chest, and we went straight to the shoreline. The sun was about to set and it glowed red, purple, and orange across the horizon. I felt that I saw a painting of my heart splashed across sea and sky.

Seth touched the clip, and twirled my hair in his fingers. I caught my breath as he leaned in to kiss me full on the lips, gentle at first, then with more emotion. The warmth of him went down through me, and I could feel his heart beating in the palm of my hands where I was holding his neck.

"You are my life, Jazzline. I'll cherish you forever." He continued to kiss me, my cheeks, my nose, and my eyes.

I sighed into his chest and felt the world was at peace with me. I'd never been as happy in my life as I was at that moment. Without having to ask him, I knew that he had spoken with his family about his feelings for me.

"I have to talk to my momma. I need to make all of this right with her like it is with your family."

If I could have called her on the phone that would have been best. But that would have been chicken, and I was a bridge. I couldn't do that. I would need to face this and be strong about it.

Seth said, "What about? I told you not to worry about how she feels about me. In time, I do know for a fact she'll come around and accept me one day. I see that. It'll take her a while. She knows she's losing you."

"Losing me?"

"She's losing you to me, and it scares her. She's also concerned what you and I will mean for Alex. She's worried how much Alex is dependent upon you. And I even know there's a hint of jealousy there. She wishes that she could be that person for him, but she knows that she's not." He trailed off realizing that he was telling me the whole play by play.

"My momma? Jealous? You must be mistaken. She told you all this? That's why I've got to talk with her tonight."

"These are your mother's thoughts, if you really want to know them. You're too young to be serious. She doesn't want you to end rushing in like she did with your father. You're going to culinary school in Charlotte and live with him. You'll take over Chica's. You will not be with me." He didn't like the sound of the last one because I saw him grimace.

My heart fluttered. "She's so wrong. Three strikes. She's out. Seth, how can I do this with her? I don't know where to begin."

"At the beginning." He spoke so plain like I could go back that far. I couldn't.

"Maybe at the middle. No, just right now. I'll tell her the truth."

"And what is that?"

"I won't leave you, Seth. I'm not going to Charlotte. I'm not going to culinary school. I have no desire to run a restaurant. All my heart wants is to be yours and maybe be on a stage somewhere singing."

As soon as I spoke, his mouth covered mine in the sweetest kiss that I'd ever known. All of his kisses were all I'd ever known and they were so unique, so different, stirring up so many emotions in me. This kiss let me know that he would never leave me, either.

He asked, pulling me back on his lap and wrapping his arms around me. "The stage, huh? I can see that for you as clearly as I see the moon dancing with the clouds. And just think, at the beginning of the summer you knew nothing about the theater. Have you thought about what college, yet?"

"Still waiting, but I guess I should decide."

"What are you waiting for? For a sudden burst of inspiration?"

I turned and snuggled against his neck, singing one of my favorite old Chicago songs, You're the Inspiration.

Look at Bree, she knew that she was going to major in dance and theater, marry Tucker, and follow him anywhere. The only part of her equation that was similar to mine was that I knew that I would follow Seth. So, I guess it was safe to leave my options open and apply to whatever colleges he did, just in case.

"Can you take me home?"

I hated to say it but I knew it couldn't wait. The talk with Momma would be now or never. The comb, the talk with his father, all of it had given me a sense of newfound strength. I felt like I needed to capitalize on the moment before I lost it.

"As long as I can stay."

I needed to talk to her and having him there might make discussing my future a lot easier. It would definitely keep me focused and not allow me to revert back to the past. As we headed home, I felt my stomach leaping clear out of its place, bumping into me. I was going to get sick. I reached for my Bible out of my purse. I turned the pages and let them fall and a passage of scripture, Jeremiah 29:11, came at me and took me by surprise. I read it for Seth to hear, " For I know the plans I have for you," says the Lord. "They are plans for good and not for disaster, to give you a future and a hope."

I said, "Amen." Momma was standing under the porch light, calling out to Alex. "Amen." Alex was running around the yard throwing up his football. He was better. "Amen."

Seth laughed. "Are you practicing to be a preacher, now?"

Alex almost clipped the car with the ball, and I watched Seth reach out his window and catch it with one hand. Alex cheered and fell on the ground. Yeah, he was better. I kissed him on the head and asked how he was doing. He said that he'd missed me. It brought back the thought of next weekend. This weekend he was sick in bed. Next weekend he'd be here while I was at the Highland Games.

Seth told me that he was staying outside to play with Alex and teach him some tackling techniques. Alex had to be eleven to play recreation ball with full pads. Seth was a star linebacker at St. James. He was supposed to back me up this evening but he was out in the yard while I stared at Momma trying my best to figure out how to start all of this.

I didn't have to wait long.

She said, "Jazzline. This is too serious for your own good."

So, that was odd. It was in the order as Seth predicted it. "I love him, Momma. What can I say?" So much more. Not enough.

"You don't know what love is, Jazzline. This family, this boy, they aren't like us. They think differently, they act like they are from another planet with all their proper ways and smooth talking. Jazzline, you are in way over your head. It reminds me so much of me when I was younger with your father. It's uncanny, really. I wish my Momma would have stopped me from..."

"Don't wish us away anymore, Momma. When you say things like that you realize you would erase me and Alex from the planet. If you regret dad, I'm sorry about that. But don't regret Alex. He's the best thing."

She bit her lip. "I'm sorry, Jazzline. Accept my apology for that. It's just it's so frustrating to see you young and in love. You're in over your head on this one, I promise you that."

"I am in over my head. I've been drowning for years. Now, I'm finally breaking free, and I'm learning who I am. Who I can be. Momma, I'm not going to culinary school." There, it was out. I did it. I did not crash.

"I know that. Do you think I'm stupid?"

"You knew? All this time."

"Of course. You aren't going anywhere without that boy. He has come in here and swept you off your feet and now nothing matters, culinary school, Alex, us or what we think." Anger was creeping into her voice, and I hated it.

She was so wrong about it all. Of course, it would look like that to her. My voice was low, surprisingly calm. I tried to step outside of my own emotions to get the level headed demeanor I would need to do this.

"I've never wanted culinary school, Momma. That was your dream. Not mine. I want to be a singer, to be honest. And I won't even comment about bringing Alex into this because you know how I feel about him."

"Well, what about us? What about my advice to you? What Luke said to you? Do you care that we're concerned about you? Don't you see that this boy is dangerous?"

"Momma, you've lost it. Seth is the kindest, most caring guy, and I'm so blessed to have him in my life." I stood up. This conversation was over. It was over when she said that Alex didn't matter. Momma and her wild fantasies.

Her voice softened, "Listen here, Jazzline Chicand. I guess you have my blessing with Seth because I don't honestly know if I ever could stop this train. I see that now, and I don't want to lose you. I'm sad because here you are, well, almost eighteen. And I've missed so much. You really don't want culinary school? Why didn't you tell me?"

Here was nice momma back. The soft-voiced one who used to tell me bedtime stories and read me Little Women.

"No. I never wanted culinary school. I will never in my life ever move to Charlotte with Dad. I love Alex like he's my own child, and wherever I go, I want him to go with me, too."

"Jazz, you need to take a step back. You are just a kid yourself. You won't take Alex anywhere. You need to focus on senior year, not this boy. You need to start applying for colleges. These kinds of decisions take planning and preparation. I understand about your father. I didn't want to live with him either."

"My summer has now been taking over by Seth MacKenzie and The Phantom. Just a few weeks ago I would have never thought that I would do either, and here I am." I looked out the window and the guys were rolling around getting dirty.

Momma stood up and dropped the remote. "Jazzline, you didn't!"

"What?"

"Momma, I haven't done that. I didn't mean it that way, good grief."

She came up and held my chin in her hands. "You better wait, Jazzline. Trust me, wait."

"I promise, Momma. I'm going to wait until I'm married. Seth and I've already talked about this."

He came in then, carrying Alex under his arm. Seth had dirt smudged on his cheek. Alex was covered and loving it.

She murmured, "That explains the rush then."

Seth put Alex down and smiled at me. My face was red, and I was sure that he could see that I had survived unharmed. If I were a swim champion, I'd be an Olympic Gold medalist at the backstroke.

"Hello, Mrs. Chicand."

"Hey, Seth."

"I hope that meeting my parents this afternoon went well?" His voice was formal again, and I thought of what Momma said about their proper ways.

At least she did seem to handle the conversation better this time, and I told her the truth about culinary school. That was a start.

"Momma, Mrs. MacKenzie said that you were very nice, too."

"They were both nice as well. Seth, I see where you get your manners from."

"Well, manners include asking can I take your daughter out again."

I asked, "What's open this late?"

I thought of something that we could do together but it was pointless. My thoughts kept circling back to one thing. He listed out midnight bowling, movies, Waffle House. We drove down the highway, and he seemed to know exactly where he was going.

"MacKenzie Observatory?"

"Are they open this late?"

"All night. For you."

I turned up the radio. "Listen."

It was Lionel Richie's, Hello.

When he said he'd never heard it I knew right then that his Broadway musical background and Gaelic singing bagpipe music was soon to be replaced with 80's hits and my favorite music of all time. I sang it to him.

When the song was over, he turned to me and smiled. "You are right about 80's lyrics. They're the best. Compare them to today. You don't get that honesty. That plain and simple feeling of love that comes out of this music. No wonder why you navigate to these songs."

"Before you, I loved to sing it. Now that I am living it, the words just seem to seep into my soul and come alive. Everything is so different now that I've found you." I held his hand and closed my eyes.

Even though the conservatory was open for business, the

button pushed, and the ceiling cleared away, I don't think that I even noticed a star in the night sky. Only the way his eyes looked in the shadows. The way his lips felt on mine, and his arms around me sheltering me from the world. I could get lost in him. So, maybe Momma was right. Maybe he was dangerous. Maybe he was stealing me away, but I was the willing victim. Let the games begin.

CHAPTER 14

Who I Am

Tucker seemed out of place and struggled on Monday morning when everyone was off-book but him. He was spending more time memorizing every move Bree made than Rao's romantic interludes. Ms. Dot moved from lines to all kinds of theater direction. With the tutorial by Bree and Seth and the enthusiastic director at our lead, I realized I was good at all of this. I wasn't growing an opera-sized ego over it. It felt free to succeed at something and know it.

We worked on blocking and stage placement, and were wrapping up Act II by Wednesday. Never in rehearsals did Seth and I practice our music. We saved that for his theater at home. Our time singing brought me closer to him than words or holding hands could ever do.

Bree was doing her duty for Tucker, coaching him and supporting him but I could tell that he was getting down over his inability to pick up the lines. When Bree and Seth went to learn technical support with the lighting crew, it left me alone with Tucker.

It was now Thursday and full-dress rehearsals were to be that evening. They had fitted us, but Ms. Dot refused any show of costumes before tonight. I was so nervous about wearing a gown and heels. Even though I tried to wear heels the past couple of dates with Seth, I still felt clumsy and foolish. Like my shoulders were too humpy, and I bent my knees way too much. But I was focused on shoes and Tucker was biting his lip trying to balance the script on his head.

"Osmosis. It doesn't work, though. Darn it, Jazzline. I'm gonna look like a fool." The script fell down, and he put his face in his hands.

"Who are you doing this for?"

"You know that, Love Shack."

"Okay, then. You could never look like a fool to her. She loves you so much, Tucker. She's so proud to have you here. To have this time with you. Don't you know it?"

"I'll hate when it ends." I watched his hands begin to twist and turn. I'd never seen this from him before. "When school starts back, and she's down here, and we're up there."

I knew how he felt. "I know. But we always have the afternoons after school. It's not so far away, and I'm sure they have the gas money to come around our way. Where did my Tuck go?"

Lives change. His had.

"Tuck is gone. Tucker Lane is here. At your service." He kissed me on the cheek. "I've always loved you, you know. You've never looked so beautiful or happy. Now that you have Seth, you seemed to have found your voice. I'm sorry for being such a jerk about it at the beginning. Seth is good for you. I see that now, no matter what."

His eyes followed Bree and she turned to him and waved. He smiled back to her and raised his hand.

"Thank you for everything."

"Are you saying that as a joke or do you mean it? I know I've neglected you since I found Bree?"

He took that one wrong. I had to work on my lines not found in a script. Maybe that I was why I loved the play so much. I didn't have to plan what I would say or how someone would take it. I could hide behind somebody else's lines and their story.

"No, it's not that. Thank you for finding Bree."

I looked at her and smiled. She had me wrapped me, too.

"Thank God for that, not me. I couldn't have done any of this without Him."

"If you wouldn't have found Bree ..."

Seth was coming towards us now, and Tucker smiled.

"Oh, I get it. I get the credit for you and Seth. So, one day when you are hopping grandkids on your knee you'll tell them the car story and how I brought you here to find ol' Grandpa."

He laughed, his voice shaking and he acted as if he were walking with a cane. If Tucker could improv the show, he might do well.

Seth smiled as he put his arm around me. "Who are you calling a grandpa?"

"We'll see who will score first. Football season is right around the corner."

Seth spoke low, "So are birthdays."

Bree came up beaming. "What are ya'll talking about? Birthdays? Whose birthday is it?"

I said, "Alex's birthday is in a few months. He'll be eleven."

But I was holding my breath. My birthday was one month and fourteen days.

Tucker said, "Jazz, your birthday is in a few weeks. Eighteen before me, so unfair."

Seth bent down and whispered in my ear, "I can't wait until your birthday."

Bree clapped. "Oh, we can have a party. I just love parties."

Tucker winked at me. He was still planning the after party next Friday night after our opening night. I didn't know how he would pull it off without Bree knowing about it since he spent what seemed like every waking moment with her. But Momma said that his plans were coming along, and they had already sent invitations out last week.

Thinking of Tucker handwriting invitations made me giggle. "I already know what I'm getting for my birthday."

Seth's eyes reverted to Bree's, and her blue eyes widened. Her hands went up in an exaggerated movement, and then she looked to Tucker. He rocked his head, and then it was out there. Sitting between us and I smiled. I knew that there were more plans for a secret party. This one in my honor. Tucker had kept nothing secret from me before, but I was sure that Seth and Bree were behind it. I'd let them have their fun. Besides, it was all for a good cause.

Seth said, "You know? Who told?"

"I don't know what car, yet. I haven't decided. Maybe we can drive around at some dealerships later to check out my options?"

All three sighed in unison, and I laughed. They were so bad at keeping secrets. With the three of them so shaken, I knew that it must have been a big deal. Eighteen, it was more than my sixteenth. I could only drive at that one, and we all know how that one turned out. This one I could declare my rights, my independence, get my license without the course, pick my car out on the way out the door, vote, and get married all in one day.

Our house never celebrated birthdays. Momma would always say she was cooking us a special dinner at Chica's, but it was always her cooking and never enjoying it with us. We'd have dessert with a candle, the wait staff would sing to us, and then it would be over. Nothing different than any other birthday celebration at Chica's for every other customer in the world that thought it was grand to go out to eat on their birthday. I hoped this year would be special. No restaurants, no tiny slice of chocolate cake. By the looks on their faces, it seemed like it would be.

I left them to their little secrets and went to find Ms. Dot to ask her advice on how I should enter and exit. Just because I knew my lines didn't mean that I knew what in the heck I was doing. It was more than the lines. It was the facial expressions, the body language, the subtle movements, the positioning. I could go on and on. And here I was, Christy, the leading lady.

Alex loved rehearsals the best when they locked us away for the day, with a full course catering company at our disposal. Mrs.

MacKenzie was even here, escorting a designer who had racks and racks of costumes and props still being wheeled through the auditorium in large black wardrobe cases. Alex kept sneaking banana pudding and putting it on a pushcart as if he were delivering, then he'd add it to his reserve pile.

Ms. Dot announced that tonight's full-dress rehearsal was the beginning of a long next week of extended practices. We were to run through the full set this evening, then take a break until Monday morning. I wondered if that had anything to do with the main characters all running off to some other costume party with a bunch of Scottish clans. Possibly.

Next week was it. I had one more week and this 1,600-seat auditorium would seat Pawley's Island finest. Momma put notices at Chica's, along with ticket information inside every menu. The show sales would be donated to The Lupus Foundation of America. We were sure it would be a full house. It was all over the local news, and commercials were even made for the local news. The weeks leading up to the show were a whirlwind.

Everyone was running around like maniacs, yet I stood still. Letting all of the noise and the hustling move around me in harmony with my soul. Laughter, nervous jitters, heels clicking as I stood downstage. Seth and Alex's conversation about football teams. Tucker swirling Bree around the stage in an exaggerated dance. Ms. Dot with her megaphone trying to organize the chaos that exploded.

Then, he was beside me, and my body leaned into him. His strength. His muscular frame. The scent of him. I was so aware of everything.

He said, "What's that look you have just now?"

"I'm taking it all in. I see this as my life now. I want all of this feeling to stay."

"I want to take you in the prop room where we first met and..."

Ms. Dot yelled into the megaphone about costume preparation. Everything felt so surreal as I changed into my costume. Bree and Mrs. MacKenzie were there with me and their help was needed because the prom scene required a fancy dress. The gown was a crystal shimmer of light, with pearl drop beading covering the entire bust.

"I've worn nothing so lovely."

Mrs. MacKenzie winked at me and smiled. "You are stunning in it, dear. Bree, outstanding design. Wait until Seth sees this."

Bree was in a simple white chorus girl costume with her hair tied in a ponytail held by a white ribbon. She seemed unearthly, regal, and angelic. She was so beautiful, and I knew that Seth wouldn't be the only one to be pleased this evening. There was something always so different about Bree. It was as if she were carrying around such a precious secret that only her heart could hold. Like she was carrying inside of her a glowing candle that radiated through her even in the brightest of days she was brighter. Like life had meaning for her because of some unseen love.

I wasn't too thrilled about my crystal, beaded six-inch heels and could barely walk in them. They pinched my toes with their pointy fronts, and I felt my ankles breaking side to side.

Bree laughed. "Maybe you should try sleeping in your shoes. I mean, really Jazzline. They were almost as much as the dress."

"I will break a leg. Isn't that what they say?"

Mrs. MacKenzie said, "Don't worry about the shoes, dear. Nobody will be looking at your feet. Trust me." She adjusted the comb in my hair. "I see you're still wearing it."

"Thank you. I love it." I hadn't taken it off since Mr. MacKenzie had given it to me. "I promise to always wear it."

"Make sure you do, love. Especially this weekend. No exceptions, okay."

The way she said it made me want to question her about what was so different about this weekend that would call for a butterfly pin, but the music started over the speaker system, and it broke into my thoughts.

The dress rehearsal had started and the prom scene was underway. I didn't feel sickness coming on. There was no need for smelling salts. I raised my head and the music carried me to the stage. As I walked on it with the lights and the props set in place, I felt myself transform to Christy. I was timid, confused, passionate, loved, and to everyone's surprise, loud. My voice was steady and strong as I spoke my lines and held out my hand to my phantom to sing with me.

The applause from the staff, parents, and cast members was like a fire being lit in my soul. It was funny to see Mrs. MacKenzie and Ms. Dot laughing and hugging, shedding tears. And when Seth was out of costume taking my hand and leading me to the silence of the night, there were no words between us. I couldn't have found my voice even if I tried. I was more in love with Seth than I could have ever imagined. And words wouldn't have done it justice.

He took me to his beach and held me. Just like every other night the past week. But this night was different. His mood was dark, eyes like liquid fire when he looked at me, and he was so hard to read. I thought about a song I'd sung a thousand times. I wondered why my brain worked best with background music. A song's word meant nothing to me before. Now, music was a connection of soul and feelings, Seth and me. Words meant something. Music made me alive.

I sang to him one of my favorite songs by the Goo Goo Dolls, Iris.

"Beautiful. How do these songs come from you?"

"It's easy to hide behind their words. The songwriters. But now it's like every song I sing they wrote it because of you."

"You are my mo anam caran. My soul mate. I was to wait for this. But I can't wait any longer."

His hands were shaking as he reached into his jeans pocket and pulled out a tiny black box. He knelt before me in the sand and held it open for me. My eyes focused on the ring. His hand was on mine. I could smell the ocean, the salt spray a mist around us, and feel God's breath on my face. It heightened my senses. My spirit was on fire, and I felt the confirmation of a yes before Seth could even ask.

He whispered, "Jazzline Chicand, will you be my wife?"

Words would not come. Only images and pictures of our life together. Flashes of my past, of how I felt before him evaded me and I pushed those aside. He was still kneeling before me with his hand outstretched with the box resting in the middle of his palm. The ring was amazing. A Celtic knot band and one solitaire diamond resting in the center of Scottish Gold. His eyes were the color of the band. Praying, my hand went to my heart. I wanted to make sure that it was still beating, and I could feel the soft thud, thud, thud beneath my fingers.

From within my soul, I felt burning. A voice that I could only account for as being the Holy Spirit and its soft whisper urging me on. God made him for you. God blesses this union. Breathe. Say yes. Love him.

Tears fell down my cheeks as my voice spoke what my heart knew was coming all along. "Yes, Seth. Yes. I will marry you."

His hand trembled as he grabbed my ring finger and slid it on. It was a promise. I knew he would be mine forever, and I cried out in happiness. He pulled me up off the blanket and spun me around in the sand.

The stars were exploding around us out the evening to witness our engagement. He announced. "Thank you, God, for letting me find her."

Then, he crushed me against him, bringing my face up to his where my feet weren't even touching the sand, and he kissed me. My heart was singing, head spinning, and my soul was like a million fallen stars hitting my center at once.

Seth sat down on the blanket first, and then pulled me by my waist to sit close to him. His arms circled around me, and I fell against his chest. His one hand came up to hold the ring like he had done so many times before with the prop ring from the performance. I wore it until Alice Flagg asked for it. She would not get this one, and I would never take it off again. His words came back to me, "I'll replace it soon." He did not fail.

Bree came to my mind, and I wondered if she knew. Most people would've considered what happened between us ridiculous and without merit. But I knew what my heart was telling me, and I knew Bree and his family would understand. The outside world didn't have that one-way vision like I did. That view inside my heart. They could see us. The days that we'd been together. Senior year in high school. They could see what they wanted. Seth was mine.

Alex would gain another big brother and would be in heaven. Momma would flip, faint, and die. How was I to explain this to her? I'd already put one foot in the door of my mausoleum by telling her that I didn't want to be a chef and take over Chica's. This? At my age? That would push me in and slam the door. I was sure.

"Our parents?"

He held me tighter. "My parents know, Jazzline. That was why my father gave you this." He touched the hair clip. "I had to wait for this. It was something that had to be done first. My parents and I have spoken to your mother."

"What! When?"

Then, it all came back to me. I could see Seth and Momma out on the patio talking, her voice rising then hushing. Her words to me, his words to his parents – blessings - their coffee visit at Chica's. It was more than just decaf and pleasantries. It was a plea for our future.

"It will be fine, Jazzline. I promise you. I know it will."

I wanted to ask him more. I had so many more questions but I knew that tonight wasn't one of those nights. It was a night to praise God and feel the blessings as he held me in his arms. Holding on to my ring that promised me forever.

CHAPTER 15

We Belong

I stuffed my suitcase to the max, and I strained to close it. I didn't even know what I was supposed to take to a campfire. Marshmallows? Bug spray? My fancy high heels I needed practice walking in? After another sleepless night staring at my ring, hearing his words resonate all around my room as if he were still there with me, my mind was not clear. I didn't even hear Momma walk in.

"Jazz, you need help?"

She plopped down on the suitcase, and all of her weight pushed it down enough for the zipper to close. I twisted my ring where she would not see the diamond and felt it cut into me. All of the words to explain this to her would not be available at eight o'clock in the morning with no sleep. It wouldn't happen. I didn't know what time in the day would be the best time, but not before the trip. She didn't seem to notice.

"Thank you for letting me go with the MacKenzie family."

I'm sure that it took a lot for someone to convince her. Not to mention her full-time babysitter for Alex was replaced by Luke. Wonder what that conversation looked like? I couldn't even imagine what ours would look like when she found out that I was engaged.

"You better promise me that you'll stay by Mrs. MacKenzie and Bree. If anything were to happen, you make Tucker bring you home. The only reason I'm letting you go is because I know Tucker won't let anything happen to you."

"Seth won't let anything happen to me either."

She snapped. "I know. You've found you a big, strong, young man. You've found the love of your life."

I ignored her tone and pulled the suitcase off the bed, and it hit with a thud, startling me. What did I pack?

"He really is, Momma. After what happened before, I never thought that it was possible for me."

"Before? I thought that he was your first boyfriend? Have you ever had another guy other than Tucker in your life?"

She could have kept going. Inexperienced. Naïve. Immature. But I might not be schooled in the love department but what I felt for Seth was real.

"I didn't mean another guy." I wanted to say it. I touched the comb, breathed, and then said it. Release. "I meant after you and daddy. I never thought that I could find love."

Now, I was alive and bursting with the feelings of love and commitment, trust and forever until it was seeping out of my pores.

She stared at me. Her mouth opened but there was no sound. I'd never spoken about the divorce. I'd never spoken about my feelings. When they tried to force me to talk about it, I went dead. Family counseling, quiet. Family talk night, quiet. The going away night, silent. Never again to speak about feelings or dreams or wishes or wants or me.

Her voice softened, "I never thought it was possible either, Jazzline. Until Luke. You never said..."

"No, I didn't. I haven't said a lot of things."

Like how I felt abandoned by both of them. Momma drowning herself in her work. Daddy leaving and pretty much losing all contact. Watching her move from boyfriend after boyfriend, filling her free time with a man instead of her little girl and baby boy. I was only eleven. Alex was a baby.

But I wouldn't say any of that because the past was behind me. I'd crossed that bridge, and now I had built a new one. The words of Mr. MacKenzie resounded in my ear, and I smiled. A bridge for my son to get his life back. He was a bridge for me to find mine. My heart was full. There was no need to travel back in time. I was ready for the future.

She whispered, "I hope you have a nice time. Be careful. Call me."

"I'll try. Take care of Alex for me."

Alex was still asleep, and I needed it to be that way. I'd talked with him about going away for the weekend during rehearsals yesterday. He demanded that he get to go, too. I told him that if he went, he would have to wear a kilt, which I explained was a skirt, just like Tucker. After that, he laughed, grabbed more banana pudding, and the conversation was over.

Seth was already outside, his hand about to ring the doorbell when I opened it. "Let's not wake him up."

I saw Tucker and Bree driving out, and I waved to them. Tucker would know soon enough because I was sure that he had announced it to his entire family after he took me home last night. That would be his thing to do. Waking them up at one a.m. to shout I'd said yes. They probably celebrated.

"Hey, sweetheart. Are you ready?" He pointed to the suitcase and seemed surprised. "Is that it?"

"Sorry. Is it too much? I didn't know."

"No. It's not that. Bree has tripled this with a wardrobe bag, and a whole suitcase filled with shoes and handbags. Ridiculous."

"Should I go back inside and get more?" I bit my lip, trying to figure out if I had anything else to get.

He grinned and raised an eyebrow at me. "No, silly. Should I talk with your momma?"

I bit my lip harder. "No. That's okay. It's not the right time."

"Not the right time for what?"

Seth held out his hand and shook hers. "Good morning, Mrs. Chicand. It's very early to be taking your daughter off, I know. But my family likes to prepare everything for my family members arriving from Scotland."

He would let me tell her in my own time. Maybe when I turned eighteen. Then, she would have no room for discussion with me. I would be capable of making my own decisions. I could leave if I had to, and if it came down to that there was nothing that her, Luke, or my dad could do about it.

"That's okay. How are rehearsals coming?"

Momma still hadn't noticed the ring. Maybe it was because I had been wearing one since the first day of auditions, and she didn't know about our ghostly encounter. But I was ready to flee the scene, hop in the car, and zoom away like a high chase movie.

Seth looked down at me. His eyes grew soft after remembering our dress rehearsal last night, and I was sure he also remembered our proposal.

"Wait until you see Jazzline. You won't believe it."

"I'm sure that it will shock me. Just for her to speak to a crowd. Is she loud? For her to be in the lead? Are you sure you can sing? You can do this in front of an audience?"

She wouldn't know. And it hit me right at that moment how sad that was.

"I guess so."

Seth frowned. Why couldn't he see that my house wasn't equipped with a theater room, a musical loving mother, a supportive family unit who prided themselves on togetherness?

"We'll make sure we call you and check in."

Seth grabbed the suitcase, and then we were gone. No explosives. No detonators. It was a clean getaway. We were out on the main highway when Seth began to speak.

"She doesn't know you can sing? Are you serious?"

"No. I don't go singing through the house with her around. I'm usually asleep when she gets off work."

"But she doesn't know you can sing? Jazzline, music is so

important to you. Your voice called to me in the darkness. Music is a part of you, and your momma doesn't even know that?"

That conjured up a song, Bohemian Rhapsody by Queen.

He raised his hands. "See what I mean. You can't help yourself. Jazzline, I'm sorry that your mother and father don't know you."

I tried to change the subject. "About the engagement? I was hoping we could wait a little bit." One month and twelve days to be exact.

"I wasn't speaking about our engagement. But now that you've brought that to my attention. When are you planning to tell them? Your mother has already given me her blessing."

It was so hard to believe. I tried to imagine the look on her face when he asked her for my hand in marriage. For them to meet her. For his father to give me the jeweled clip. It had to have been very shocking to her system. She'd never had to deal with one boyfriend with me. Let alone the thought of a fiancée. I could see where it would be a tad bit overwhelming. It still was for me.

I had decided. "On my birthday."

"So, you plan to get a car from her, stuff Alex in the trunk, and drive off with me in the sunset?"

This broke the gloomy mood. His face was radiant. He was so self-conscious about his scars but he had no clue how gorgeous he was to me.

"Something like that."

"My parents can't wait to see you. Bree didn't sleep any last night."

I leaned back in the seat and stretched. "Let me guess. Was she planning our wedding, too?"

"Probably. Bree wouldn't let me in the room, but I could hear her in there, pacing around. I imagined her with a sketch pad in her hand designing your gown or something." He squeezed my hand. "I hope you can handle my family."

"They're so wonderful to me. I know that I'll try my best to belong."

"That's what's so special about you, Jazzline. You don't have to try at all. You belong with me."

I started to sing Pat Benatar's song, We Belong.

"What's got you singing so much this morning?"

My eyes met his, and the look he gave me was grand.

"I told you I sing when I'm happy."

"Do I really make you happy?"

"I am the happiest girl in the world. My whole insides are about to burst open."

"Wow, that would be a sight. One I wouldn't want to see."

I laughed. "I told you I'm terrible with words."

His laughter fell in with mine. Perfect harmony. "Don't go putting words like that in the vows. My family might get mental imagery of a scary movie or a nightmare and run screaming down the aisle."

"Ha, ha, very funny. With your mom's latest movie concept, I doubt that."

With the talk of wedding gowns and vows, my stomach did a somersault. I hadn't had one of my old Jazzline episodes in a long time, thank God. Now wasn't the time. So, I tried to think back to his family.

"What can I expect this weekend?"

"Crazy. Strange. Home."

"How many are coming over from Scotland?"

I'd seen videos and photo albums. I'd heard about Aunt Shea, Bree's favorite and Douglas who was to stay after his family returned, and the notorious Uncle Colin. He went into the full detailed family history.

Next year, I might travel to Scotland as his wife. Or what if he would want to be married there? We could fly Alex, Momma, and Luke over with us. Momma always dreamed of traveling. This could be her ticket to ride.

It didn't take us long to drive to the Southdale Highland Games and Clan Gathering. I'd seen the banners for it before we turned into the park's long entryway. Tartan flags of every plaid and color were lined along the sides of the winding dirt road. I pointed out the MacKenzie colors, and he smiled.

Vendor tents were lined as far as the eye could see. Arenas and stages were still being constructed, and large buses and trucks were being pulled in with equipment. Banners signaled sections of the park, Sheepdog trials, heavy game competitions, a national dance competition, birds of prey exhibit, it went on and on. This wasn't a little dress-up party. This was turning out to be a grand affair. And who sponsored the event? The MacKenzie family. Their clan name was on the archway as we entered. I should have known. Money can buy a park and turn it into a faraway land any day of the week. Friday seemed like a good day for a transformation.

We pulled up to the section that held fancy RVs, and Seth opened the door.

I asked, "What's this?"

"It's home for the weekend. I hope that it'll suit you."

He pulled my bag and his out of the car and set them down on the paved patio.

"I thought we were camping?"

"Did you think tents? Come on, Jazzline. Think of Bree in a little mesh tent. With sleeping bags and mosquitoes?"

I laughed at the thought of it. So unlike Bree. I should've known.

Tucker stepped out of the RV. He said, "Come on over here, and give me a hug. You went off and got engaged and didn't tell me."

It was so proper that he'd be the first one to congratulate me.

He didn't shake Seth's hand, but reach out and gave him a huge bear hug, lifting him off the ground.

Tucker said, "I've got me a little brother with Alex. Now, I guess I have to adopt a big brother, too. Soon enough you'll be my brother-in-law anyway."

He winked at Bree as she skipped down the narrow steps of the RV and landed perfectly on her feet beside Tucker.

She had tears in her eyes as she looked at me. "Jazz, welcome to my family. I love you."

I hugged her tightly, blushing. Emotions were running wild. "I love you, too. Thanks for being so nice to me."

She turned to Seth. "She acts like it's a chore or something. When are you going to get it through to her that she's wonderful?"

"I thought I was working on it."

The door to the second RV opened, and Mr. MacKenzie walked down. He held out his arms for Mrs. MacKenzie to fall into them.

She said, "I thought that I heard talking out here. Jazzline, Seth honey, come here."

They held out their arms to us and gave us both a hug. I thought that I'd suffocate between the bodies of those two MacKenzie men, and when I came up for air, I felt my face flushed with excitement.

Mrs. MacKenzie smoothed back my hair from my cheek. "Dear, we're so happy for you and Seth. We adore you."

Mr. MacKenzie patted me on the back, a little rougher than he meant to. "Welcome to our family, dear. We can't wait to spread the news this evening. I'm sure there will be more than one toast in your honor. Maybe a few rounds."

Mrs. MacKenzie took my arm and led me to the RV. "Will this be fine for you, dear?"

When I peeked inside, I saw luxury accommodations, a flat-screen TV suspended from the ceiling, leather sectional, and baskets of food lining the counters.

"It'll be fine."

Seth set the suitcase down inside the RV and told me that he had to get changed. We needed to be ready when the family arrived. That meant me as well. Bree was sidestepping on her feet like a little schoolgirl. When I went down the steps, not as elegant as Bree, I was so relieved that Seth was there to take my hand or I would have fallen right on my face.

His whisper caressed my cheek. "You look so lovely in my plaid. So beautiful."

I looked to him in the kilt, and I caught my breath. It wasn't the reaction like Tucker. Tucker and his dreads and his corn dog attitude messed me up. But, Seth. He looked regal, almost like he'd stepped out of a cover of one of those romance novels Tucker's mom kept around the house. His long black hair flowed down past his shoulders, making a stark contrast with the crisp white shirt that he wore. His eyes glowed against the green, and he seemed taller, more masculine somehow. Like he'd just stepped out to sweep me off my feet.

His parents came down the steps and walked towards us, and I felt myself being transported to another place. To another time when a world like this existed. This held a language of its own, a shared history, a shared tradition, a family bloodline that was sacred and held with the utmost respect and reverence.

There was something more as they stood together in the circle on the park grounds at the opening ceremony. The bagpipes began to play and in marched a Battalion of pipers and drummers parading in unison. Seth whispered to me that he knew how to play, and it didn't surprise me one bit. Nothing about him could surprise me. He'd already loved me. That was the biggest shock of my life. I could deal with anything.

The calling of the clans came just in time as the MacKenzie brood fresh from the airport escorted in Hummer limos, sauntered up to fall in line around us like royalty. Hugs and laughter mingled in with the sounds of the clans. I swear the MacKenzie clan were the loudest of the bunch. Seth said crazy in his description, and I winked at him as I surveyed the lot. They were a bunch of rowdy men and women who seemed eager to be on American soil. I counted seven adults and three children. Cat and Douglas were around my age.

After singing and parading and calling out names and opening ceremony announcing, we were off. The excitement mounted because as soon as everyone began to disperse towards the fair, I was tackled by the MacKenzie clan in the middle of the park.

"Let me get a good look a' the lass."

"Mind yer' elbows. Come oan, get off!"

Something about what would "bairns" look like with both of us with curly, long locks. The kids were standing around giggling. As I was introduced to them all at once, I wondered if I would be able to ever understand their thick accents. Let alone remember their names.

"Well, it's nice to see all of you, too. I am standing right here, you know. I'm the one who proposed. Don't I get any attention?" I think he was laughing more at me as I looked pure terrified at him through the heads and armpits that had surrounded me. "Let me formally introduce my bride to be, Jazzline Chicand."

More cheers from the MacKenzie's. More cheers from passerby clans. I was sure that by nightfall everyone in the camp would know about our engagement. Maybe everybody all the way to Scotland. Maybe it would travel across the sea and not down Highway 17. All I could do was strain my ears to pick up on their strange talking. Okay, I got crazy when they stepped out of the cars. Strange when they opened their mouth. My mind smiled at the next descriptive word Seth used, home. He was right.

In all honesty, Tucker seemed right at home from the beginning. But Tucker's personality was loud, to the point of sometimes being obnoxious. He didn't stand out, except for his hair. If his dreads were out, he could have passed for one of the MacKenzie men with his broad shoulders and shining eyes. Bree was telling Cat all about him I was sure, by the look of jealousy on her newly arrived cousin's face. I pitied Bree for one split pea second. Everyone I ever saw look at Bree did so with a green eye. Yes, Bree was beautiful. Yes, she was graceful and poised, confident and bold. Yes, she had Tucker on her arm dotting after her. But that was just what she was, and I loved all of that about her. There was no jealousy over her. Only love.

The sheer force of numbers from his family physically pulled

Seth away, and I found myself beside Mrs. MacKenzie where she was introducing me to Aunt Shea, her sister. The same eyes, pale skin, and strawberry-blonde hair. Aunt Shea was not married, and had no children of her own, but was the family's official godmother.

Mr. MacKenzie's brother, Colin, whose Seth's brother was named after, had a wife, Sarah, with the twins Devon and Donell who had turned teenagers and were scoping out the park for girls. Mr. MacKenzie's sister, Aileanna, married Fergus and had Catriona, Bree's favorite, and the older brother Douglas who I would get to know since he was staying behind to attend senior year here.

Mr. MacKenzie's youngest brother had passed away a few years back, with what I hated to hear - Lupus related heart disease. His name had been Abhainn, but they called him Abbey. Mr. MacKenzie's eyes teared when he saw Maggie bring forth Alasdair, who was ten, the youngest of the MacKenzie clan. He attempted to give Mr. MacKenzie a bear hug. He looked at Maggie, and she smiled at him. I saw the exchange and knew that the loss haunted Mr. MacKenzie. He saw Abbey in little Alasdair. He held on to his game bag the same way that Alex would have if he were here.

Seth was introducing Tucker to Douglas. What was it with this MacKenzie family? Were they all from supermodel stock? Douglas was an athletic star, and had national status in Scottish football.

The last person to meet was the most formidable. He was a few inches taller than Seth. His weathered face was weary, and his eyes were gray as a rolling storm cloud. Mr. MacKenzie stepped forward, grabbed my hand through his arm and went over to his father as some of the younger members of their family moved towards the line of RVs rented for the occasion. The man before me was still so vibrant and strong, with muscles rippling against his wrinkled skin as if they were fighting off old age.

Seth was standing behind us. Something about this seemed heavy. More than the normal introductions. Mr. MacKenzie squeezed my arm, and then released me. I wanted the support back, and then Seth was there beside me nodding his head at the old man in respect.

Mr. MacKenzie said, "Father, you're looking well."

"Aye. Seth, I didn't know of yer' snatching up a pretty one."

My eyes narrowed from the strain it took for my brain to process his words but the conversation continued in like manner, a formal exchange. Every now and then, I heard a Gaelic word thrown in there. I heard soul mate. That was the only word that I'd learned from Seth. I needed the lessons that Bree got for Tucker, and I wondered why one was not given to me?

"Jazzline Chicand. I would like for you to meet my grandfather, Gillivary MacKenzie."

His head cocked to the side, and his gaze was intent on me. Those gray clouds turning into a storm. Then passing.

He spoke, "Clever, son. I see ye've given the lass my jewel. I can judge her, ya know. Ah, but it suits ye, miss."

He winked at me, and I smiled. My voice would not come, but his wink assured me that it would be fine between us. The talk between them was safely on the topics of castle conditions, travel arrangements, and the state of affairs between the estates. I could pick up bits and pieces of it as they flowed from English to Gaelic and back again. It was not on me anymore. It was as if the minute that Gillivary MacKenzie began to speak the whole family scattered with the four winds. Just as soon as I started to catch on, the old man turned away and walked up to a separate, smaller RV and went inside.

"That's my father for you. But you passed judgment, both of you, so have fun. We'll meet back later at seven for dinner."

I asked, "What would have happened if we didn't?"

Mr. MacKenzie said, "Don't worry about that, dear. What matters is that you did."

We moved on towards the vendor section of the park, far away from the eyes and ears of his family. Seth's hand never left my back as we walked around the grounds. He told me how his family purchased the property years ago. How having these games as a part of their family history was important to honor their heritage in America. The MacKenzie's did not blend in. They seemed a bit bigger. Larger than life.

When I would catch a glimpse of Alasdair or Douglas, I knew who they were in the crowd. When Maggie brushed by us and squeezed my arm, it wasn't the color of her plaid. It was the feel of her. That was when I understood what home meant. They were all the same, with some unspoken thread between them that held them together, and drew me in with them as if I were now one of them.

The day passed quick, as it always did when Seth was beside me, and it was time for the dinner. They had a large tent circled by bonfires in banquet style with a stage set up for highland musicians playing harps, mandolins, and other instruments that I didn't quite know what they were.

The dinner was extravagant with lamb and grouse. I'm sure that Momma would have been in heaven here among the food and the atmosphere. I looked across the table at Tucker and Bree. He caught my eye, and his face lit up. He was so happy to be there with Bree and her family. His family was beyond dysfunctional, and I knew he always dreamed of this. Funny how he fell right into a brood of muscle men who loved games and their women and their family more than life itself. Tucker's kind of people. I watched Bree how she held on to his hand even as they ate. What if they had never met? What if Tucker wouldn't have been out on the beach that day?

I shuddered at the thought and felt my body tremble. Seth looked down at me and frowned. "Are you okay? Do you not like the food?"

My plate was still full. My nerves were still on edge being around all of his family, being here, taking it all in made me have no appetite at all. It was hard enough to breathe beside him, let alone think about all of the food and smells swirling around me. Everyone was holding out their electronics, recording the music, each other and sending videos out to family that couldn't make it.

I tried to focus on the sounds of the strings and the flutes, but it was all becoming a blur and my head started to spin.

"I need a minute. Can you please excuse me?" I looked up to his father more than to Seth. Mr. MacKenzie nodded to me, and I found a dark place to hide.

Seth was there behind me in the dark. I felt him hold back my hair as I got sick again. I was so embarrassed.

He said, "Can I do something? Please tell me?" His concern was thick in his voice, and I hated to be a bother.

"I'm so sorry. I didn't mean to do this." I straightened up and smoothed down my dress, checking to see if I'd cleared it and thank God, I had.

"Do you think you're getting sick?" He pulled my hair away from my face and pressed his palm against my cheek.

My stomach lurched again. "I think it's just my nerves. It's nothing, really. Maybe I need some time to adjust to everything all at once. It's so fast, and loud, and everyone is so happy. It's hard for me to put into words."

His arms wrapped around me, and I felt the warmth from his body, comforting me and calming my soul. "If you need to go rest, I'll stay with you."

I whispered, "No. Give me a minute. Maybe we can take a walk."

He buried his face in my hair. "I've got to tell you something, Jazzline. I can't keep it a secret from you any longer. Because if I lose you over this like I think I will, then it is better now before we're married."

I pulled from him, my eyes searching him out. But I saw Bree approaching and pulled away. She smiled at us.

"I'm in there about to give you both a surprise, and you're out here necking. Come on."

Seth breathed. He was relieved. My heart sunk to the ocean. Secrets. What secrets?

She glided across the stage in front of five hundred people and gave us a gift of a Scottish traditional dance to celebrate her future sister-in-law and brother's engagement. Her sweetness could not erase the talk of a secret between Seth and me. I couldn't concentrate on her dance, and when it was over the crowd cheered. Seth stood up for her and pulled me along beside him. My hand rose over my heart. I felt panic and frantic heat rising in me. My eyes were tearing. She thought that it was for her but it was for the talk that would be forced between soon. I felt the room spinning, and I knew that if I didn't escape, I would faint.

Tucker must have sensed my dread, and he came over to whisper to Seth to take me out. Seth took me by the arm, and I tried my best to force a weak smile at Tucker to apologize to Bree. When we made it outside, we didn't head back to the RVs. He carried me in his arms clear across the park, sat me down on the grass and paced back and forth. The moon hid, then showed itself, then hid again. Minutes passed as I watched the shadows play around me, and I couldn't find the words to ask him his fear? Had he realized that I was not good for him?

He sat down beside me and took my hands in his. I knew what he was doing. He was trying to plan the approach. His words hit me in the face, and he hadn't even spoken yet. He said that he knew how to be smart at these things.

"Seth, whatever you have to tell me, please say it."

"I don't know how."

"Nothing you can say can surprise me."

He looked right into my eyes gathering his strength to say it. "I can see things. I can see death."

Now, that surprised me.

CHAPTER 16

The Broken Road

There was no crashing. He didn't say, "I can't marry you." He didn't say, "My family doesn't approve."

"You see death? Like dead people?"

"Some say it is like a prophet from the Bible. That's how dad describes it for me. Some might say I have a psychic ability. I just see things. People. Energies. Whatever. I know things."

"I don't understand what you mean? What do you know?"

"Whatever this thing is, this gift, helps me to communicate with the dead."

"Like a ghost hunter? Some paranormal investigator?"

"I guess the television shows make it easier for me to talk about. At least you know I'm not the only one."

"But I always thought most of that was fake."

"What I have is not fake. Trust me on that."

"So, why didn't you want to tell me? Seth, I thought you would leave me! I thought you were about to break up with me."

"Seriously? I thought you would leave me when you found out that I can see dead people. It isn't a movie or a show. It's my life and that means this curse will affect you. You'll be with me, by my side, and I'll see things. I'll know things, and when they speak to me sometimes it isn't nice, Jazzline. Not all things left behind were loved."

"I love you. That's what matters to me."

"And you won't run at this? You stayed when you saw me scarred. You'll stay when you know my darkest secret?"

"I'm not going anywhere."

He pulled me into him and I felt his body trembling against mine. "How can you love me when I see things?"

"Do you see us? Like things that affect us."

He didn't answer me at first. The silence let me know.

Then, he whispered, "I do."

"Well, what do you see? Tell me." My voice broke. Would it be divorce? Would we even make it to our wedding day? Or die of old age with ten grandchildren at our feet?

"I can't tell you all of that. All I can say is that I'll love you forever, and you'll be mine. I know that for certain."

His finger was twirling my ring again, letting me know that it would be. Did I want to know everything about our future? Did he see it all or flashes of us?

"So, that's why we saw Alice Flagg. How does it happen for you? What happens?"

That night came back to me, and I felt the chill running down my spine. He spoke with her and reached out unafraid. He had seen death before.

"It's hard to say. Speaking about that."

"Tell me, Seth."

His hand went to his face in that self-conscious movement that he sometimes made. "I see death before it comes. And afterward, if it still lingers on, I connect to it like a current. Of those I love, it hurts the most. To those I can't save it almost kills me because there's nothing I can do about it. Death does not even stop for me."

"How does it happen to you?" I wanted to keep questioning him because I felt that once this was over, he would never want to bridge this conversation again.

"In dreams or flashes. Images. And I do not have the power to change the future. I tried only once but realized I'm forced only to see it. If one thing could be different, would it change it? Could I change the course of life?"

I could feel him drifting away in the current.

"You are not responsible for the world."

"I'm responsible for the ones I love. Yet, I can't tell. What would a warning do? What would I cause? A chain reaction that would change God's plan? I'm not God, and there's so much of this that I don't understand. I do know I'm not some messenger of death, an angel of death. I'm just me. And the truth of it all is killing me. My grandfather has tried to instruct me in these matters, but his words fall short and are as cold as I feel."

"Does the rest of your family know?"

"We all have, what you would call them, special gifts. We have documented it in our family bloodline for centuries. I don't consider mine a gift, only a curse. I'd love to have Bree's. But then, God no, because then she would have had mine."

The thought of Bree having a gift didn't surprise me. The gift that she had was to be like an angel I was sure. Maybe she had beautiful white wings stitched away and when she and Tucker were alone, they would go flying over the ocean. It seemed as if she was always wearing white.

"Does Tucker know? Why hasn't he told me?"

"Yes. Bree told him, but my father asked him not to speak of it to you. He felt that it was my place to discuss this with you. To tell you what you were stepping into. I understand if you want to walk away. I never will understand how you can even look at me, let alone love me. Now, with this. I know that I should've told you. But if it's just too much for you, I swear I'll leave you alone."

It filled his eyes with tears, and my heart shredded like paper. Seth was always so strong, but now that his secret was out, he was fragile and broken.

"I'll admit that what you've told me is a little too much. It's too much for you to handle alone. I'll never leave you, Seth. I'll never walk away. Let me try this without you judging my accent, beannaithe ag Dé."

His first smile. He was breaking through the riptide. He was coming back to me, and my heart beat again.

He kissed me on the cheek. "Blessed by God. Who taught you that?"

"I asked Aunt Shea tonight. I wanted to show you I would learn Gaelic for you. I'd do anything for you." My mind hit the jukebox, and I began to sing a Bryan Adam's song.

"So, you're singing now?"

"What's Bree's gift? What does Tucker have to deal with? Let me guess. Can she fly?"

"Why don't you ask her? She's coming. They're all coming."

"They?"

I turned to see his family, and their arms were entwined. They stopped by the entry gate and Mr. and Mrs. MacKenzie stepped forward in front of the crowd of beautiful, gifted and talented Scots, and a tag-along Tucker who had that guilt-ridden look all over his face. I'd let him ride it out for a while then tell him that I understood why he felt obligated not to tell.

Mrs. MacKenzie was the first to speak, "We hope that we aren't intruding, but we felt the need to come."

Seth stood up, pulling me along with him. "No, Momma. I told her. She knows, and she didn't run."

Mrs. MacKenzie frowned. "Everything?"

"Enough. And she is, well, ask her how she is."

"I love him."

That had to be enough for his family to get that I wasn't going anywhere. I couldn't tell them that I understood because that would be a lie. And with all of them standing there in front of me, waiting, I could say what I knew.

I saw that Mr. MacKenzie's father, Gillivary, was not among them. Maybe he didn't see the need for his presence here. Based on what I could read of him this afternoon he wasn't one too impressed with words. Speaking of this out in the open might not have been his wish. The others didn't seem to mind. They seemed almost eager to take another person into their tangled vine of family secrets.

Bree sat beside me, then Tucker. He still wouldn't look at me, and I decided I better let him off the hook. I couldn't relax with him worrying. I leaned over Bree's legs and whispered, "I know why you didn't tell me. It's okay. I love you."

Bree's face was radiant. "What did Seth tell you, exactly?"

I looked to Seth and he spoke, "I told her about me. That's all."

Bree clapped. "Good, because I wanted to be the one to tell Jazz."

Mr. MacKenzie looked straight at me, and his eyes held an intense stare. "Are you sure you can handle this, sweetheart?"

"Yes."

Bree rocked back and forth on her knees. "I have a special gift, Jazzline. Guess what it is?"

I told them my first thought of Bree when I found out about his family. "You are an angel whose wings spread over the ocean." I left out the part of Tucker holding on for dear life, but I smiled because of it.

She burst with laughter. So did the rest of the family. My face reddened.

Mrs. MacKenzie reached over to squeeze my hand. "That's precious, dear. Bree, tell her about you. No more games."

Thank God. It would take all night at this rate. Her hand went to Tucker's, and she looked at him for a moment before she let the words pour out of her like a sweet melody. "I have the gift of true love."

"I don't understand?"

I knew that her love for Tucker was true, I knew that. Anybody would see it by watching them. Was she like a modern-day Cupid? Did she put Tucker under some love spell? Was I under her same spell over Seth because from the minute I laid eyes on him I knew he was the one?

Seth's smile was dazzling under the full moonlight, and I was in awe of him sitting among his family. For the first time since I knew him, it was as if he were free of his scars, his insecurities. He was just Seth, the man that I loved. No more secrets between us. Or I hoped not. I hoped this was it.

Bree said, "I can see true love. I know it. I feel it. When I see people, I see their soul mate. I can see their lives connecting from within, and it is a power that I discovered the day that I saw Tucker. Then, with you and Seth. Now, when soul mates are near, I can sense their presence, and it's the most wonderful feeling in the world."

I whispered, "That explains it."

It explained many things. Me and Seth. I knew that something stronger connected us. Even though I knew it, the overwhelming sense of freedom lit my soul on fire when I heard Bree tell her gift. A soul mate sensor. And she saw the love between us. An unseen force or power she could see, connecting our spirits. It also explained who Bree was. A light.

Bree asked, "Explains what?"

"How you can be so lovely and special. Having all of that love inside of you and knowing that it exists must give you peace."

There was no laughter this time with the crowd. I wanted to say more. That I had doubted it and questioned it from my childhood. To be like Bree and see it between souls must be the most awesome power in the world. I could see why Seth would say he wished he had her power to see love instead of seeing death. If she lived with this power of love within her how did it feel to Seth to have the loss there?

Bree frowned. "But now that you know Seth's, you see how the words, 'til death do us part,' really sting for him. I would rather have his gift so that he would not feel pain."

Seth tugged at her hair. "And I would never trade that for anything. You're the light between us, Bree. I've grown accustomed to the dark."

But I knew that was just a front for him to be strong in front of his family. He had not gotten used to the gift, and it haunted him.

He said, "Dad, how should we do this?"

"It has been done before, Seth. Let our family speak and tell their powers to her themselves if they wish. If not, understand that. It's their secret to tell not mine."

Some were comfortable with the reveal. I could tell it by their gestures. Only Cat and Douglas seemed out of place. Maybe it was that they were young and had not had long to process their abilities. Maybe they were like Bree before the summer. Her power came when she saw her own true love. That made me wonder what brought on Seth's curse. I'd have to continue that conversation with him when we were alone.

Mrs. MacKenzie said, "Maura means the star of the sea. In my life, I can witness the stories of people's lives as they come and go, wash away and break free. I see how we all connect, in life, in death. I see the vast ocean, yet every elemental force in between. Their wants and needs, their potential. I can see their story. Maybe that's why I am as successful as a screenwriter. I have seen these little dramas unfold all around me since I was a child and they have impacted me so."

She knew my story. I was broken and now healed and that meant she knew from the beginning. She knew Tucker and what pain he endured through his childhood with his family. She knew me and Tucker and that kind of knowing scared me. It was as if I could keep no secrets from his family. I was an open book. She saw my story with Seth, and knew that I loved him. I looked at Tucker. He was hearing all of this for the first time, too and I could tell that he was hurting at the thought of Mrs. MacKenzie knowing his past.

Tucker frowned. "So, you know about me? About everything that happened to me when I was younger?"

Bree squeezed his hand and put her head on his shoulder. He must have told her his secrets, too. Years of therapy led up to him being able to speak even that sentence aloud.

Mrs. MacKenzie said, "Yes, son. I could see it."

"And you still let me date your daughter?"

"You are her soul mate. Besides that, Tucker, you are your own man now. Your past does not define you. You have lived a tough life, son, but times are changing. You're one of us now. Never forget that."

Tucker wouldn't meet anyone's gaze, and I knew that his emotions were raw. Dear God, please give Tucker peace.

Mr. MacKenzie was next to speak. "My name is Monroe. I don't think that I ever formally introduced myself to you. Monroe means out of the river's mouth. Please, Jazzline, forgive me for our conversation in the study the other night. It was with good intention, I promise you."

Did he expect me to understand what his gift was? I thought we weren't playing games anymore. He didn't apologize to Tucker, and I figured whatever he pulled on me, he did to Tucker but relished the thought of it because of Bree, his baby girl.

"My gift is to bring forth the truth. When I am near someone, they cannot help themselves but be honest with me. Often forgetting that they should probably keep their mouth closed, and they speak whatever is on their mind or heart to say."

My hand went to my mouth. "Oh."

That was why I was so open with Mr. MacKenzie when he gave me the jewelry. My mind went straight to that meeting that they had with Momma over coffee at Chica's. What I would have given to have been there to witness and hear that one? Wonder what truths he extracted out of Tucker without him knowing?

Mr. MacKenzie's sister spoke, "Ah am Aileanna, the light bearer. I'll bring hope fer MacKenzie's in times of darkness with just a touch."

She lowered her eyes and did not speak anymore. She was beautiful and fragile, shimmering as a light under the glow of the moon. Her husband, Fergus, was holding her hand and Catrione was picking the grass. Neither one of them spoke.

Colin was next. His eyes warm as he held on to Sarah's waist,

"A don't know how tae say it. Ah am Colin, the young creature. No matter how old I be, down the centuries, I'll always live young. Thank God, Shea also has a true love sensor an' rummeled me Sarah tae love and coorie down wit."

Shea hit him upside the head, and he winced. "It was my place tae say mine, ye bam pot."

I held up my hand. "English, please? Ah have no gift of Scottish words."

Mr. MacKenzie laughed. "Sorry, dear. They need to come with a translator. You know them and their tones, you can figure out what they are implying."

I wasn't so sure of that. Knowing what a bam pot was would need a Scottish urban dictionary.

Seth leaned in and said, "Pretty much, Shea called Colin an idiot for telling her gift. She wanted to make a formal announcement. Colin will never grow old and neither will Sarah, his wife. Shea found the soul match for Colin, and she never lets him live it down."

I smiled up at him for the quick rundown because I was a complete bam pot once they all began talking all at once overloading my senses until my brain hurt.

Mr. MacKenzie raised his hand, and when they still did not quiet down, he yelled, "Enough!"

A soft voice spoke in the crowd, and with the sound, Mr. MacKenzie froze. It was from Maggie. "May ah speak fur Abhainn?"

Mrs. MacKenzie said, "Of course, dear."

She said, "Abhainn, my dear husband. Abhainn means river. His gift was a rushing river of sadness and death. He knew when times were near, even his own. I'm sorry ye touched him, Seth."

Everyone's head dropped and eyes reverted to the ground. Seth and I stared at this broken widow who was clinging onto Alasdair for air.

"I'm not sorry, Aunt Maggie. I'm grateful."

"Grateful tae have scars? Tae have sickness? Death?"

Seth's voice was calm. His hand was warm against mine. I could feel the tension being released from his body as he spoke. As if he had bottled this up for a long time, and it was fizzing over and spewing forth from the pressure. This had never been discussed before now, and by the feel of Seth it was about time.

"I loved Abhainn like a father. He wasn't just an uncle to me. He was like me. When he passed, it went through me. If that's what I have left of him, and what was meant for my gift, then I can deal with that. You have Alasdair, and one day he will defend our name in Abhainn's honor and yours, Aunt Maggie. You still have Abhainn with you when you look at Alasdair."

She rose then, bringing Alasdair with her, tears falling down her cheeks. Her body was trembling. "I'm so sorry I brought this up now."

Mr. MacKenzie stood up to approach her, "It's time, lass. We love you and Alasdair so much. We love Abhainn still. Just take Aileanna's hand. The joy will come for you again."

Maggie held out her hand as if she were about to, and then let it drop to her side clinching her fists. "I cannot. It'll let him go."

Seth stood up then and moved closer to Maggie. His eyes were glowing. He towered over her and his presence there was shrinking her back from him as if she were afraid of him.

"It's been three years. He'll always be here. He's always here. Trust what I say."

I wondered if that meant he was here with us now. Could Seth see his ghost? He said that it was worst when it was family. Three years. The pictures stopped of him in the hallway three years ago. His uncle passed Lupus to him. I remembered the chapter on heredity and Lupus, but I think that they omitted this part of the passing between souls for the sake of normalcy and an accurate medical diagnosis.

She started to back away when Mr. MacKenzie stepped forward.

She pulled Alasdair behind her as they went back towards the main park. "I'm so sorry."

What had started off as amazing and awe-inspiring turned into a dark night.

Everyone else rose and nodded to me as they left the circle that we had made. Colin was the only one that approached me and Seth. He gave me a quick hug and looked to Seth. "She's a mighty braw Sassenach, if ye ask me. Have we met before, lass?"

"No. Trust me, I would have remembered. And what's a Sassenach? Is it like bam pot?"

Seth put his arm around me. "He said that you were pretty fine as far as English standards go."

"Thank you, I guess."

Colin winked at me then went off to run behind Sarah. She swatted at him as they swung hands together. I wondered how old they were, but those questions could come later. I knew that Seth needed my full attention right now, and I was trying my best to think of words to say to him that could comfort him.

We stood alone in the arena again. The stars were dancing above us. The moon was peeking in and out of clouds. Abhainn was still surrounding us. I might not have been able to see his spirit, but I could feel the heaviness of Seth. I wanted to know the whole story, but I wouldn't ask. He would tell me in his own time. I could respect that. But what could I do to calm him? We stood there, with his arm awkwardly around my waist as if he didn't know what to do with it, so I took his other arm, circled my waist and leaned into his chest.

He buried his head in my hair.

I sang Rascal Flatts, *God Blessed the Broken Road*. All I could do was sing to him. Nothing else would do.

His kiss let me know that he was coming back to me, and I wrapped my arms tighter around his neck and pulled him closer. But closer was never close enough with him.

I blushed at the thought of how close we had become so fast. The soul mate connection. It was real. I knew that, but now, really knowing it, sealed it.

"Do you know what I'm thinking right now?"

"I'm not a mind reader, Jazzline. But for those who are here that is why my father gave you the jewel. Something in the elemental properties of the shell serves as a blocker with the family and the others. Wear it always. It will keep our secrets safe."

He would have to give me a " How to Deal with SLS: Scottish Language and Superpowers" to get me through this relationship without being clueless.

"Those that are here? There are more?"

"All of the Scots here have special gifts. This is the only place where we meet together and can be in full power without fear of being discovered by an outsider."

I was beginning to accept that people like the MacKenzie's could exist. But to know there were more?

He held me close to his side as we made our way back towards the long line of RVs that now bordered the four perimeters. I guessed people with gifts all came with luxury accommodations. I wondered if they were all covered with abalone. To think that snails could be so useful.

"Now, what were you thinking back there that was bad?"

"I was having thoughts of us being so close."

"Baby, we're not close enough. Soon our time will come. Time continues to roll. You'll be eighteen in ..."

We spoke in unison, "One month and twelve days."

I said, "So, you've been counting."

He tried his best to put on the deep slur of his Uncle Colin. "Aye, Sassenach. I'm countin' down th' days til' ye ur mine forever."

He kissed me again to the point of sighing. The kind of kiss that makes a girl want just one more, and one more after that.

"That means I really need to have a talk with Momma if you're planning to steal me away on my birthday."

"You best do that because it will be really difficult to explain tickets to Scotland."

"Scotland? You want to get married in Scotland?"

"Aye. At Eilean Castle. Our family home." His voice was far away as if he were already there.

"I would follow you anywhere."

And I meant it. Scotland, the ends of the earth. It would all be the same to me as long as I had him.

"Then, let's apply for expedited passports for you and your family first thing Monday morning. Guaranteed and ready for the stamp."

It was his turn to sing. His voice was beautiful and strong. His eyes shown light again as he spun me around in his arms. I had no clue what he was singing, some musical apparently about how he would do anything for me.

"And you pick at all of my oldies. What was that?"

"I was in Oliver a few years ago. Those musical numbers stay with you and become something when you find a love of your own. It all makes sense."

"What does?"

"Everything. Music. Experiences. Touches. Moments. Memories. It all just makes sense now. I wondered when I would get to this place because it brings purpose to my madness, and I have finally arrived."

"I understand. All of my lyrics are you."

I'd forgotten about the musical, the rehearsals, about Murrell's Inlet being here with him at the Scottish Magic Powers Highland Games. If Alex had been here and witnessed the circle of superheroes he would flip, knowing that stuff like this existed from his video games and comic books. He would be sure to get some to pass through him. Then, I thought of Abhainn again. and I felt the sadness wash over me.

"Are you okay?"

"I'm tired."

My head was in a daze as he sat me down in front of the narrow steps leading into the RV. All of the lights were on down the line and even though it was close to my twelve am drop off maybe during this festival, they all had a late-night curfew.

"I wonder what my momma would say if I stayed with you tonight?" He kissed me on the cheek, then my nose.

"I..."

"I don't mean like that. I'd be away from you. I'd stay on a pullout. I need you closer to me tonight."

His momma opened the door. "Come on in, Seth. But you'll be between Jazzline and me. I promised her momma. Come on in, baby. I know."

His eyes found mine, and he winked. He knew that the walls of the RV were paper-thin, and his mother could hear our conversation at the door. I had a lot to learn from him. I would also have to learn how to snore like him after everything we'd been through because I could hear the steady rise and fall of him through the narrow hallway of the RV and tossed and turned again in another restless night.

CHAPTER 17

Love Is A Battlefield

I woke to the sounds of pots clinking and clanking. After only about two hours of sleep, I needed more than eggs and toast to get me ready. Seth was in his kilt, ready for the day. Bree was singing and dancing around him, holding on to the back of his shoulders trying to jump higher in some kind of dance move. I leaned against the doorframe and watched the two of them together, and my stomach churned.

When we married, what would happen to Alex? Where would we live? With his family? The house was big enough to get lost in it.

He seemed a little taken back that I was standing there, and his face reddened. What was he thinking? I wasn't a morning person, and he was. I didn't have powers, and he did. Just another opposite on our list.

He handed me a soda from the fridge, and I smiled at him. He said he wasn't a mind reader but sometimes I wondered.

"Where's Tucker?"

Bree pouted. "Momma wouldn't let him stay on the pullout. He had to sleep with Daddy. I fear for him, and hope that he comes out alive."

Seth drew back a breath and turned from us, his body leaning against the tiny counter. I put my hand on his back and felt his body trembling. "Are you okay?"

He sighed, and I knew he wasn't. "Yes. I'm going out to check on everything. I need to make sure we have all of our equipment ready."

"Equipment? For what?"

Bree circled me with an elegant bow. "It's competition day, Lassie. Not only am I up for a dance title, but Seth competes in the games."

I looked out of the tiny glass window and saw Mr. MacKenzie unloading a battle ax, claymore, and some primitive looking weaponry that looked like something you'd see on a medieval knight. Were they serious?

Seth asked, "Are you hungry? I made us breakfast."

He'd burnt some eggs that looked like rubber tire tracks had made their mark. The smells hit me like a blow to the stomach, and I made it to the bathroom just in blessed time.

He knocked on the door. "Are you okay?"

I was sure he'd heard everything through the paneled walls. I was weak. He was strong. Another for the list of opposites.

"Seth, you can't."

He laughed. "I know. I can't cook, but I tried. We don't have our chef with us. She might not understand the whole clan thing like this. And we wouldn't want to be responsible for anything happening to her."

I came out of the bathroom but couldn't look him in the eye. "No. It's not that. I mean, you can't fight like that. I saw those weapons."

"Nothing will happen. It's for sport."

"So, it's like MMA?"

"Well, I guess so," he grinned. "But we fight for more than a rank or a belt. Our clan must stand their ground against greater forces, and this is what I call our training ground for that. We fight here as if we would if our time comes to face the darkness."

"I think there's more to your family than what I learned last night."

"Time will reveal all, Jazzline. Don't worry. Just know I love you and would never put you in harm's way."

He did his best to reassure me and as we made our way towards the arena. Rival clan members were yelling curses and ranting at each other like a televised wrestling match. Obscene gestures were flying and painted faces of warrior men were on the verge of appearing as if they were savage animals soon to be let out of their cages. Some were even crouched down in animal-like positions, beasts ready to pounce, when the MacKenzie's walked by. I saw men in chains and shackles being held back because they appeared to be uncontrollable without restraints. What was happening? Where was I again?

I felt my fingernails dig into his arm. Fear seized my soul as we moved closer to the MacKenzie tartan colors. Not only was my Seth involved in this mayhem, but all of the men, including young Alasdair, were dressed up in the yellow war tunics that had the strangest smell to them.

I pressed my face against his sleeve trying to figure it out. "What's that?"

"It's dyed with horse pee, Jazzline."

My stomach did a flip.

Aunt Shea said, "Ye're lookin' awfy peely-wally, lassie."

Seth's grin turned into concern. "You do look pale. If you need to go back, Jazzline. I need to walk with you. But honestly, I'd much rather feel safer with you here with my family than back at the RV alone. It's safer here than there. Okay, you aren't going back. This won't take long. I promise. I'll finish them off soon enough."

I caught the warning behind his words and goosebumps rose on my neck. "You make it sound like I'm not safe. I thought you said nothing would happen."

"As long as you are by my side, nothing will."

There was a hint of seriousness in his voice. A protective plea for me to please pull it together and stick by his momma.

She squeezed my hand. "Soon enough you'll be able to cheer them instead of fear for their life. We haven't had a real threat in many moons. Let us not think of this as anything other than a battle of skill and a bunch of brutes going at it in the ring. It will get better, dear. Each time you attend the games, you'll understand more and more the purpose of what we do."

But it only got worse as the time went on. Blood was spilled in the very same spot where I danced with Seth the night before.

Roars erupted as McDougal's fought Moody's. Gordon's took on McLeod's. Burns' versus the Stewart's. My men were clanging and banging swords against shields, raising their arms in protest, looking as if they were about to charge at any minute. Even the twins and Alasdair were throwing out some slang that sounded close to sinning. But nothing more than pure anarchy erupted in the stands, along the wooden fencing, among the warriors, than when they announced the MacKenzie and MacDonald's clans.

I looked to Tucker and anxiety crashed over me like a tidal wave. Bree whispered to Tucker and they switched seats. Would Tucker ever be out there with them, defending the McKenzie name? Fighting for Bree? These men were fighting for something, and I was sure it was not for competition. It was for rage and anger and blood and guts. A story that was waiting to be told. Maybe I didn't want to hear about it.

The clans circled each other, picking off the weaker ones first. Going after children. I screamed as I saw Alasdair being knocked to the ground by the sheer force of a six-foot five heathen barreling at him with a sword. No one was paying the least bit attention to my terror. All eyes were on the arena and mine rose up to God.

I prayed, " Please God, please God."

I could find no other words.

Tucker yelled, "Seth, watch out!"

That meant Seth was being attacked. I peeked from under Tucker's arm as he moved me back and forth with him in his excitement. Seth was battling a shorter man, but full of weapons - a spear and a battle ax swinging as Seth dodged and danced around him. Another man was sneaking up to his back. Seth's claymore rose in the air and with full force struck the man down to the ground, then swung it with one hand behind him to send his unseen assailant paces back.

As sweat tangled his long hair crossing over his face, I could see his eyes that had become a predator. Not the eyes of the man that I loved. Not the eyes of the man that cried tears to me the night before. The eyes of a man consumed by fire and wrath. No matter how bad I wanted to turn away from him I couldn't. My eyes would not revert, my breath was ragged, and I felt my heart barely able to contain itself. He was there at Alasdair's side now, defending him. He was the champion.

Douglas and Seth stood side by side, as they struck the final two men to the ground. They clasped each other, arm in arm, then broke away. Monroe MacKenzie came and put his arm around Seth and led him through the carnage of bloodied MacDonald's. Blood was pouring out of Seth's arm, and he didn't even seem to notice. Dirt and sweat covered his war-painted face. His clothing was torn. His hair was a tangled mess. He was standing over me. I knew he was there and my hand reached out for him. I could see my hand move out towards him. I could see my fingers shaking. Then, all I saw was black.

CHAPTER 18

When You Say Nothing

I knew I had fainted. God, give me the strength to love this man.

Then, I heard him whisper, "Baby, it's all right. I'm so sorry you had to see that. But it had to be done."

I felt his fingers touch my cheek, and I opened my eyes. His eyes were soft and golden. He had changed, and he pulled his hair back in a ponytail. He had a deep cut above the corner of his eye. A scar to remember this day.

"Don't ever fight like that again, Seth MacKenzie."

His eyes narrowed. "Don't worry about that now. The fighting is over for today."

Thank God, it was just him and me. I hated feeling weak but having others witness it was beyond embarrassment.

"Seth, I thought you would die."

He grinned. "I'm not going to die, Jazzline. And when I do, I think I'll be the first to know."

I tried to swat at him but I felt all of the movement in my body unable to keep up with my thoughts. "Don't make a joke out of this, Seth. That was not a competition out there. You lied to me."

"Yes, it was. Douglas and I tied for first place. For both of us that is a great accomplishment. Our fathers are very proud. There will be a lot of toasting in our honor tonight."

"I'm glad Alex wasn't here."

He smiled. "Yeah, knowing him he would have wanted to join Alasdair. They would have made a great team."

"People were getting hurt out there. You were getting hurt out there. Those were not fake blood packets."

"Nobody was seriously injured. I think broken arms, a concussion here or there, and a couple of gashes on the MacDonald side, but for our side Colin had two ribs crack, but that is all. As you know, he will survive."

He made it sound so normal. He spoke about this as if he'd seen worse. He wasn't hurt. But he could have been.

I kissed him, and when he pulled away from me, this time he was breathless. Funny how he'd just mutilated about twenty gigantic Scottish looking warriors, and then I could bring him to this with a kiss. His face was soft and his touch was tender.

"I want you to promise me you will get some rest. I really want you to come with me to the Ceilidh."

"Translate, please." My head could not handle much more.

"It's a formal dance. And it's in two hours."

Great. I needed more beauty sleep than that to get me ready for an event. I wondered what in the world would be inside my suitcase to prepare me for a dance but then I remembered that I had Bree with me. She would take care of all of that.

"Tell Bree to come wake me up to help me."

He stood up but did not move from the side of the bed. I felt his presence still in the room. He whispered in that thick Scottish slang, "Ah can't wait tae hold ye in my arms tonight."

I whispered, "Aye."

He chuckled as he left me to dream. But my sleep was not a peaceful one. After walking away from a battlefield, fake or real, how could one have any peace about them?

Bree shook me and said, "Wake up! We've got to hurry!"

I groaned. "Bree? I thought it was in a couple of hours."

She clapped and pulled me up by my arm, "It is. That's why we have to hurry! Go take a shower. You'll feel so much better. Then, we can get ready."

She was right. The hot water made me feel better. She had a sandwich waiting for me, and I ate as I opened up my suitcase.

Bree entered with two dress bags, makeup cases, and hair products that she dumped all over the counter. Gel and a curling wand hit the floor missing my toe.

She turned to me and said, "Why do you seem so shocked? This is only half of my stuff."

"I don't even own any of this stuff. I wouldn't know what to do with it even if I did."

Bree's mother came in. She was already wearing a beautiful satin gown of forest green. Maura MacKenzie was stunning. If makeup and hair curlers would do that for me then I was up for some revitalization. I felt like one of those contestants from a makeover reality show. Down to fingernails and toes, hair spun up in an elegant twist. My beautiful butterfly clip was clamped in place. Bree applied my makeup, giving me a tutorial along the way. I tried my best to remember the tips of the trade that she and her mother were giving me.

The dress was simple. I admired how brilliant Bree was at all of this. She chose a color that was like the way Seth's eyes were when he looked at me after a kiss. It was deep gold.

"Did you put a love spell on this dress?"

"No, but Seth sure will be powerless when he sees you in it."

She held up her dress for my inspection. It was similar in cut to mine, but a sapphire blue, the color of Tucker's eyes. Instead of dyed, jeweled high heels, we fastened ballet type slippers on my feet. Thank goodness.

Bree was next to get ready, and she was a master. I hated to hear that I missed her twirling around on the dance stage that afternoon after the battle was over. She told me all about it, and it was as if I had been there myself. But I felt like a fool for missing something that was so important to her. She had won first place again in the dancing competition. I was sure that my behavior had embarrassed the entire MacKenzie's. Here they were strong fighters, free-spirited beautiful creatures, and I was the ugly duckling waddling around throwing up and fainting since I'd been here. How did I ever feel like I belonged to this family?

Mrs. MacKenzie stepped back in. "It's time, my lovely daughters."

Seth would be waiting. I stopped in the hallway as they walked gracefully in front of me. My feet would not move.

Bree turned and asked, "What's wrong? Did you forget something?"

"I can't go."

"Stop this nonsense. You'll be fine. Seth loves this part. I don't care how manly he seems. My brother loves to dance."

"But I don't know how to dance." I held my head down in shame. I was a constant disappointment. I was so sure of it.

Mrs. MacKenzie stepped forward and said, "Don't be silly. We know that you won't know any of the dances. Just follow along and have a wonderful time. No worries."

"You mean you have dances, too?"

Bree laughed. "Ceilidh's have special Scottish dances that we all perform as clans and groups. We all move in formation, or in lines, or with couples. You'll see. It's so awesome."

Of course, it was to the little dancer in the family. To me, it seemed like a barn dance ready for hillbilly disaster. I would be the only outsider that didn't know how to move before them. I couldn't understand them when they talked. I wouldn't be able to do an organized, choreographed dance.

Tucker told Bree how beautiful she was as she stepped down to meet him. I heard Mr. MacKenzie speak some Gaelic words to his lovely wife. I felt so rooted to the spot. Seth called out to me but I still couldn't move toward the door.

He bounded up the steps and the RV shook with the massiveness of him. "Baby, let's go and..."

He stopped. His eyes grew wide then softer, narrowing. Twinkling. His formal attire was that of a wedding day. One that would come up so that my mind went there instead of a dance. My feet found their rhythm to him, and I stood before him smiling. I was proud to be his as he took my hand and kissed my fingertips, then the palm of my hand, giving me shivers again.

"Ah, Jazzline. You're so beautiful. You're my angel."

I found myself stepping closer, wanting to feel safe in his arms. He held me until we heard his father cough and call out. The door was still opened wide and the blinds were up at the tiny window. I could see the whole clan standing there pushing against each other to see as we shared our moment.

Seth stepped out first, speaking something in Gaelic to his awaiting family. Tucker laughed so I was sure that it had to be some crack. My face was still flushed as he helped me down the stairs, then took my arm. Every woman there was beyond beautiful. Ethereal and angelic. It was like a fashion spread in Vogue magazine, each woman sharing a similar pattern matching the eyes of their soul mates. Hair wispy, adorned with priceless abalone jewels. The men, all dashing and larger than life. Even Tucker looked regal in his kilt, standing there awe-struck by Bree. My man was the most handsome of all, and his large hand covered the opening of my dress at the back, sending chills down me even though he was always so warm to the touch.

Mrs. MacKenzie beamed at Bree. "Darling, you did a magnificent job at the dress designs. Your gifts are immeasurable."

I watched Gillivary MacKenzie, the leader of the clan, and how he would eye each clan member as they approached us. Once they made it past him, they could come closer to the other MacKenzie's who had formed a tight circle in the dance hall tent.

"You've got to tell me his power. I need to know."

Seth danced me slightly away from the group and whispered back, fear he would be bashed if found out that he told the secret that was not his to tell. "He casts judgment. You passed. No worries."

The chieftain MacKenzie's eyes were gray. That was what

stood out for him the most. Seth explained that he'd lost his wife a few years back, and the Ceilidh was his grandmother's favorite part of the Highland festival. I would have to say they were mine, too, if I had to rank it up there with blood and gory slaughtering. But it surprised us both when I felt a strong hand on my arm applying small pressure there.

I looked into the eyes of Mr. Gillivary MacKenzie, and he smiled at me. "I'd loch tae dance wi' ye, if 'at is okay wi' yer fiancé."

Seth was pleased by the request.

"Yes, grandfather. It would be my honor."

He winked at me as Mr. MacKenzie put my arm through his and took me to the corner of the dance floor. They had not started the traditional dances yet and were playing fiddle and pipe music as the guests were all arriving. I could sway. Manageable. But with a judge? Still intimidating.

If he were a judge, could he judge character or my mood? I wasn't sure of his powers, and I was timid with him. Did he know that I could not talk? Did he know that I was weak? He would not want that for his grandson. I could judge that just by the way he was. Formidable. Larger than any other.

His voice was more English now that we were alone. Thank God, I could half-way understand him. My mind was reeling with trying to remember his words so I could recount to Seth later as I tried not to step on his shoe. He told me that Seth was the appointed one. The chosen one to lead the clan and someday would become a chieftain. He would rule Clan MacKenzie when his father, Monroe would pass on. I didn't know that, and I didn't know what responsibilities came with that, either. I knew that Gillivary was the leader of this unruly bunch but to think of one day Seth taking on that role was striking to me. Did these things happen this day and age?

Gillivary touched the hair clip and smiled. A faraway look surfaced on his face making him look vulnerable but only for a brief second. "This reminds me of Renna. Ah gave this tae 'er, did ye know? Ye remind me of her, wi' yer dark locks and yer silence. She had a quiet way. Seth is a lucky one."

I turned to find Seth in the crowd. He was standing next to Douglas and his father, Fergus. They were going over the moves of the day. There were handclaps on the back, nudges in the side, yet the whole time Seth's eyes kept reverting to me. I could feel his protective shield from across the room. He would do anything for me. Without a doubt.

"I'm the lucky one, sir. I know that."

And I did. No matter what our future would hold for us, I was sure that Seth MacKenzie loved me more than any other person ever could on the face of this Earth. He was my soul mate.

Gillivary asked me all about my name meaning, my father, and started in on my family history. I didn't have much to share, and I could tell that he was curious about it all. I didn't know how to tell him that my family was so different from theirs. I guess he figured that out on his own. The dance was over, and Mr. MacKenzie led me back to Seth. He nodded to Seth then turned to find his seat at the head of the clan table.

Seth's arm circled my waist and he moved me away from the talk of the victory today. He knew that I didn't need a recap of today's events. My mind had them etched there forever. He took me back to the present with the smell of him as he lingered over me.

"That seemed to have gone well."

"Yes. He told me about Renna. That I reminded him of her." I smiled at him as he caressed my arm with his fingertips.

"You do. My grandmother was an exquisite, special woman. It was a compliment for him to say so. I have always known that you were this way, too. I have a surprise for you. I couldn't let my sister upstage me with a gift for you. I thought I could sing you a song this evening. Is that okay with you?"

I closed my eyes and leaned into him not even aware that another person was in the room or on the planet. "I would love that."

Then, I wondered what he would sing for me. A show tune? A song from one of his mother's musicals? He said no more but motioned for the band. Heads turned, nodded, sheet music pulled from the side and replaced the one playing. His family took their places, and all of the clans seemed to wait in anticipation, along with me, as Seth took the center stage and held the microphone in his hand. Here, his scars did not matter. He did not have to wear a mask. They accepted him. Free. As he was with me.

He sang a song I knew by heart. When You Say Nothing At All by Keith Whitley. As the music began to play, I imagined him searching up old love songs to find one that would be right to sing for me. He found the perfect one.

The night was alive with the sounds of the band playing on well into the late hours. They raised toasts for our champions, for our dancers, and our engagement. The fiddlers and accordion players raged on as the dancers twirled to The Flying Scotsman, The Packhorse Rant, and the requests went on and on. I found out that I didn't need to even know the steps as I was led by all of the Scots around me, pulling me close then weaving between and spiraling around until I was breathless and blissful and blushing. Face red. Joy elated. Life renewed.

Seth was always there even as I was out of control among the crowds. His hand was there. His eyes were there. He watched me as he did his part. He was always present. And then the night wore thin, and the crowds moved away. It was over. I felt exhilarated and burning and did not want it to end. I knew why Renna loved the Ceilidh the best. So did I.

His family went ahead of us and we trailed behind. As soon as we were away from earshot, I whispered to him, "Can we be alone?"

"Aye, Lassie." He turned me away, leading me in the opposite direction of the RV line.

I heard Bree call out in that sweet little whine. "Momma, look at them. You better get back here, you two. Can me and Tucker go off together for a little bit of privacy?"

As if they all knew every single MacKenzie yelled out a resounding, "NO!"

I couldn't help but laugh and bury myself in his chest. I sighed against him then wondered where he would take me.

"Don't take me there."

He knew that I meant the arena. It would remind me, and I didn't need that.

"I know the place. There's more you should know."

"More secrets?"

"Maybe just one more."

His steps grew quicker as he led me past the clearing. I felt his arms tighten around me as if he were shielding me from the battle scenes as they were still being played out by ghost Scots. The sounds of the cheers mixed with cries and screams were still ringing in my ears. We went to the edge of the perimeter and he stepped into a wooded area. I thought of what they had said before about their place to have a safe union with other powerful clans. No one would ever find them here. After what seemed like a mile deep of forest, it broke suddenly to a worn bridge over a rushing river.

"Your family owns all of this land?"

"Yes. And this bridge. There is more that I must tell you. It can't all be tonight. I could not tell you our whole story over a weekend."

I knew how to start. "What does it mean that you will be chieftain?"

"Aye. I will be one day. We'll one day have to move to Scotland. Just like my father will before me, when Gillivary...well, you know. But that will be some time far off from now." He would not speak of his grandfather's death, but with the way his voice shook I knew he could see it.

Moving away to Scotland would mean what for Alex? Could he tell me what he saw about Alex? What would happen to us?

"Do you know everything?"

"No. I only see us in dreams. So, how can I know what is real and what is what I imagine us to be? I see us in love. I see us happy. That's enough for me."

I sighed and kissed him, feeling the sweetness of the moment. "Happy. Loved. Treasured."

"You truly are, my love. Will you follow me when the time comes?"

Did he still question that? I thought that I made myself clear when I said I'd follow him off to any college he attended, that included continents.

"Anywhere with you."

He pointed to the bridge. "Well, I want to show you something. But don't go falling in now. I would have to follow you, and then we might have a potential problem."

He took me closer to the worn wood and stone bridge and I hesitated. The rocks were slippery and I held on to him. His warning made no sense but I trusted it. "What's this?"

"My plane ticket to Scotland. Let's just say we don't need a passport."

Did he expect me to play these games with him again? "Tell me, Seth. You're making no sense."

I bit my lip and held on to my stomach. Looking down I saw dark waters. Still waters. Nothing but black ripples under an old stone bridge.

"We travel here. And at Pawley's Island. We have one there, too. Bridges carry us home."

"Home? Seth, seriously?" I found myself unable to follow him.

"I don't know a word for it. Transportation? A conduit? MacKenzie's need bridges. This bridge takes us to Scotland. To our home at Eilean. The bridge that leads to our castle connects to this somehow."

"So, your family? They stepped through here?"

I was still skeptical, and I tried to get a closer look to see if I saw a glimpse of a Scottish moon or a castle. But nothing. I felt his arms tighten around me and pull me back and away from the bridge.

"All of the clans come through this way. But we don't know what will happen..."

"What? If I go through?"

"Aye. Yet, they trust it. I do not."

"Well, then I don't trust it. I'll fly over to Scotland for our marriage besides Momma, Luke, and Alex. I don't think I'll mind it so much now." I would want to make it to my wedding night.

"That's for the best. I hate to be away from you. I hate that you can't travel with the whole family, but I'll fly with you to protect you. I trust that better than having you fall through and never to be found again or crash against rocks."

"How does your family go through? Are they all with powers then?" I remembered that Fergus and Sarah never spoke during the circle meeting.

"No. But their marriage and birth of children somehow have protected and sealed them through the travel. We only speculate that binds them together when they cross. Maybe it's the soul mate connection, but Bree hasn't seen that with every family couple so we're not sure about that either. We don't know for certain. And I know that I can't take that chance with you ever. So, promise me you will never cross. No matter what happens. Promise me." His voice grew dark and his hand began to tremble against his face.

"I won't."

"I swear, Jazzline Chicand. If anything ever happens, swear to me that you'll never cross."

"Seth, I won't cross." That's when I knew he had seen a vision of me jumping a bridge or he wouldn't have been so adamant about it.

He crushed himself against me and kissed me as if there would be a chance he would never see me again. Like he was trying to brand me in his memory.

He tried smoothing down the hair that had fallen out of the

clasps that were binding it. I reached up and let the clips fall, all except my jewel, and my hair cascaded around me.

He hands fell through my curls. This time his kiss was gentle. He whispered, "I will marry you. Do you hear me? You're mine."

"I'm counting on it."

I kissed him back, pulling his hand off my waist and entwined my hands with his. Seth's hair fell with mine, and his breath was on my cheek.

He sighed. "When Bree told me you were my soul mate, I wanted to not believe her at first, because that meant I would live my whole life knowing you existed, and I couldn't have you."

"Why?"

"I didn't want you to have a life like this, with a scarred man, and all of this. With death hanging over me like a shroud. And with the powers and position I have, everyone that knows wants a piece of me. It isn't safe for you. It's a dark place I go to, many days."

"Then, let me be your light."

"And you know what you're getting into, and you still want me?"

"Can we stop a soul from crashing into another? Can you stop the tide? Even if we tried to deny it or run from it? I am yours, and yours I'll always be. It's settled, Seth. You belong to me."

"Yes. You're my soul mate. God made you for me. This is true."

"If it takes our whole life with me standing by your side for you to understand why I'm here, then so be it. I want you just the way you are. I want you with all of your faults and all of your strengths. I want you, Seth. I love you. And I will love your family as my own, and I'll pledge my life to you."

His finger twirled my ring, and he pulled my hand to his lips. "It sounds like you're practicing your vows. That's what you can say to me on our wedding day."

"Soon."

"I've already expressed my desire to marry you on your birthday. Bree wanted a party and so be it. She shall get one."

I felt my eyes blur, trying to picture our wedding day at their home. Would their castle have a moat and crocodiles? Would I stand by their bridge, waiting for him to walk towards me and carry me up to his family? I sighed. All of my questions would find their answers, and I was okay with that. I was sure different from the girl that I once was. What would it be? How could I stand up for what I wanted? I was new. I could be strong because he loved me.

"Does Momma know about you?"

"No. And we would like it to stay like that, please."

"What do we tell her?" I knew that they had already discussed the engagement. He'd told me that, anyway. But, now to tell her that our wedding date would be August 24th. That would be a little of a shock.

He always made complicated things sound so simple. "The truth. We tell her that we love each other, and we see no reason to wait. That's the truth, isn't it? Let's get our story straight right here and now."

I grinned. "Well, I can't very well tell her that I'm ready to marry you now so I can have you in my bed and still be on good speaking terms with God, now can I?"

He laughed. "So, that's why you agreed to marry me? I'll give you some of me right now if that is all you are after."

I hit him. "Seth, you know what I mean."

His voice was as smooth as silk. "Aye, lass. I ken exactly what ye' mean."

"I love it when you talk to me like that."

Then his tone turned serious and he whispered to me, stopping the laughter in my throat. "Honestly, Jazzline. When you've seen death as I have. When you've stepped right up to it and touched it, then life seems fleeting, and raw. It seems too vulnerable, unbearable at most. But you make it all worth living. You calm every storm in me. That's why I can't wait. I see life short. A blink. And I don't want to miss a single day or change of happiness with you."

There were no words for me to speak to him after that. I was his and I needed to bring him back to me. I would need to learn these sudden twists in his emotions and would need to sense the signs. I knew he had so much more to tell me. Maybe I would never know. Would I be able to live with that, always left one step behind? I would have to try.

CHAPTER 19

I'll Be There for You

I hated that we had to say goodbye early Sunday morning. Seth explained that his mother told the family we would be there in one month to be married. They were to stay on in Pawley's Island at the MacKenzie estate for a much-needed vacation but when they knew that the wedding was soon approaching, Aunt Shea demanded they all return, even Douglas, to help with the arrangements. Bree promised she would begin the shipment of dresses as soon as my mother was sized. Maybe she would be supportive. She'd get a beautiful gown and a trip.

Seth seemed disappointed that his family would not be there to watch our performance on stage Friday night because he wanted his family to witness me singing like an angel. His words, not mine. Only six nights away. He made me swear in front of them all that I would sing at our wedding together. I promised. How I would carry it out without falling completely apart, I had no clue. But I promised him all the same. I would worry about that another day.

They were all standing by the bridge, and the next second, they were gone. No trace of them existing. The water did not ripple. It was a dark pool of murky depths leading to the other side of the world.

As we were driving back to Murrell's Inlet, I felt an intense sadness take over my body. The most perfect weekend I had ever spent in my life was over, and I must face reality. Yet, I still did not have all of the answers. I was sure that Momma would go combat mode. I wasn't ready to battle, just yet. But I knew someone who would be.

"Seth, will you please stay with me to talk with Momma?"

"Yes. I know it has to be done. But Jazzline, you need to use your voice so she'll not think I'm pressuring you into this. She needs to hear it from you. I'll be there to support you but I'll remain the silent one unless I have to step in."

He took my hand in his and fiddled with my ring.

"I have a question about something your grandfather said to me when we were dancing. What did he mean about my name? About my dad naming me Jazzline? He was questioning me about my father and my name history."

"Gillivary names us all. With his power comes judgment. Comes recognition. He names us as we are to become. My name Seeth, Seth, meaning appointed. I would be appointed to lead the clan. But Seeth, to see, he did not know what I would see. Maybe see the truth, justice, or hope. Instead, when Abhainn passed through me, I now see death. I think that's why they look at me with this lingering question in their mind. If it wouldn't have happened in that way, what would my gifts have developed to be? Maybe the same. I don't know. Brianna means strong. We were all surprised at that one, no offense but look at how tiny Bree is. Strong? Strong-willed maybe. But what is stronger than love? It can tear down any defense. But she has the gift of true love like Aunt Shea. As we have found out, maybe we're special because my mother and father both have gifts, giving us a double portion. We're still learning these things, Jazzline. It's not like we're a science."

"But what does all that have to do with me?"

"My grandfather was amazed at your name because an outsider named you in perfect complement to your gift from

God. How many Jazzline's do you know? You're my first. Your father named you for who were to be. A singer, learning lines, even though we pronounce it lean, look at your spelling. Your career has been in your name since your birth, and you say you have always struggled with what you see yourself becoming. It has been right before you since the day you were born. I know it even if you don't see it yet. Your name is like ours. It makes my grandfather wonder."

"At least I have something in common with your family."

"My family loves you. No more feeling that you don't belong. You are one of us."

"Aye, laddie, I know. Now, let's see to me Momma." I tried but I sounded ridiculous.

"Your Southern accent doesn't cut it, sweetheart. But I love the effort."

"The thought of Tucker picking up Gaelic surprises me."

"He's trying. I have to give him credit. He's always been this way, I guess?"

"Always. Tucker is one amazing guy, and just thinking of how he found Bree, and it all brought me to you...I owe him yet again."

"What else do you owe him for?"

"Tucker has done so much for me, Seth. He's been there for me when I had no one else. I can't even tell you the way we are. It's perfect we have all of this together."

How wonderful it was to share this new chapter with him. We were already home. How dare Seth speed under these circumstances? She didn't attend church and the restaurant was closed. Her Sunday afternoons consisted of naps and suntanning. Alex was splashing on the slip and slide, skirting across it on his board. Tucker had gotten it for him for his birthday last year. So much would happen in one month. Fall in love, get engaged, birthdays. Get married.

I stepped out on the patio. "Momma, can I talk with you a minute."

Alex came running towards us, his face wet, hair matted down and body dripping. I didn't mind that he tackled me. I missed him.

She sat up and put on her wrap, reaching for a tall glass, and gulped it down.

Momma said, "How was your weekend?"

She held up her cell phone that she had sitting by the table and waved it to me.

"Oh, Momma. I'm so sorry. I forgot to call."

"You could have at least let me know that you were okay."

"I'm fine."

Her eyes were on it. She was looking dead at my finger. The band. The diamond. And she knew. Her voice was shrill, "Luke, get out here! Alex, you're wrinkled. Go on in and take a shower."

"But I'll still be getting wet, more wrinkles."

Momma gave him the look, and he sulked inside.

Luke said, "What's wrong?"

"Look at her finger."

"Momma, let me explain."

Luke said, "Let me see? What is it? What's this about?"

Momma hit him on the arm. "She's got on a ring. Seth MacKenzie, you promised me you'd wait."

"Aye, I did. I said I would wait. And I am waiting to marry her." His voice was calm against her rage.

"Momma, he asked me to marry him, and I said yes."

Alex flew through the glass doors landing on Seth's arm. "You're going to be my new brother? Sweet!"

Momma and Luke glared at him, and spoke in unison, "Alex!"

He ran back in the house hollering his congratulations. I was so glad that he was happy for me. That made the rest more bearable.

"We're getting married on my birthday. And we're all flying to Scotland for the wedding. So, please try to plan at Chica for a vacation for you and Luke. Oh, and we need passports. It's not like there's a bridge that can take us there."

Seth chuckled.

For the first time in my life, Momma was speechless.

Luke asked, "Let me get this straight. You're getting married at eighteen? Jazzline, come on. Get serious. You just met this boy."

"He's my soul mate. I will marry him, and I would really like your support. I want you both to be there. Luke, I would like for you to walk me down the aisle."

I hadn't planned that, but it felt right to say it. He was more of a father to me than my absent one who spent more time running after women than checking on his children.

"But your father? He would want to do that." She picked up the cell phone as if she were about to call him now.

I stopped her. "No. I don't even want my father at the wedding so no phone calls, and don't speak to him about my plans. He abandoned us long ago. He doesn't care to be a part of mine or Alex's life."

I turned to Luke and held out my hand to him. He was not the affectionate type but I knew that he loved us in his own way. I knew that he loved my momma. I didn't have to ask Bree that.

"Luke, you've always been good to me and Alex. It would honor me if you would please give me away at my wedding."

He smiled at me. "I would love to, Jazzline."

Momma gasped, hitting him in the arm. "Luke! Whose side are you on anyway?"

He shrugged, smiling at me. "There are no sides. She'll be eighteen in..."

Seth said, "One month and eleven days."

Luke chuckled. "One month and eleven days. She'll be legal. She can marry who she wants. We might as well accept this boy and fly off to Scotland or you'll lose your daughter. And I know you don't want that. And besides, if I would have met you at eighteen, I would've married you the second you said yes, my dear, and we could've lived a longer life together."

She sighed and leaned back against the chair, placing her hands across her stomach. "I guess Luke is right. I won't act as if I am happy about this. I don't agree with it one bit, Jazzline. You're so young. Baby, you're still in high school. What's Scotland like this time of year? What should I wear?"

I had won. Only God could've helped me through that one, and I gave credit to Luke. He stepped up. Seth and I had won. Now, I knew what Seth felt like on the battlefield.

"I know you have reservations about us, still about Seth. But I tell you now, Momma, he's the best thing that's ever happened to my life and I can't let him go. We may not have everything all figured out yet. But I'm okay with that."

Seth said, "And I will swear to take care of her as long as I live."

She swatted at Luke again, and then handed me the phone. "At least tell him."

I pushed it back to her. "No. I don't see the point."

She frowned. "He's coming for your play. That'll be a good time to tell him."

I said, "Honestly, he probably won't come to that, either."

My mind raced behind me at all of the times that he promised he would come for this or for that. What would make him come now? But I would not let it push me in a dark corner or force myself to a game of silent ball. I would live my life with Seth and move on.

"I guess we need to make plans for the wedding. If it's only one month away, then that isn't long."

"Don't worry about your travel plans. My family has that already taken care of that as a wedding gift to your family."

She frowned. "That's too much to ask." Then, she turned to Luke and asked, "Do you really think we can take a vacation in the middle of the summer?"

He reassured her. "I'm actually looking forward to it. We haven't been away since our honeymoon cruise to Jamaica."

His arm came around her. There it was. The look. Was that what Bree saw when she saw us together?

Later that evening, Seth was giving me the look as we were standing by his car. His arms were around me. "I didn't know you could be so forceful. Telling your Momma the way you did. Where did that come from?"

It still surprised me. "I guess I've never had to fight for something until now, until you. And you're worth fighting for."

"I'm proud of you."

"Me, too."

Tucker was there beside me, and I didn't hear him approach. He shook Seth's hand again and Bree came beside me and put her arms around my waist. I smiled at her. My soon to be sweet sister, Bree. I was getting more than Seth was in this arrangement. I was getting a wonderful family with all of their mystery and intrigue, their language and folklore. And even though the thought of it should have intimidated me, I was prepared for anything as long as Seth was holding my hand.

Bree asked, "Well, how did that go?"

"She's ready to make plans."

Bree danced from one foot to the other in her Highland way. "Oh, let's go. Bye, Tucker. Love you, honey."

She pulled her laptop bag out of the car and gave Tucker a kiss that made me blush. I heard her screaming for Momma as she stepped through the door that Alex opened for her. The Calvary had arrived.

Two long hours of watching Momma and Bree hash out the intricate details of my wedding had me pulling out a bottle of Ibuprofen. I giggled when I thought about how Aunt Shea was already at her computer checking the emails that Bree was sending, switching over to video chat.

It all sounded glorious to me, down to the bagpipes and harpists. The virtual tour of Eilean showed a magnificent castle, straight out of a fairytale. The pictures of another family home two miles from the castle reminded me of their mansion by the sea, but this time there was a backdrop of a mountain range in the distance.

I needed a break from all of the traditional Scottish wedding talks. Bree was successful at dancing, wedding planning, designing, the girlie stuff. I shuffled out, feeling a little dazed to find my three favorite guys lounging on the couch playing video games. I sat down beside Alex and tried to hug him, but he shrugged me off.

"Stop it, Jazzy. You'll break my concentration. I've never beat this level but look I'm doing it. I did it! I did it! All by myself!"

He began to jump around. I felt the tears well up in my eyes. Alex did it all by himself. Soon, he would be by himself. Where was the beginning of my summer? Where did it go? Sitting with Tucker and Alex, now with Seth holding my hand, brought me back to where I was and even though I was sure I never wanted to go back there again, I didn't want to abandon Alex either.

I didn't want Alex to see me cry so I made my way out on the patio and closed the doors behind me. He was so excited that he'd accomplished his level I don't think that he even noticed me leave the room. Tucker came up behind me. He held out his arms to me, and I fell in. Like always, my sun. I wondered what was the meaning behind his name, Tucker Lane. To me it meant sunshine. I didn't care what the internet said.

"Look up your name meaning," I asked.

"You're weird. Why?"

"Let me know what it says."

He started to search it and laughed. "In French, it means all heart."

"Oh, that's a perfect name for you. I guess you had to be all heart to walk up to Bree on the first day. She's a beauty that probably was a little intimidating to you but then again she could sense your heart a mile away."

"A little intimidating? What are you talking about? A lot! But she was the one that approached me. She danced up to me and light glowed from her, and I thought it was the way the sun was highlighting her on the beach, but it was her. She said she found me, and took my hand. I didn't have to do a thing, so I wasn't the brave one. She was."

I smiled as I envisioned the scene before me. "Can you believe that we stepped into this family? Tucker, it was all something this weekend, huh?"

"I'm sorry I tried to push you away from Seth at the beginning. I knew about his disease, and how sick he is..."

"It's okay. Maybe we shouldn't talk about him being sick. How about let's talk about him being mine."

"You do know he's really sick, don't you, Jazzline."

"You just said my name."

"Maybe I did. Because it's serious."

"And I love him regardless. I know the vows say in sickness and in health in there somewhere."

"Bree convinced me to let the two of you love each other. She was right."

"I'm glad you listened."

Tucker laughed. "With that woman, I have no other choice. She's relentless, that one. But my baby, all the same."

"You guys are adorable, you know that? Thinking back on our first chaperone dates. Oh, my goodness, Tucker. I thought I would rather crawl in a hole if I had to watch the love pass between y'all. And then...Seth...I totally got it. I get it."

It was wonderful to share it all with him. It was how it should be. Just like Bree and Seth were opposites, seeing love and death, we were the sun and moon. I let that roll around my head for a few minutes as I felt the sweat pick up speed down my cheeks. Tucker was enormous and radiated heat, but I wasn't ready to go back inside. I needed time with him.

"The dancing, the song, you in that kilt, the fighting..." I shivered as I pulled away, taking his hand with me as we sat down on the lawn chairs.

"That was the best part. I can't wait until next year when I'm allowed in the arena. Seth has to teach me, and with Douglas coming this fall I'll have another practice partner."

I tried to remain calm. "No, Seth will not. You won't get out there to fight. For what?"

"For Bree." He looked back to the window of my room as if he could see through the walls and smiled.

"Bree doesn't need you to fight for her." What was this? Some medieval concept of war and fighting for those you loved. It was the twenty-first century for crying out loud.

"Yes, she does."

Did he know something I didn't? What all had Bree told him about their family? I wished that I were a mind reader. What was it Seth kept saying about protecting me? From what or who, for that matter? If Tucker knew more about the MacKenzie's, he didn't seem ready to tell me. Alex and Seth joined us, and Tucker rehashed the whole warrior smackdown event for Alex. As they play wrestled, Alex pushed Tucker on the waterslide, and he fell right on his butt in the leftover water.

I cheered for Alex. "Defeated by the ten-year-old. And the champion is Alexander Dumas Chicand."

Dad named him after the writer. Would he ever be one? I thought it always strange that he named him after the author of The Three Musketeers since he seemed the leading man in my and Tucker's lives for so long.

I wanted to hide again but there was nowhere else to go. So, I held in my tears until he went back to the house again for a soda. Tucker frowned as he followed me, grabbing a towel off the counter.

"What's wrong, mop top?"

"I was thinking about how things will never be the same" I turned to see Alex settling back down on the sofa again with Seth.

"Exactly the point of life, Jazzline. It changes. We move or we stand still. We grow or we shrink. I'm not planning on looking back. It's messy when we live like that. I want to live free."

"What'll happen to Alex?" My heart broke into a million pieces and scattered with the wind. I felt sickness rising up in me.

"Stop that, Jazzline. He'll be fine. We're about to move on anyway. College is right around the corner for all of us."

He sounded like Seth. Alex would be better to stay with Momma, Luke, and everything he knew here. His school and friends. It was not my responsibility to worry about Alex the way I did, but I couldn't help myself. Maybe when he could take better care of himself, then I wouldn't be so worried. But ten was still a baby.

"I'll be right next door, Jazzline. I'm not going anywhere."

Bree interrupted us. "Can you take me home? Momma and I need to make some calls. I've got measurements."

Life had changed. And I knew that I could not wallow in the darkness over thoughts about Alex. A year was a long time for Alex to grow and mature a little more. It would be okay, I told myself, but something kept nagging underneath the surface, telling me I had every reason to worry.

CHAPTER 20

Here Comes the Sun

Rehearsals were long and exhausting. The mental energy it took to face the challenges of each new scene was exhilarating yet overwhelming. Funny how Tucker could learn Gaelic for Bree but have trouble stumbling over lines on stage with me. The singing was not improving, but he didn't seem to care that he sounded like a tortured soul hitting high notes. Neither did anyone else. None of the other guys in the cast could sing either, except for Seth. They scheduled us for two more late night practices.

I imagined Ms. Dot with purple war paint across her cheeks in the middle of the battle arena taking down wild-eyed Scots. She could handle her own after putting up with the cast the summer.

The gash on Seth's arm from a sword wound had sliced the skin and was swollen and bright red, still. It looked like it might get infected.

"Does this hurt?"

He looked down at me and smiled. "No, I've had worse."

He didn't go into detail, and I was glad. What life had Seth lived? What would it feel like to have all of that in his family? It was so packed down hidden from the world. I thought about Colin and how he seemed so out of place from the rest of the

Clan and had to ask when we were on lunch break, hiding away in the prop room where we first met.

"I can't see your brother Colin with your family like that."

I couldn't imagine his lanky frame and wire-rimmed glasses anywhere near that ring, on a dance floor, or yelling toasts.

"I guess there's something you need to know. They adopted Colin. My parents, well, they weren't sure about having children. They were the first of our generation to find two soul mates with gifts. But one year later, I was unexpected. And when my momma held me, she knew that it was right to conceive us, and Bree came soon after. You didn't notice we come in pairs?"

I hadn't ever thought about it until he brought it up. The twins, Douglas and Cat, but Alasdair. "Alasdair doesn't have another?"

His eyes turned dark. "He would've if Abhainn would have lived, but then again, they always knew there could never be another."

"Why?"

"He is the protector of mankind. If they would have had another child, well then, think about it. He or she would have been ..."

"A destroyer? So, you mean you're all opposites?"

"Look at Bree and me. She sees love. I see the loss of it. 'Til death do us part."

"What does your brother Colin think of all this?"

"Colin is special in his own way. He's a tech genius. One day he may be the one to save the world by discovering some cure or create some high-tech computerized gadget. I knew they'd accept him to MIT but he worried anyway."

"But I thought you couldn't tell what you see? You told him?"

"My father has tried his best to instruct me on how I should responsibly use my gifts. It's been very difficult for me since we discovered my gift. The only person we knew to possess it had already passed. Uncle Abhainn had the sight. And I never got the chance..."

His mind was not on the play for the rest of the day. I wished I could discover the answers for him. He seemed so tired as he spoke his lines, and he apologized to Mrs. Dot for his lack of enthusiasm. Seeing them over the weekend brought everything to the surface again,

and instead of a joyous reunion, he was faced with young Alasdair, fatherless. I wondered if that was all that was bothering him? He seemed to shut himself away as time drew closer to our performance.

MY FATHER CALLED THE NEXT DAY TO GIVE HIS EXCUSE why he could not make it to opening night. His new girlfriend had the flu. No matter. Alex shrugged when Momma told us that he would not come as if he could have cared less. He needed his father. He wanted to have that connection with him. I knew the end of that story without having to read the future, and I didn't care to see how that would play out.

I was filled with anticipation and hoped I wouldn't embarrass Seth's family or myself. His mother took such pride in these grand productions. Looking through her eyes, it must have been a way to involve her family and community with her passion. It also was not small when I found out that the nights sold out within the first week of ticket sales.

I felt transported to another place and time and I could close my eyes for one brief second and feel myself becoming Christy. I'd remembered watching actors being interviewed about what it felt to star in a certain role and I'd hear words like, it would take over, they'd get lost in it, or they felt the connection. That was me. I felt a connection to the stage. I felt like my Spirit could hit a panel switch, and I would be on autopilot. My body moved across the floor fluidly and with purpose. My mind cleared and focused. My voice was loud and confident. But it was somebody else's' life I was living. In my own, I could feel something else rising. Was it fear?

When I was holding Seth's hand, I felt that I had the strength to face whatever came my way. Momma, fears, my future. The thought of Momma buying me a car when all of this started was my driving motivation. Now, a greater force was compelling me to shine. My sense of self-worth was bursting forth on the stage. The thought that I could be alive standing on my two feet in front of the world. Unashamed, smiling, secure. Now it was my time. My turn.

We had to let Seth and his family in on the secret of the cast party planned after opening night. Tucker stole away to make final arrangements and was gone for the rest of the day. Mrs. Dot would only wink and tell us he was working on his wardrobe. I could only think that he probably busted through the seams of his shirt, that big old weightlifter and need to be refitted like the Hulk.

Seeing Alex with his newspaper boy costume on, squirming under the steady hands of the makeup artists was precious to me. He clenched his eyes together but when he looked at himself in the mirror, he moved his head side to side admiring his stylish flair. Then, he ran off to go play on the rafters.

Bree said that it was important for our mental state to separate ourselves from Seth and Tucker for the day. She didn't understand that I needed to draw from Seth's strength to be able to move. Since her name meant strong, she was enough for her and Tucker both. What a perfect match made in heaven. Even in her tiny, petite dancer frame, she was the strength of us all. I would never underestimate Brianna Rain MacKenzie.

A soft knock rapped on the ladies' dressing room. Seth peeked in then shut it when he saw some of the girls still changing in costumes. I snuck out of the door with Bree yelling at me about my blocking out the present and stepping into the past of the character. Whatever. Seth was there in his black suit. His hair was falling down around him. His newly fitted black phantom mask in place.

I was already in my first costume and he told me it was his favorite. It was a soft blue gown with rose petal embroidery with pearl droplets covering the corset. My hair hung in tighter ringlets instead of the tangles I usually wore. I felt beautiful. And when he stared at me, I knew that I was, at least to him. I was okay with that.

He put his arms around me. "Are you ready, my love?"

"Ready? Nervous doesn't even cut it. I'm a little terrified."

He kissed me, then I felt the soft jerk of Bree's hand trying to pull me back into the dressing room.

"You leave her alone. We've already spent an hour on her makeup, and we can't start over. Get on, shoo." She was pushing him back down the hallway. Then, as if she couldn't help herself, she asked, "Where's Tucker?"

He winked at me. "You'll be so surprised. But don't faint. We don't really have time for that today."

"Ha-ha. Very funny."

The orchestra music began to play and that was when the chaos hit. It was like lightning striking. People were frantic, and I stood motionless as they moved around me in panic and fear, excitement and nervousness. I saw heads ducking and disappearing behind curtains, and heard calls for places and last-minute checkups but my eyes never left Seth. He stood at the end of the hallway staring at me. His soft eyes calling me to be his angel.

The curtain rose, and I found my place on stage with the lights glaring, and my throat constricted. Lord, be with me, I whispered. I let out a slow breath and moved. Bree bounded up to me with her line, and I blinked.

Time stood still. Could I do this? Would I be enough?

She repeated her line, stepping closer to me and catching my gaze. She touched my arm as if to share her strength with me. I smiled and my line flowed out, a nervous laugh followed, and I brushed back her hair that had escaped out of her bow. I didn't remember practicing that, but it felt right.

I found my rhythm. "Did you hear there was a phantom? Have you seen him? If I tell you a secret will you promise not to tell?"

Bree smiled. "You can trust me, Christy."

I looked around to see if Seth was near me, and he gave me a slight wave from the rafters. He was going to be lowered down soon enough. And then we would have our time to share the stage together.

I turned to the Bree. "I think I know him. I think he is my muse."

And the songs began, and everything we worked for, all of the hours, and practices, and late-night memorizing, all came together in one perfect night.

The applause was the thunder after each song and act. It was heralded as the most impressive since the theater opened its grand doors five years earlier. Mrs. Dot claimed that it was the passion between me and the phantom and how our voices will be in her head as long as she lived. And I overcame my fright. My fears. And I found my voice.

I had a voice.

I knew the tears in my eyes were more than how the walk down the ramp leading us off stage right made me feel. It was how proud I was to have stepped over my fear and faced it head on. I'd come so far, and Tucker knew it more than anyone.

Tucker bowed to me as I made my way past him and whispered, "That's my girl, right there."

Momma cried. I could see the look of astonishment on her and Luke's faces. They'd never heard me sing. Momma even hugged Seth. Tucker was glowing. And Bree was the happiest of them all, it seemed. It wasn't that she was magnificent on stage and stood out among all of the other girls. It wasn't that her costumes were getting rave reviews by audience members. It was that Tucker had taken out his dreads for her and walked on that stage as a true Rao, with a sandy blonde short haircut. Looking like a gentleman. His face was so handsome, with his strong set jaw. He looked sophisticated and more suited to be with Bree. It also pleased her parents. But none other than Bree. She kept touching his hair as they congratulated the cast. I thought she saw nothing else but Tucker. There was an unusual glow about her tonight. More than usual.

In all of the madness, I saw something flash in Seth's eyes that looked like a spark of fear. He tried to lighten his expression but it didn't work. Momma and Tucker were rushing out the back exits so that Bree wouldn't notice their leaving. Tucker winked at me as he was going out of the side door and blew me a kiss. Then, they were gone, still in costume, and that was my cue to keep Bree preoccupied with changing in our after-party clothes. I acted like I had no clue what to wear to an event like that, which was near the truth.

Seth found me, his voice pleading, "Where's Alex?"

I smiled at him for his concern. "He's with Luke and Momma. They left to go back to Chica's for you know what."

Bree bounded up then and I hushed. She could not hear me with all of the screaming and noise.

"Seth!" She flung her arms around him. "Did you see Jazzline out there? Girl, this is for you. I've seen no one as beautiful, so magnetic on the stage. Jazzline, you were amazing."

Mrs. Dot hugged us all. "All of you were amazing." Then, she turned to me and asked, "Have you never done this before? I mean, really Jazzline. I know what you said to me earlier, but still. You can tell me the truth."

"I promise you. It was all your direction, Mrs. Dot. You were the one that pulled all of this together."

She fanned herself and batted her eyes. "Stop it! Enough of that or I'll start up crying again. Just hearing you and Seth sing was enough to hold me for a lifetime, darlings. Two more nights to go, and they only get better after opening night because all of the nerves fly away."

She kissed us on the cheeks then went off to bask in her director's glory.

Seth spoke low, "Momma is going to take Bree. Let's go."

Mrs. MacKenzie was still holding onto a delicate, lace handkerchief, that she used to wipe her tears. "That was a treasure, dear. All of you. I'm so proud. This is one of the proudest moments of my life, next to bringing you both into the world."

She hugged us all and took Bree by the arm.

"We have some celebrating to do. Why don't we all go down to Chica's for some dinner? I'm starving."

Bree looked around her, and asked, "Where's my short-haired cutie?"

Mr. MacKenzie coughed. "He'll meet us there. We wanted you to ride with us to discuss the performance. You know how your mother wants a complete critique rundown afterward with you."

She beamed. "Wonderful! Come on, Momma. Well, what do you think about the costumes? Weren't they divine?" Their voices trailed away down the mass of people still in the backstage area.

Seth took me by the arm a little more forcefully than I would have liked, and we maneuvered through to the parking lot. His hands were shaking as he tried to open the car door for me, and I stopped his hand and pulled him back.

"What is it?"

He stammered, "I ... I ..."

This was so unlike him. "What's wrong?"

A sick feeling began to rise, and I knew something wasn't right. Death was staring him in the face. His eyes were darker and stone. His hands were continuing to shake, and his body grew rigid. I didn't want him to answer me, and I was glad that he didn't as we made it in the car, and turned out on the road towards Chica's.

The Beatles song, Here Comes the Sun, was playing on the radio and I sang along, thinking of my Tucker.

Then, I heard it. A low growl from the bottom of Seth's throat that turned into a grunted scream.

His eyes were frenzied with fear. I tried to reach out my hand. He jerked to the side of the road, almost running into a minivan. The horn honked at us, and my stomach lurched. He beat his head against the steering wheel, over and over, as I sat there shocked. Fear was washing over me, crashing into me.

His body trembled and convulsed. His eyes wide and fixed ahead of him.

I whispered, "Seth, what is it? Please God." I kept praying over and over.

He put his face in his hands and began to cry.

"What is it?"

I didn't want to know. I didn't want to hear what he saw. He saw death so that meant ... and I lunged out of the doorway, throwing up on the gravel. He didn't get out of the car to save me this time. He sat in the driver's seat looking at me. His eyes told me he was sorry.

"Who?"

I choked out as I felt the gravel cutting into my hands. That was when I heard the sounds of sirens. I looked up to see the Pawley's Island Heavy Rescue Team swerving through traffic. I saw a fire truck right behind it. My face hit the ground, and I felt the scratch against me. Crash.

He picked me up and sat me in the seat. Seatbelt on. Who? He closed the door. Everything in slow motion. Everything missing sound. Lights blurring. I knew he was driving fast to show me who he saw, or saw no more.

My eyes focused on the lights flashing, the red in the night was so beautiful. The red bounced around me. Then, I saw them. They were all standing there. No, not all of them. I saw Mr. and Mrs. MacKenzie. Bree was there with her hair wild as if she had been in a catfight. I saw her eyeliner streaking down her face. She wouldn't be able to go to the party looking like that. I saw Momma and Luke. Momma was hiding her face in the crook of

Luke's arm, and he was crying, too. What was Tucker's Momma doing here?

What was this? Seth was pacing in front, his hands clenched in tight fists at his side.

We didn't look like we'd made it to Chica's. I didn't recognize the place. It was so dark. I saw the road. When the lights blared around me, highlighting the world like a disco ball. I saw tire tracks. That's when I turned my head. I saw the bridge. I saw the blocks of cement broken away.

My hand somehow opened up the car door, and I felt my body stepping out. My gown was pulled under my feet, and I knew I would trip.

Seth said, "Get back in the car, Jazzline."

I pulled myself back up and kept walking. He said it again as he was racing towards me, sprinting.

"Baby, get back in the car!"

That's when I saw it. It was bobbing up and down in the water like one of those fishing lures red and white on the end of our fishing line when we took Alex fishing of the Marshwalk Pier. It was metal, bobbing, then going down further and further. And I knew. And I couldn't breathe. And I fell to the ground hitting the pavement hard smacking my knees and hands when a cracking sound exploded in my brain.

I heard myself yet I didn't know that I was speaking. "It's Tucker. Oh, God, no. Seth! Tucker!" I felt the yell rip out of my throat. "Tucker!" I cried. "You stupid fool! Tucker!"

Seth bent down beside me but I pushed him away. He fell back against the pavement.

"You knew, and you didn't tell me!"

He held up his hand to me but did not speak. What could he say? He knew.

I bit my lip until I could taste blood on my tongue. "What is it? Go ahead, tell me."

He couldn't. His hands covered his face and he began to cry

again. I looked and counted again. Mr. and Mrs. MacKenzie. Bree. Momma and Luke. Seth. Me. Oh, dear God. No.

"Alex? Where's Alex?" I spoke his name, and my heart died. Along with him.

Mr. MacKenzie stepped towards me as I sat on the ground. Seth would not look at me. The coward. Mr. MacKenzie held out his hand to me, and when I did not take it, he grabbed me by the arm and pulled me to my feet. I searched his face. What truth did he want to hear from me right now? That Alex and Tucker were dead? That Seth had killed them? He let them die without warning them, and to me, that was the same thing.

Mr. MacKenzie didn't speak. Just pulled me along with him towards Momma who fell apart again when she saw me. None of us could speak, as we stood huddled together as the rescue workers and dive teams searched until after two a.m. When the last diver came out shaking his head at the police captain, he started to approach us. I knew what his words would be before he spoke them. All of us did. Even the ones without gifts.

"I'm sorry. We'll begin again in the morning."

He turned from us and would go back to his life where his family was waiting at home for him to hear the news if he'd found the people that barreled over the bridge.

Mr. MacKenzie picked Bree up who began to fight him with small fists, doing no harm. She wanted to stay here at this place but her father walked back towards the car, dragging her with him, and she was helpless. Momma and Luke passed us. She sounded as wretched as I felt. No, I was beyond feeling. I was ripped apart, and my other halves were somewhere out there. Somewhere in the inlet either lost and cold, tired and wet, or floating.

I shook my head. I sat down on the blocked lane until construction crews could come and clean up the broken pieces of concrete massed along the road. What a mess? My baby. My baby was gone. How could you do this to me, God? How could you take them away from me knowing that they were my sun, my heart? What did He need Alex for? And Bree for Tucker? Bree. I put my hand over my heart and rocked back and forth on the ground, then beat the pavement. Bree without Tucker.

I turned to him then. Me without Seth. How could one soul mate exist without the other? Alex would never get the chance to find his soul mate. To have love and a family. Did he know how much I loved him? Did he know that I thought of him as my baby? I'd never told him. God, I never told him that I wanted him to come stay with me and Seth. If I had him back. If only I could have Tucker back for Bree and for me.

I crawled over to Seth. I blamed him. And I knew that I was wrong. I didn't understand it but I couldn't blame him. He loved Bree. He loved Tucker. He loved my baby. He swore to me that he would always protect him, yet he had failed.

I fell into him then, rocking him backward. His arms did not come around me. They lay there beside his crossed legs. But I forced him to look at me. I forced his eyes to see mine. I tried to tell him that I didn't blame him. That I knew that it was out of his control. But the words would not come. So, I held him, and his arms came around mine but they were not the strong ones I was accustomed to. And I needed them to be.

"Seth."

He pulled me against him then, burying his head in my hair, rocking with me as I closed my eyes against him. I tried to imagine that none of this ever happened. He wasn't holding me on this pavement. We were at my beach. I could make the whole night disappear from my mind. Erase it. Start it over again. That would be my gift. I could be an eraser. I could turn back time.

He spoke, "I'm so sorry, Jazzline. I'm so sorry."

I knew that a part of him, maybe all of him felt the responsibility. I knew that he was sorry they were gone. But sorry wouldn't bring them back.

We waited. Sat right in the middle of the road as the sun came up. I could feel Seth's arms around me trying their best to comfort me but I felt frozen. My mind would jump to names. Not images.

Just names. Bree to Momma. Momma to Luke. Seth to me. All the people who were still here and waiting. Only waiting.

Mr. MacKenzie opened the car door, and Bree was still dressed in her costume from the night before. Momma and Luke arrived, with my daddy with them. We beat the team of workers who were slowly piling in. They had recruited more. And more than emergency personnel. TV reporters, camera crews, church members, our preacher, many of Tucker's friends from Seaside were there standing back against the police tape. We were inside the sealed off perimeter, and for what it was worth, the yellow tape would shield us from outsiders.

The clan walked up and stood at the police tape as if it could hold them back. But they kept their distance, eyes tearing with worried faces. They grieved for two boys they didn't even know because they were mine. Because he was Bree's. I would never forget their presence here. They were all here. Even old Gillivary. I looked at all of them and sighed. They would have been back in Scotland making plans for our day.

And now. Now there could be no wedding. There could not be a day for celebration and a union of our souls when part of my soul had disappeared. Or so we were told after twelve more hours of search and rescue, and combing the waters. More and more workers came and went, back and forth, moving across the bridge. Up and over. Nothing. I didn't want to hear about the chance of survival after forty-five minutes. It had been twenty hours. I didn't want to hear anymore, and I stood up to leave. I couldn't be here anymore. I couldn't stay where death lingered.

I looked to Seth and searched his face. Did he see them?

"Are they? You know? Are they here?"

I held my breath. Please say no, because that would mean they were not dead. Please say no, because I would still have a chance to find them.

He shook his head and whispered, "No."

I felt it. It made sense now because they weren't here. I knew their love for us, and they would linger here. They were not. Feelings came back and the relief flooding my senses. Then, I understood it all as it crashed into my brain. They were alive.

My voice was louder than I wanted it to be, and I sounded on the verge of madness. "Don't you see, Seth? Don't you see?"

"Jazzline, baby. I told you, they're not here. Do you want to go?"

"Yes. And I'm going. I love you, Seth MacKenzie."

I turned from him and walked to the bridge. He took two strides and was in front of me. This time his strength had returned, and he held me back. My will was stronger than my body, but I could not will his massive body from in front of me.

His voice came in a hushed whisper, "No, you can't."

"Yes, I can. And I will. They went, Seth. Don't you see? They aren't dead. They did whatever it is that you do. That's why they haven't found the bodies. That's why they'll never find them. Don't you think that if they died, they would be here with us now? I have to go."

"Not all stay behind who've died, Jazzline. It doesn't work that way."

A flicker of hope crossed Bree's face, and I smiled at her. "Look at Bree, Seth. See, she believes me. Come on, Bree. Let's go. Help me cross."

Seth would not let my arms go. "Stop this, Jazzline. I've seen them go. They're gone now. And not to Scotland. They are gone. I watched it play out, baby. They went over."

"I don't care what you say. I know Alex and Tucker are not dead." I started to scream, "Momma, Alex is alive. He's just lost. I'll find him, and bring him home."

Momma began to cry hysterically, and Luke took her to the car. I turned to Gillivary who was standing like stone. A rock fortress. I shouted at him. "They've not gone. They're just away. Please tell Seth to let me go."

He shook his head no. His gaze fixed on me.

Mrs. MacKenzie came up to me then and put her shaking arms around me. Her voice was soothing, fluid. "I know that is what you would want to believe, dear. We would all hope it to be true. But the family is here. They would have passed them on the way or seen. They used this bridge for that very purpose."

I began to panic. They would not believe me. "They wouldn't have recognized him. Dressed up, dreads gone. He would've looked like any other Scot. They never met Alex. They wouldn't know. I swear I feel it. They're alive. They are there. Let me go. We have to go there."

"Please, Jazzline. Let's go home. Come home with us, dear. Bree needs you. Please, for Bree."

I needed someone to believe me but there was no one. Mr. MacKenzie was silent. The family did not move to jump in and try to find them. Seth would not jump in to find them. No matter what they said, I would find a way to go to them. I would bring them home. And I didn't care what promise I'd made to Seth about never crossing. I knew that I would have to. Someday I would have to. For Bree's sake. For my sake. It would be.

CHAPTER 21

Two Hearts

I allowed them to take me back to the house because I couldn't walk back into mine. I couldn't see the light on in Tucker's house, and not see his jeep in the yard. I couldn't open my door to see Alex's game sitting there with cords still tangled across the coffee table with our controllers resting on the couch. I couldn't walk down the hallway and pass his room. I didn't know how Momma went back but I wouldn't do it.

Bree never spoke. Her face was ashen and blank. She stole glances at me but they were only for brief seconds to make sure that I was still close to her then she would revert to her head down, hands twisting and trembling over her stomach. Her finger twirled as if she were tracing a smile.

I gasped. "Bree? You're pregnant?"

Mr. MacKenzie dropped the whiskey glass that he was holding, and it shattered on the ground. I'd forgotten we weren't alone. The family was all there. Silence. Waiting.

Bree never spoke. She held her stomach, looking down at the Persian rug that covered the entire wooden floor of the family room. I couldn't believe that I had spoken it. But I was beyond propriety right now. Then, the words that Seth had told me hit me square in the face, and I shot up from the floor where I'd been sitting, fiddling with Seth's shoestring.

"That's it! Listen to me."

Sarah stood up and dashed the children from the room. Shooing them as if they were a bunch of chicks escaped from the henhouse. I kept going, taking on the rambling of Tucker. For a girl that would not speak, I had a lot to say.

"That's why Tucker's alive. He's fathered this child. Bree is pregnant. Aren't you, Bree? I see it on you. Tucker grabbed onto Alex as they went over the bridge. Is that true, Seth? What did you see? Tell me, now!"

Seth stood up beside me and put his arm around my waist. "Please, Jazzline. You're crossing the line here. You need to stop this crazy talk of yours, and try your best to stay calm."

"Calm! Calm! You think my brother is dead! You think my best friend is dead! And now, Tucker is Bree's soul mate. The father of this child. The connection has been made. What did you see?"

"Don't make me tell you? Don't do this. I can't do this."

He looked to his father, then to his grandfather as if he were pleading for them to make me stop. But everyone was silent. Letting me rage on.

"The connection has been made between Bree and Tucker. Now, Tucker has the transfer of this gift or this power that makes you guys jump bridges without falling. Don't you see he wouldn't let Alex go? He would have grabbed hold of him. What happens when you fall through? Really? Tell me everything."

Bree whispered, "You just fall and then you stand. And you are here or you are there."

It sounded like a Dr. Seuss rhyme. "More. Tell me more."

"Daddy, I'm so sorry. I'm going to have Tucker's baby. I'm so sorry. But, no. I'm not." It was her turn to stand, still holding on to her stomach. "If this baby saved his life. Saved Alex's life. Then this baby is a miracle She is a miracle anyway."

Mrs. MacKenzie looked to the others, never once looking at

Bree. "I can't believe this. I'm so shocked. I can't believe that she would, you would..."

Bree laughed. "What? Be with him? Momma, he's my soul mate. I knew it from the second that I saw him. I wouldn't waste a day without him in it. I will not end up like Aunt Shea."

Aunt Shea cried out and ran from the room.

I said, "Now, I'm telling all of you the truth. Alex is alive. Tucker is alive. We've got to get them."

Mr. MacKenzie sat down beside Bree and took her hand. "I sent your Uncle Colin through. He's gone back and forth twice. He has word out on the lands. If they show up, we'll hear about it. We'll know it. We're so sorry that you must face this. But we have to speak rationally here."

I said, "When has this family ever been rational? You live in fantasy every day. You, with your gifts, and your closeness and your connections, and your rich heritage. You're telling me to be rational and you can bring light and peace, see love, speak truth and see stories, and judge others. I'll tell you what I see. I see now that anything is possible. Between this life and the next. I see God in all of this. And I know that God has not taken them from me just as I know that I love Seth MacKenzie."

I was breaking them down, too. I could see their doubt and would win. Round one - Momma accepting my marriage. Round two - MacKenzie's accepting that an unknown could be true. Doubt would lead to searching and seeking ye shall find.

I walked over to Bree and touched her stomach and reassured her with my voice as calm and peaceful as the ocean wind against my face. "You don't worry about a thing, Brianna Rain. I'll find Tucker for you and for this child. You'll be married and live the life you know is meant to be yours."

Mr. MacKenzie looked to his wife and motioned for her to follow him to the study. That left the others in the room to their own back and forth debates. I heard the words daft and loony and off rockers and knew that they were referring to me. Maybe I had gone a little crazy. Maybe this was grief. But if hope were all I had, then I would hold on to it with all my might.

Seth put his arm around me as he stared down at Bree. "Why couldn't you wait? Bree, you knew what could happen. Why didn't you wait?"

Tears fell down her cheeks and she whispered to Seth, "I couldn't. Just like you can't wait to be with Jazzline. You only have one month left. I had two and a half years, Seth."

"You still could have waited. You know what this could mean."

I turned to Seth. There was something more. "What happened to Aunt Shea? What could happen? What are the risks?"

Aunt Shea walked up to Bree and whispered to her. "I know, Aunt Shea. I'm so sorry. Yes. Thank you." She turned to us. "I'm going tonight with Aunt Shea. She'll take care of me until the baby comes. I know Daddy will not allow me to stay here. I have an excuse. Douglas is to stay here. I'll be the exchange. Not Seth. No one will know the difference."

I said, "Bree, I need you to stay with me. I need you to help me cross. Seth won't help me jump."

She held out her arms to me and circled my waist. "And he shouldn't. Jazzline. You can't tear yourself away from Seth. I'll be in Scotland, and Tucker can find me there. If you jump, Seth may never find you again. I do believe what you say about Tucker, whether or not anybody else believes you, and I'll hold on to that hope with all of my heart. Seth can't lose you. Don't do to him what Tucker did to me. Cross your heart to me that you won't go. I'll see you in a month's time."

Seth's tears flowed. "She won't go through. I won't let her. You'd better take care of yourself, Bree. I love you."

Aunt Shea took Bree by the hand. They moved towards the door. They were going? Now? She would not say goodbye to her parents? I cried out, "Wait!" But she kept moving with Aunt

Shea's arm supporting her, probably to go jump off some bridge. Lucky ducks.

"Can someone please tell me what's going on with Aunt Shea?"

Mr. and Mrs. MacKenzie came back into the room. "She's gone."

It wasn't a question. It was a statement of fact.

Gillivary spoke, "Do not judge 'er. It's not yer place."

Mr. MacKenzie retorted, "Aye. We know it's yours."

Gillivary's eyes narrowed. "Watch it, now."

Mr. MacKenzie stood up to face those grey eyes, and said, "Remember you're in my house. This is my daughter who, need I remind everyone in this room, is only fifteen years old. And after what happened to Shea, what will become of Brianna? And who else could she hurt? What would become of the child if it's anything like our past? This is beyond our understanding, and I'm at a loss here. I can't protect Brianna or the child."

Gillivary held out that MacKenzie hand of calmness and peace. "Bree knew th' consequences. She'll have to face her Maker."

Mr. MacKenzie's face was on fire. "Bree is only a child herself. How will she ever be able to take care of a baby? Her future? What will it be now?"

It was Seth's turn to defend his sister's honor. "Happy. Bree will be happy. Give her that, Dad. Give her your blessing when you see her. Don't live with regrets because trust me, you will."

Gillivary said, "Well spoken, child."

The discussion was over. I wasn't sure if I had any supporters in the room, and I knew there was so much they weren't telling me.

I asked Mrs. MacKenzie could I please stay with them. I couldn't go to the house. They would have to understand. She nodded, and I knew that I would have a place here.

Mr. MacKenzie said, "We all understand if you'd like to postpone the wedding, dear. Under the circumstances, with your brother and…"

I interrupted him. "There's no need to change our plans. Tucker and Alex are still alive. Seth and I will be married because the connection will be stronger. We'll go to Scotland as planned. I'm sure they are there, somehow. Somewhere. Can we still be married, Seth?" I turned to Seth then, hoping that he would agree.

"Whatever you wish."

He must have thought, well, I thought it, too, when the accident first happened and I was drowning on the road, that I wouldn't want him. But now I realized the truth. I must be married to him. That would be my way to go to Scotland to find them. Starting a marriage on lies would not be a sound decision so we could travel to Scotland without bridges.

"I wish it very much."

~

WHEN I WAS TUCKED INTO BREE'S ROOM, AND THE lights were out, I caught my breath when I heard the closet door open.

Seth whispered in the dark, "Shh, it's me."

"How long have you been hiding in there?"

He said, "There is a secret passageway that connects our rooms. Castles always have them. When the house was built Dad wanted it to be as much like Eilean without it being overstated."

It was overstated but I said nothing.

"Seth. I can't go back there. To my house. Without Tucker beside me and Alex right there. I'd see his things. I can't do it. How are we going to explain all of this? Don't make me."

"You have to go back. For your mother's sake. She's already lost one child. She can't lose you, too."

"You still don't believe me?"

Why couldn't he trust me? Then, I thought about how his

gift was limiting his ability to see the possibilities. He'd seen the accident. So, to him this was permanent. To me, it was just a transition that would soon be reconciled.

He kissed me on the cheek. "Try to get some sleep, please."

"I can't sleep. Not when you're right here."

"Do you want me to go?"

"No."

"Then, let's go down to the beach."

"I don't think I can. I want to be still. I need to think this through."

"Jazzline, I saw them wreck. What else do you need to think through? You act like you can formulate a plan."

I sat up, determined to convince him. "I need to go through like Tucker and Alex did at the same location to find them in the right spot, don't I? They claimed they came through the bridge, but went further down for fear the police teams would see them crossing. When your Uncle Colin went back for them, I'm sure he wouldn't have recognized them."

I had tried to think of everything.

He got down on his knees and leaned over the bed, pulling the covers over me. His voice was filled with sadness. "Don't you dare jump. You'd better swear to me. Promise me that you'll not do that alone. You don't know what you're saying. Jazzline, I couldn't. I will not. I won't live without you. So, swear right now. If you jump, you change."

My voice was shaking. "If I don't jump, I'll have given up. That's something I'll never do."

He shuddered, "But when you jump, you could hurt yourself. Hit against the rocks. The concrete foundations. It's too unpredictable. It's not safe. You could die. Or get lost. Either way, you're bound to be separated from me."

The dream. Weeks ago. "You knew, didn't you? The nightmare. Tell me, Seth?"

"Aye. I knew it. I dreamed of a Tucker with short hair and Alex was there beside him. I made you tell me you'd always keep

Alex with us when we drove. I didn't know he would take out his dreads. I asked you that night where was Alex and you said he was with your mother and Luke."

His eyes filled with tears again. "I really thought Alex was with them. Then, I knew it was going to change. That what I saw wouldn't come to pass."

"There was nothing you could've done, Seth. This is not your fault." I believed that.

"How can you say that? I thought that if I made sure one part of the event missed that it could never happen. Yet, it all happened as I saw. And I see it every time I close my eyes."

"You have nothing to feel guilty about anyway. They didn't die. I know it, Seth. Believe me."

He stood up. "Get some sleep. In the morning, things may look differently to you."

I held out my hand to him. "Will you stay with me until I fall asleep?"

"You better keep your promises. Every promise you ever made to me."

I sighed and let my eyes close. "I'll try," was all I could whisper.

I would jump. He knew that I would do it, too. He would have to see that in his visions because I would surely do it. I had to figure out how would be the best way. How, when, and where.

When I woke up, Seth was gone. His mother was knocking on the door, and I called for her to come in.

She came over and sat at Bree's desk, pushing papers aside and trying to straighten up frilly pencils and stacking her notebooks in a pile. "Your mother is downstairs."

"I can't go back to that house. I want to stay here until we go to Scotland. When can we go to Scotland?"

"Jazzline, I'm not sure that you'd want to do this. Sweetheart, I know this must be hard for you. But the next couple of days will be some of the hardest days you'll ever have to face in your life.

Then, the days will turn to weeks, will turn to months, and these things...well, they take time."

My eyes were clear. My mind was focused on truth and nothing more. Seth was right. The morning brought a sharper perspective. "I know they're still alive, Mrs. MacKenzie. And I still want to marry your son."

"I know you do, dear. But your mother. She'll not understand that."

"Do you understand it?" I needed to know that I had someone who could hope and pray with me, other than Bree.

"Yes. I know how much you love them. And I know what you want for them. I want that, too. But you must continue with this day and the next days. You must go on with our secret hidden from the world."

She was right about secrets. I'd have to keep theirs. Who could I go running to tell about magical bridges and gifts of sight? Even if I did, nobody would believe me.

I breathed deeply, stepped forward and walked down the stairs with Mrs. MacKenzie to go and meet my mother. Seth was nowhere around. I had to handle Momma on my own. She had my dad with her. They were both sitting on the couches opposite each other. Neither one looking at the other. Neither one talking. I figured it was because maybe my daddy blamed her.

When I entered the room, Mrs. MacKenzie said, "I'll leave you alone."

Momma looked at me. Her eyes were void of all feeling. "Your father and I want you back at the house. Now."

I sat in the chair that belonged to Mr. MacKenzie. Just sitting in it might rub off some of his strength. "No."

"Jazzline, don't be ridiculous. We have people coming. We have arrangements."

"No, Momma. I have to stay here. I can't go back there. I can't see that they aren't there anymore."

"I see it. I'm there. I need you there, Jazzline."

I couldn't tell her the truth. I had to keep the secret. But I couldn't go back in fear I would let my mind take my hope hostage. The best way to stay strong was to stay by Seth.

"I'm sorry, Momma. But I can't go in the house with Alex's stuff. I can't do it. I won't do it."

She stood up wobbling, with her arms dangling lifeless at her side, and I could tell that her muscle control was lacking. Valium. Something heavy.

"You will do it. You'll come home, young lady. We've got to go to the funeral home, and I need you there."

"Momma, they never found his body. Why would we go to a funeral home? What will you do? Buy an empty casket."

I shuddered at the thought of having to pick out a casket for my baby brother. How could she even think I could go? Maybe she wanted me to handle everything while she broke down. Well, not this time.

"Shut up, Jazzline. Just shut up, and come on." She came towards me but hit her leg on the ottoman and cursed.

My father stood up then. "Stop it, Jackie. She can't deal with it. How do you expect her to handle this? Maybe it's better that she stays here." He turned to look at me then. "Why didn't you tell me you were getting married?"

Momma scowled, "This is not about her. This is about my baby. Oh, Alex."

She crumbled right down to the floor. I watched the whole scene play out. I wanted to scream at her if she would've shown us a little bit of this emotion when he was alive.

"I'm sorry that I'm not going home. I'm sorry that I can't go to the funeral home. I can't handle that."

Just let them believe I was over here wounded and needing Seth and his parents to take care of me. That followed more in line with the story that I would have to portray for the sake of secrets. Let them think I was weak. And maybe I was before but I could not be any longer because I had to save Alex. And Tucker for Bree and that sweet baby.

Daddy grabbed Momma, and they were ready to leave now.

He didn't want confrontation. Funny how he used to always start it. "I'm so sorry, Jazzline. Let's go, Jackie. She'll stay here."

I wanted to say I was sorry for him that he never had the chance to know his son. I wanted to ask him twenty questions, starting with what was Alex's favorite game? What were his friends' names at school? Who were his teachers last year? What did he have bad dreams about? And what made him laugh? But it was pointless. He wouldn't know any of the answers, and I wasn't a cruel person. I had Jesus.

As he held Momma up to leave, I wanted to reach out and comfort her. Tell her everything would be all right. I'd get Alex back. But I said nothing.

She turned around as they were leaving. "And don't think that you're going off to Scotland. You won't marry him, Jazzline."

"I will marry him. We're still going next month."

"Are you serious? If you do this. If you leave to run off and marry him..."

"What? What, Momma? You'll disown me? Never speak to me again?"

"You'll not be my daughter. You'll not leave me with all of this and walk away. If you do, never come back."

But I could not tell her that I needed Scotland to find Alex. Secrets.

"She doesn't mean what she's saying, Jazzline. As you can see, the doctor had to give her something. Are you okay?"

"I'll be okay as long as I can stay away from there. To stay here. Please tell her for me when she can understand."

"I will. I'm really sorry that I've done the things that I have with you and with Alex. I'm so sorry and now it's too late. But I have my reasons. Ones you'll never know." He continued to pull her down the front steps and out towards his truck.

I walked back into the house as if it were already my family home and went to the theater room. I knew I would find Mrs. MacKenzie there. She was sitting at the piano, pushing through papers, using a black marker to make notes on the blank sheet music.

"Am I bothering you?"

She looked up, pushing her glasses that had fallen down her nose. "No, no, dear. Did everything go okay with your family?"

"Is it okay that I stay here? I never formally asked. I pleaded and begged Seth, and he agreed. But can I stay here? I can't go back."

She stood up from the piano and the papers went flying, "Sure, dear. Sure, you can stay."

"Can I ask a favor? Can I not go home to get any of my things? Do you think Bree will mind?"

"No. She'd be happy to share everything that she has with you. She has loved you from the start."

"I love her, too. I'm worried about her."

Seth came up behind us and touched my shoulder. "Worried about who?"

"Bree. Will she be okay?"

"I went."

"Seeth MacKenzie! Where?"

He nodded to her and took me upstairs to his room. "I tried to find Alex and Tucker for you because I knew you would jump."

"And? What happened? Where were they?"

He sighed, rubbing his face. "Jazzline, I don't know? I didn't see a trace. Nobody has seen anything out of the ordinary. No strangers in the town. No newcomers. No signs. I'm so sorry, Jazzline."

I wrapped my arms around him. "Thank you for going for me, Seth. I love you. That means you believe me."

He held his head up and a look of fear crossed his eyes. "You would still jump?"

"I promised you I won't jump." I crossed my fingers behind my back. He loved me enough to forgive me when the time came.

I'll jump, find them, and come back before he even woke up. That was my plan anyway.

He changed the subject. "What did your mother say?"

"You should know." I wished that I knew how his brain worked.

"No. I don't. I just knew she'd be coming over to get you. But I see that you're still here."

"I'm not going anywhere." I sighed into him as he kissed me.

His cell phone rang, and I panicked. Could it be news?

He reached for it and growled. "Bree."

I smiled at him. She always seemed to interrupt us at the wrong time. It was as if she were right with us. I could hear bits and pieces of her side of the conversation because she was screaming. I heard Tucker's name, some panting, something about tombstones, and then I heard my baby's name, Alexander Dumas Chicand. Crash.

I heard the thunder, like a storm brewing in my brain. Everything went black.

Bree shook me. I could feel her hands on my shoulders. "Jazzline, what did you do? How did you get here? Jazzline, wake up."

I sat up with a bolt, an electrical feeling as if it were charging my system like a pulsing station raced through my body. I rubbed my temples. A sharp pain stabbed me in the head, and I groaned as I laid back down.

"What happened? Where's Seth? Where are we?"

I felt the warm tickling of thick grass. The faint smell of lavender wafted all around me. My eyes were still closed. I felt every sensation coursing through my body. Then, I heard a voice. It was faint at first, then grew closer. It was Seth. When I lifted my head, I saw him running through a field with mountains behind him in the distance.

Bree? What was she doing here? I didn't recognize this place. It was in such stark contrast to the black of Seth's room that I felt disoriented. The picturesque clouds were hiding the most brilliant sun. And there was my man. Seth, wearing his kilt, kneeling down beside me. His eyes were a glowing heat of fire, and the shimmering of gold took my breath away as I reached up to move his hair away from his face.

"Seth? Where are we?"

Bree was laughing hysterically, and I wondered if I were in a dream. She held on to Seth's arm trying to catch her breath. I smiled as I recalled the extra little somebody she was carrying around. Seth held me in one arm and put his other one around his little sister.

Seth said, "Jazzline, baby. We're in Scotland. You crossed. How did you do it? One second we were talking to Bree on the phone, and the next you were gone."

When I tried to sit up, I felt my body weaken and collapse against him.

A smile like lightning flashed across Bree's beautiful, tear-stained face. "You did it, Jazzline. I don't know how, but you did it. You're going to find them."

I could hear the strong beat of Seth's heart and felt the arms come around me that I loved so much. I smiled to myself as I leaned into Seth. I would find them safe. I would bring them home.

Sneak Peak of Crossings: Book Two of The Lightbearers Series

CHAPTER 22

Free Falling

There is a tricky thing about fainting. And not just the faint where you stumble, hold on to a chair, regain your composure and keep at it. The fainting that was always so prone to attack me came with no warning and when it hit everything went black. When I would come out of it, I felt as if I was still in the black even though the brightness of the world would shine all around me. But not this time. When I came out of it, I swore I was in a dream. Things like this just can't be real.

I heard his voice. I took a minute just to feel Seth's huge hand caressing my face. He was so present even with the light touch of his fingers against me. His voice was rough with emotion, strained, as if he, too, might have had an attack.

"Baby, oh God. What did you do, Bree?"

Bree was my little angel, calling me home. I didn't have to open my eyes to see what she would look like right now. She was like a little love fairy and I couldn't help feel the smile twitch at the corners of my lips.

I couldn't find my voice still but the words kept reverberating in my brain, hitting in my core. Because wherever my Tucker was, so was Alex. My eyes flew open.

Seth said, "Jazzline, you're alive. Oh, God. I thought..."

Bree's laughter was melodic, "Let her up for some air, for crying out loud."

I felt my body being moved from his chest but not too far away. He smelled so good. He positioned me on his leg and my head had nowhere to go but drop to stare at the dark blue jeans he was wearing. My favorites on him. Funny when you wake up from a dream you notice even the stitches.

Who fainted these days anyway? Oh, yeah, me. I knew that he had told me we were in Scotland. Bree was rambling. I buried my head in his long hair. Just give me one more minute to sit here like this before the world crashes.

I felt the touch of Bree's hand on my arm. She was always breaking up our little love sessions. Somebody should have been paying more close attention to her and Tucker.

I felt her tiny hand on me and the strength that was tingling right below the surface was different. She had something coursing through her that felt like an electrical shock had just coursed through my body.

"What was that?"

She smiled. "Well, you finally got your voice back. I think the first time I crossed, it felt like I had the flu for a week. It's the baby. She's trying to tell me something. She's excited that I'm talking about her daddy."

How could she know the sex of the baby? How could the baby tell her anything? I looked to Seth and he was frowning, too.

"You don't know if it's a girl yet. Just calm down. Let's take Jazzline to the house."

I put my hand around his neck and whispered, "Not yet, please. Just a minute. I need to get a grip on where I am."

Bree's said, "You are in Scotland, at Loch Duich. You're home."

She had taken her hand off of my arm but I could still feel her power through me and I felt stronger. Somehow, just by her touch, she made my head cleared off all thoughts of sickness. And all of the memories came back. And all of the pain, and the hope, and the doubt, and the planning.

"Seth, where are Tucker and Alex?"

He didn't answer me. His hands were now cold when they were once so warm. I knew the signs his body made when he was close to death. I recognized the change even if I didn't understand it all.

Acknowledgments

I am so thankful to God for all of His blessings. My children are my greatest joy, and I pray they will always hold God and hope in their hearts. When they see me day by day pursuing writing, I pray it serves an example to them to go after everything their heart desires because the Lord will supply their every need.

I miss my parents dearly and know when I get to Heaven there will be a reunion like I can't even imagine. They supported my dreams of being an author. If only they had the chance to see my name on a cover, I bet they would have been proud.

For all of my readers who have found The Lightbearers Series, welcome. I'm so glad you're here.

Author Bio

Jen Lowry lives outside of Raleigh, North Carolina and is a proud native of Robeson County. You'll find her enjoying every second of life spent with her family (preferably in pajamas). If you ask her what she's reading it's probably more than one book.

Learn More About Lupus

If you would like to learn more about lupus, please visit the Lupus Foundation of America site to understand more about the chronic autoimmune disease.

https://www.lupus.org/

You can become an advocate, join a Walk to End Lupus Now event or start your own!

Donate today at https://www.lupus.org/give/ways-to-give

Author's Note

If you, a friend, or a loved one needs help, please don't keep it inside.

There are family members, guidance counselors, teachers, community organizations, and nationwide organizations that can offer help.

National Alliance on Mental Illness (NAMI): https://www.nami.org/

1-800-950-6264

TEXT NAMI to 741741

988 Suicide & Crisis Lifeline:

Call or text 988, or chat at 988lifeline.org.

Crisis Text Line: Text HOME to 741741.

Atrium Health Call Center

1-704-444-2400

Mental Health Resources http://www.mhresources.org

American Psychology Association http://www.psychiatry.org/mental-health/